I0550561

Guardian of Fate

The Fate Trilogy

L.J. Kentowski

L.J. Kentowski
laurakentowski@yahoo.com
http://www.laurakentowski.com/

Editing by: http://www.editingfairy.com

More books by L.J. Kentowski

Fate Trilogy:

Guardian of Fate (Book 1)
Seeker of Fate (Book 2)
Angel of Fate (Book 3)

Lexie Pearce Series
Descended in Vengeance (Book 1)

Heart of Seeton Series:
Love Owned (Book 1)
Full Potential (Book 2

Learn more about these books at
http://www.laurakentowski.com/

<u>Get a FREE Urban Fantasy Short Story!</u>

When you sign up for my VIP Newsletter, you'll receive access to release news, upcoming events, and exclusive content and giveaways!

As a thank you for joining, you'll also receive a FREE bonus short story companion to the Lexie Pearce Series!

Get started here:

https://preview.mailerlite.io/forms/1675703/1604802888
34586588/share

Prologue

I knew I should try to free myself, but he drew me closer with an uncanny magnetism. His beauty enticed me like no other man ever tempted me before. While his body was perfect masculinity, with broad shoulders, lean muscular arms, and a taut stomach, his face possessed a mesmerizing softness. Dimples outlined his lush lips, making the hard lines of his jaw seem less intimidating, and promising a smile to warm even the iciest of hearts.

Every feature seemed created for perfection, but it was his eyes that locked me in. The lightest shade of blue, they seemed to glow in the darkness of the night. Unable to break away, I gazed into those eyes with tears in my own, as he brought his lips to mine. The kiss was gentle, but held a power that seemed to possess my very soul with its caress. He held me close, and I could feel the hard muscles of his chest press against me.

A cool wind brushed across my wet lips as he ended the kiss, and emptiness came over me. With his face only inches away, his fingers caressed my cheeks.

"Tell me you love me."

CHAPTER ONE

I was crouched on the hood of a car, unaffected by its steady speed down the road. Peering through the windshield, I looked into the faces of the men in the front seat. I should have been blocking their view, but they were oblivious to me on the other side of the windshield. The driver sang along with the radio as if it were just another day. But I knew better; if I were here, someone was going to die. I only needed to figure out who it was, and how it would happen.

Searching for a shadow, my clue of who the next victim would be, I strained my eyes, seeking it out around the men in the car. While I could find no shadows near either of them, my attention was drawn to the passenger. Clean-cut and strong in appearance, he was an exceptionally handsome man; more attractive than any I'd ever met. But there was also something hauntingly evil about him. His eyes, an intense, light shade of blue, held a compelling power, as if they could reel me into their depths. I was so drawn to them I had to remind myself he couldn't see me.

He leaned over and whispered into the driver's ear. Whatever he said, transformed the man behind the wheel. His eyes glazed over, lips pressed shut, jaw clenched, and his hands tightened on the steering wheel.

The wind whipped the hair from my face as the car rocketed forward. I turned to see where we were going and immediately spotted the signal ahead as it turned red. The driver made no effort to slow down. In fact, he seemed hell-bent on racing straight through it. Driving at a devastatingly fast speed into traffic, we were clearly going to crash.

A woman stepped off the curb to cross the street ahead of us, and then I truly knew who the victim would be. I screamed at her to run back, but she couldn't hear me. No one could. I turned my head back to the windshield and tried to get the driver's attention, but it was useless; he continued to stare right through me. I closed my eyes, dreading the sound of the woman's screams before I felt the horrible thump of her body colliding with the car, and then crashing into the concrete several feet away. When the car finally came to a stop, the sound of the passenger's laughter sent chills through my body.

***

Having a vision about someone dying wasn't new to me. I'd been having them since I was sixteen. As a Guardian of Fate, it was my job to prevent the innocent deaths of people whose souls Hell targeted. My visions showed me who needed to be saved; at least, they did until recently. Needless to say, I'd seen various modes of death, but I never got used to it. Death was still death; it was never pretty.

I learned long ago that after having a vision, time was of the essence. My first failed assignment, before I knew anything about the Guardians, was my best friend, Tiffany. It wasn't my fault she died, but that hasn't stopped me from feeling guilty about her soul imprisoned eternally in Hell.

I'll never forget the day. I think of it almost as if it were the day I was born. Before then, my visions meant nothing to me. They had never been about tragedy, but hindsight being twenty/twenty stopped being a cliché the minute my mom sat me down at the kitchen table to relay the dreaded news from Tiffany's father. It was then that I learned my visions were prophesies...and Tiffany was dead.

That night, my mom taught me about who I really was and what my purpose was in the world. From then on, my visions held meaning. More importantly, they held the fate of people's lives, and ultimately, their souls.

"We are called Guardians of Fate, Cassie," she told me. "We are few, but we are powerful, and very important. You will need to pay special attention to your visions now. Every one of them will lead to the fate of someone's soul."

I learned about Shadows, the Underworld, and demons. It didn't matter my reality was more like a bad horror movie, or that it scared the hell out of me. My mom was telling me the awful truth. These things *did* exist, and I was going to have to play the heroine.

Shadows were immortal demons from a place called the Underworld. They were sent to this earth to collect souls, forcing them into an eternal life in some hellish world. The victims were never meant to die and never suspected a thing out of the ordinary. The demons were devious entities that made deaths appear as natural, accidental events.

While the Shadows were invisible to the human eye, they couldn't hide from our Guardian visions. They appeared near the victim, as if a mere shadow, but blatantly inappropriate to the setting. Once we knew exactly how the person's death would take place, we could create an alternate ending. As far as Mom knew, the Shadows could not sense us; therefore, we could step in without fear of being attacked. Once the victim's fate was diverted from its destructive path, our job was done. In most cases, the Shadows did not stick around and try again. Once their fatal attempts were thwarted, they disappeared, and the person went along their merry way to live their merry life.

When I first found out I was a Guardian, I felt like Cassie, the Demon Slayer, only without the slaying part. I had these special powers that would help me save the world. I was a superhero, but I also knew the burden I would bear if I missed just one step, if I wasted just one minute. I didn't like how heavy that weight felt on my shoulders. I vowed, from the day Tiffany died, to master my calling and never lose another victim to the Underworld.

I drove to the scene while mulling over the vision in my head. Twenty minutes later, I pulled up near State Street and spotted the woman from my vision walking down the sidewalk toward the intersection. I parked in the nearest lot, which turned out to be some corner bar's dimly lit parking area. Deciding to go with my *bump and dump* method, the rescue technique I'd come up with after realizing the shadows were quite predictable, I grabbed my purse to use as my prop and ran toward the woman.

As I got closer to the intersection, I glanced down the road, looking for the speeding car I knew was coming. Just as I spotted it, I ran into the woman, knocking her off the curb and into the street. So much for the *bump and dump* method.

The woman swore at me as she picked herself up. While I half-heartedly offered to help her, I watched the car down the street pitch forward and gain speed. Her rants stopped abruptly as we both watched the speeding car careen into traffic, swerve to avoid another car driving through the intersection, and slam head-on into a telephone pole.

An eerie silence followed the deafening crash of crunching metal. It was as if a storm appeared on the horizon and everyone stopped to look at it before reacting. When everyone realized what happened, there was panic. People from every direction raced toward the car. Others stood nearby on their cell phones, most likely calling 9-1-1. Lights turned on in upstairs apartment windows, occupants sticking their heads out to glimpse the event. Businesses came to a standstill as customers and employees rushed to the windows, some venturing out to become witnesses, others jumping right in, offering help.

A hand lightly touched my arm, and I turned to see the woman with whom I had collided. She stared at me with wide eyes, shock apparent on her face. The grip on my arm tightened as I moved to leave. "You...you saved my life. If you hadn't knocked me down I would have..." Her hand flew up and covered her trembling lips.

"It wasn't your time." I took off toward the car, leaving the woman to deal with the emotions that came along with a near death experience.

I was compelled to see the condition of the men in the car. I had to know if I'd made the right choice. Would the woman have saved herself from being hit by the speeding car? Should I have stopped the car somehow, saving all of them? Was that even possible?

As I neared the wreck, my heart fell, fearing the worst. Smoke and steam poured out of the hood, the steel concavely wrapped around the wooden pole that sat at its center. Glass, from the back and side windows, was scattered all over the street surrounding the car. As I walked closer, it crunched beneath my shoes, and the smell of burning antifreeze overpowered my senses.

With so many people around the car, I couldn't get close enough to see the condition of the men inside. A sense of hopelessness set in as I realized the people closest to the car were not frantically attempting a rescue. Instead, most of them stood around with sad, downcast eyes and pursed lips, discussing the occupants' fatal demise.

Wanting to get closer to see for myself, I pushed my way through the crowd. I caught a glimpse of the driver's arm, hanging lifelessly from his body, but then a man blocked my view. He grabbed my shoulders. "Honey, you don't want to see this. It's not pretty."

"I have to." I squirmed away from his hold and cut around him. He was right. The entire front of the car had been pushed forward, causing the dashboard to pin the driver between it and the seat. He never could have survived the crushing weight. His face lay against the partially inflated airbag. Blood drained from his mouth and stained the dirty, white material with streaks of red. Shards of plastic and glass lacerated his face, neck, and arms. The blood from his wounds had already started to clot.

Sirens blared in the distance. Help was on its way, but they were too late. The man from my vision was dead. Thoughts of guilt slammed into my mind and reached my heart, where they met with ones I had stored away long ago when Tiffany died. *What had I done wrong?* I grabbed at my chest, my body too heavy for my legs to keep up. I must have staggered, because the same man that tried blocking me from the wreck wrapped his arms me.

"Hey, are you okay?" he asked. "Did you know this guy?"

I stared at him, wondering how in the world to answer what seemed like such a simple question. *Yes, I knew him. He was the guy that blew through the red light and killed the woman walking across the street.*

Wait. I ran the vision through my head once more. *What happened to the passenger?*

My focus quickly returned. I twisted out of the man's arms and ran toward the passenger's side of the car. The window was shattered, but the door remained closed. I peered inside. The seat was empty, and there was no evidence to hint someone had been injured, or even sitting there.

I ran back to the man who appeared to be the civilian in charge. Grabbing him, I asked breathlessly, "Where is the passenger?"

"Who?"

"The passenger," I screamed. "The other man in the car. There were two men in this car. Where did he go?"

"There was nobody else in that car," he said, shaking his head.

CHAPTER TWO

"But there had to be. I saw him." I gripped the man's arm hard.

His eyes softened as he peeled my hands from his arm and held them in his own. "I think you should hang tight here. It's obvious you're in shock. The person you thought was in this car isn't here. Let's have the medical unit check you out when they get here. Just stay with me."

How could this be? My visions had never been wrong before. I remembered looking directly into the eyes of that passenger. *No*, I was drawn to the eyes of that passenger. I heard his laughter. *He was there, damn it.*

It was obvious to this man, as well as everyone else, the driver was the only one in the car when it crashed. I knew there was no way I could convince him of what I'd seen. If I pushed further, I stood the chance of being forced to talk to a medical unit, and I wasn't prepared for that. I had so many thoughts in my head that I didn't trust myself to speak. So I decided to play along.

Looking up at him, I pretended to gather my composure. "I need to call my mom." I tried to step away from him, but he stopped me. "Please, I have to know if she's okay."

"Aren't you going to talk to the police? You have to identify the driver. You might be the only one here who knows him," he said.

"I'll come back, I promise. I need to call my mom and know that she's safe. I can't hear anything with all these people around, so I'm just going to run down the street to my car."

His attention jumped to something over my shoulder. I turned my head and saw the police and firemen were now walking through the crowd toward the car. When I turned back, the man was eyeing me again. "All right," he said, "you go ahead and get a hold of your mom, but come right back. I'll let the police know you have information for them."

He finally released me after I agreed, and I took off. It felt better knowing the lie I told him had some truth to it. I was going to call my mom, but it was not to find out if she was okay; I needed her to help me sort through everything, like she did when I first found out I was a Guardian.

My legs shook with every step I took as I ran to my car. As soon as I got in, I called her. Her voicemail picked up. "Mom, please call me back right away. Something's happened. My visions...they...they've changed." I felt the dam of tears break and flow down my cheeks. "I didn't know what to do, Mom, and I lost one. I lost another one. Please call..." My voice broke, and I hung up.

My mom would call me back as soon as she got the message. I knew she would. I just prayed she'd have answers for me, because I was completely lost. She was the only one I could turn to about these things; the only one who knew about them. My dad was a Guardian too, but he wasn't around anymore to help.

Troy Cosgrove, my dad, died when I was four years old. Everything I knew about him came from pictures and stories my mom told me. She described him as a brilliant psychologist who helped many people with all kinds of problems. Mom never mentioned the extent to which he helped them. The devil is in the details, I've since learned. Details were something I never overlooked anymore.

She told me I looked just like him, which explained my long, wavy, auburn hair and blue-green eyes. My features were quite a contrast to my mom's blond hair and green eyes. She tried telling me my tall, athletic figure came from my dad too, but I had nothing to really compare it with. It was hard to see my father's physique in a photo.

I was proud knowing I looked like my dad. It sounds silly, I know, but it felt like I carried a piece of him around with me. I often wondered if I would have felt the same if he hadn't died. Would I have cherished being so much like him? Or would I have rebelled to be completely opposite, like some of my friends did with their fathers?

The only tangible thing I had from my dad was a family heirloom. It was a jeweled ring, supposedly passed down through generations of his family. Mom said he planned to give it to me when I was older. From the size of it, I assumed it was passed on through the males in the family, but I wore it every day, hanging on a necklace, proud to carry on a tradition, even though I never really understood it.

With my head heavy, I fingered the ring, thinking of my father and how much I wished he could tell me more about its significance. I wanted him to help me understand everything that was happening to me. Knowing we all shared something so important, so unlike any other family, made me wish we were all together. As it was, my mom would be the one to help me through this.

All I wanted to do was go home, curl up in bed, and shut the world out. But my roommate, Nora, would be home, and she would ruthlessly pry until she found out what was wrong with me. When it came to seeing me hurt, she never gave up until I came clean. She was a great friend that way, but I knew I couldn't go home because of it.

I gazed out my windshield, thinking I would simply hang out in my car until Mom called back, when I noticed a neon sign for the bar. The more I thought about it, Luke's Pub and Grill seemed like the next best thing to home. Instead of drowning myself in a pillow, knowing I couldn't sleep anyway, I could drown myself in a beer.

As I walked up the few steps leading up to the door of Luke's, I jumped when I noticed a man's face peering out the window to my right. It was difficult to see what he was looking at, because of the dirty film on the glass, but as he stood to the far right of the window, it looked as if he were trying to see what was happening down the street. I didn't imagine he could see much from the angle, since the accident was well down the road.

When I walked in, I got the feeling Luke's Pub and Grill hadn't changed much from when it was originally established. There were about eight or nine red vinyl stools lined up at the small bar and four matching dining benches along the opposite wall. Dark carpeting and dim lighting completed the retro fifties-style atmosphere. There was even an old style jukebox in the far corner, centered between the men and women's bathrooms. I had a feeling the décor wasn't purposely designed to portray the ambience of that era, as so many newer bars and diners strove to do lately. I was pretty sure Luke's simply never changed.

As I stood near the door, assessing the place, the man from the window walked toward the bar a few feet away. I assumed he was the bartender, from the towel he wore on his shoulder, obscuring a T-shirt so faded I couldn't read what it said. He was a younger guy, not what you'd normally expect in a seedy looking bar such as this. He smiled at me, and my assumption was confirmed when he greeted me.

"Hey there. I don't think I've seen you here before. How are you doing tonight?"

The place was empty, which accounted for my car being the only one in the lot. His voice seemed to echo off the walls without the normal bar chatter to drown it. I walked toward one of the barstools in the middle of the bar.

"I could use a beer," I said, sitting down and rifling through my purse for some cash. "I'm not picky about the kind. Anything light on tap will do."

"Ah, a woman after my own heart. No complications." He grabbed a glass. As he began to pour, he looked at me and asked, "So what's your name?"

"Cassie," I answered, placing a ten on the bar at the same time he set my beer on a napkin in front of me.

"It's nice to meet you, Cassie," he said with a smile. "I'm Caleb. Welcome to Luke's."

His warm reception was a refreshing departure from the night I was having. It also emphasized his good looks. With short, blond hair, light blue eyes and a slight tan, he had that boy-next-door appeal, which made him seem even more out of place. With his lean, muscular build, however, this boy next door definitely looked like he could handle himself if a patron got out of hand.

I thanked him and slowly took my first sip, almost moaning with the gratifying indulgence. I wanted it to dull my senses, so I wouldn't have to think about being a Guardian. If only for a short time, I could ignore the deaths I felt responsible for. But there was no amount I could drink that could ever make me forget.

Lost in my indulgence for the moment, I opened my eyes and found Caleb casually leaning against the counter behind him, arms and legs crossed. I was quite certain the smile on his face this time had nothing to do with graciousness, but more my drinking performance.

Embarrassed, I said, "It's been a *really* crazy night."

"So tell me, Cassie, what was so crazy about your night that it brought you here for a make-out session with your beer?" He chuckled.

Heat burned my cheeks as I laughed at his joke, holding my hand to my face in mortification. It felt surreal to be in an empty bar, laughing after what I'd just witnessed not more than an hour ago. I wished my life could be as simple as sitting in a bar, having a beer, and joking with a guy like Caleb, but it could never happen. Reality was never that simple for me.

"It's a long story, and I wouldn't even know where to begin," I explained, realizing there was no way I could ever tell him what brought me here.

"Well, it couldn't be as crazy as what just happened down the street. Did you see that crash? I ran out earlier when I heard it. Man, that car had to have been flying to do that much damage. I haven't had anyone come in since it happened, so I'm not sure about the details. I can't even imagine how anyone in the car survived." Caleb grabbed another glass and poured himself a beer. He set it across from mine, leaned against the bar, and looked at me expectantly.

Contemplating how much I wanted to reveal, I took another drink of my beer, being careful to remain moan-less this time. I hated lying to anyone, so I always looked for ways to describe impossible explanations as truthfully as I could without sounding like I belonged in an institution.

I couldn't deny seeing or hearing what happened. Luke's was situated on Palmer, not far from the corner of the intersection with Fourth Street, which was completely shut down due to the accident. There was no way of getting into the parking lot without seeing something major was going down on Fourth. There was also a very likely possibility Caleb would have seen my empty car sitting in the lot this whole time. He may have even watched me book out of it toward Fourth right before everything happened. He did say he ran out after he heard the crash. Hell, he might have witnessed just about everything I'd done since I'd gotten there, and I wouldn't know.

"Actually," I said, "it's funny you mentioned the crash—" The front door slammed open, and I jumped, nearly biting my tongue in mid-sentence. In any other setting, possibly any other night at Luke's, it may not have been a slam at all, but because of the emptiness within, it seemed to echo louder than it should have. Caleb and I turned our heads toward the door at the same time.

~ 17 ~

The figure of a man filled the doorway. His face was shadowed from the angle of moonlight coming through the window, but his frame was tall and strong, broad shoulders filling out a hip-length, black leather jacket. He stepped away from the door and into the dim light of the bar. I was mesmerized by his dark allure, and found myself unable to look away. Short, dark, tousled hair severely contrasted silver-blue eyes, unlike any I'd ever seen, yet they seemed strangely familiar at the same time.

In my peripheral vision, I could see that Caleb seemed just as captivated by the man. We both stared as if compelled to find out who he was and what he was doing there, our penetrating gazes somehow able to unlock the mystery. I knew how ridiculous we must have appeared to the stranger. He was someone simply coming into a bar, after all. But I couldn't seem to break my trance, and it didn't help that the man was blatantly staring back at me.

Caleb finally broke the spell after what seemed an eternity of not being able to blink. He pushed back from the bar and faced the stranger at the door. I thought I heard Caleb quietly sigh before greeting him.

"What can I get you, friend?" he asked, not as graciously as the title would assume, and definitely not as pleasantly as how he welcomed me.

The man came up and stood behind the stool next to mine. Not wanting to embarrass myself further with my awkward gawking, I turned my head back to the bar and grabbed my beer.

"I'll have a whiskey straight," he said.

My head jerked up from the sound of his deep voice. *I knew that voice.* I sat with my mouth hanging open and eyes wide with shock as I stared at the profile of the man I'd had countless encounters with since I was sixteen. I was entranced as he pulled money from his wallet.

Guardian of Fate

Standing next to me was the man who'd been haunting my visions for years.

CHAPTER THREE

I charged through the woods, terror propelling me faster than I've ever run before. Branches ripped at my thin dress and lacerated exposed areas of my body, leaving bark in my skin and blood dripping from the wounds. The bottoms of my bare feet received the same torture from tree roots protruding out of the earth. I should have been in agony, but the adrenaline pumping through my veins masked any pain my body felt. It was the same thing causing me to perspire, while my breath formed puffs of steam in the chilly night air.

I looked over my shoulder, searching for the man who was chasing me. I saw nothing but the forest around me, but I knew he was there. I could feel his power energizing the air. Turning back, I slammed into something solid. Trembling, I looked up and my heart stopped as I stared into the face of the man I feared most. He grabbed my arms to hold me still, burning my skin under the pressure of his touch.

I knew I should try to free myself, but he drew me closer with an uncanny magnetism. His beauty enticed me like no other man ever tempted me before. While his body was perfect masculinity, with broad shoulders, lean muscular arms, and a taut stomach, his face possessed a mesmerizing softness. Dimples outlined his lush lips, making the hard lines of his jaw seem less intimidating, and promising a smile to warm even the iciest of hearts.

Every feature seemed created for perfection, but it was his eyes that locked me in. The lightest shade of blue, they seemed to glow in the darkness of the night. Unable to break away, I gazed into those eyes with tears in my own, as he brought his lips to mine. The kiss was gentle, but held a power that seemed to possess my very soul with its caress. He held me close, and I could feel the hard muscles of his chest press against me.

A cool wind brushed across my wet lips as he ended the kiss, and an emptiness came over me. Keeping his face inches from mine, his fingers caressed my cheeks.

"Tell me you love me."

My heart beat fast in my chest, as if it wanted to answer him on its own, binding itself to him forever. My eyes locked with his, and as much as it terrified me to tell him how I felt, I was compelled to answer.

"I love you," I said breathlessly.

A smile grew slowly from his mouth. The reaction should have pleased me, but I only felt an overwhelming sense of dread.

"Will you kill me now?" My voice shook.

His smile faded, but he did not pull back. "No," he said, softly. "You will do that yourself, Cassandra."

***

There was no doubt in my mind that the man next to me was the same one who had been in my visions for the last six years. He was real, and he was at Luke's buying a whiskey? I almost felt cheated. For so long, I wondered what the vision was all about, feeling that it held some deeper meaning I would someday grasp. Yet, here I was at some seedy bar, and the man in my dreams shows up and orders a whiskey. Now what? Save him from dying of inebriation?

"Will you kill me now?" I'd asked him in the vision. The recollection of my haunting words surfaced to the forefront of my mind. The nagging feeling it was me that needed saving crept up as I looked at the object of my recurring vision standing before me. It paralyzed me to think my time had finally come. There was no journal entry for this. I had saved countless souls at a moment's notice. Could I save my own now? Would I need to?

He turned toward me with the whiskey in his hand. His familiar angular face was just as strong and beautiful as it had always been; his eyes, just as mesmerizing, as they looked back at me. The dimple I'd seen so many times, deepened with the smirk that widened his perfect lips. I couldn't take my eyes off those lips, remembering the possession they held over mine time and again.

His eyes left mine and roamed my face, as if memorizing my every feature. They drifted down my neck and chest, caressing me with an invisible hand. My skin tingled as if it remembered his sensual touch. I shivered and found myself wanting him to take me in his arms and warm me. I knew it was wrong; I didn't even know this man, but at the same time, I felt as if I'd been in his arms forever.

"You gotta name, friend?" Caleb asked.

"Hunter," he answered, releasing me from his spell and giving Caleb his attention.

"Welcome to Luke's, Hunter. Name's Caleb." He offered his hand over the bar.

Hunter shook his hand, but held on to it when their greeting ended. They stared at each other in silent battle, their locked hands an afterthought. Did these guys know each other? What had I gotten myself into now? After the night I'd already had, I didn't feel like being caught in the middle of any crossfire. I knew I should get out while their testosterone blinded them from my exit, but I couldn't leave knowing I'd had visions of this man for years. I had to find out who he was and why he was there.

I cleared my throat. It was the only thing I could think of besides trying to arm-wrestle the two powerhouses away from each other. Their hands fell apart. Hunter turned to smile at me, but Caleb continued to glare. The tension was still in the air. I smiled and extended my hand to Hunter in an attempt to break through it.

"Hi Hunter, I'm—"

"Cassandra," he finished.

There was no draft in the bar, but shivers ran down my spine after I heard my name spoken with the deep, resonating voice I'd heard countless times. I stared at his lips, remembering the gentle pressure of them against my own. My heart began to race.

His smile captivated me. It was the kind of smile that made you lose focus in everything else around you and be content to simply sit and stare. I couldn't imagine any woman being able to turn away from it. I'd been seeing it for the last six years and even I wasn't immune.

"Do I know you?" I asked him, not bothering to tell him the nickname most people referred to me by. I liked the sound of my full name coming from his lips. It was formal, yet seductive.

Without taking his eyes off mine, Hunter slowly raised his hand to my breast. I sucked in a breath as I watched his hand nudge my open jacket aside and grab the nametag on my shirt. "Just a guess," he said in amusement.

My hand moved to the tag I had forgotten to take off after my shift at the hospital. My fingers brushed his, lingering a bit longer than I was comfortable with, sending a blast of heat into my body. When I looked up at him, he slowly let go.

"Oh, of course," I mumbled. Every ounce of my being screamed that he knew me better than he was letting on. The way he looked at me was much more intimate.

"It's a pleasure to meet you, Cassandra. Mind if I join you?" He straddled the stool and pulled off his jacket, revealing a broad chest. The black T-shirt he wore emphasized his tan, muscular arms. He was powerfully built from head to toe, which no amount of clothing could hide.

Caleb busied himself with washing glasses underneath the bar. What glasses needed washing from an empty bar, was beyond my comprehension. He seemed nervous all of a sudden. Was Hunter making him anxious? Was Caleb getting a vibe from him too?

"So, you from around here, Hunter?" Caleb asked.

"No. Just passing through."

"Oh yeah? Where you from?"

Hunter took a sip of his whiskey. "It's a little place in the middle of nowhere, really. I doubt you'd know where it is."

"Try me. I've been around quite a bit." Caleb stood straight and stared at Hunter. He sounded more like an interrogator, but if it bothered Hunter, he didn't show it.

"It's a small area near Sequoia National Forest, nothing much around. About 200 miles north of Death Valley. Ever been there?" His tone held a note of challenge.

"I've heard of the area," Caleb said, "but can't say I've ever been there. To be honest, I'm not really much of a hot weather type of guy."

Hunter smirked and nodded, as if he already knew this.

"What about you, Cassandra?" Hunter asked, turning toward me. "Ever been there?"

I was so busy watching the exchange between the two men and wondering what was really underneath it that the question threw me off.

"Uh...no. I've never been out West. I've been here pretty much all my life."

"Well, if you ever happen to get out there, you'll have to look me up. I'd love to show you the forest sometime. It can be quite beautiful at the right times."

Are you kidding me? He wanted to show me the forest? The same forest I ran through in my visions? There was no doubt that he knew me, and somehow he knew of the visions. Was it inevitable I would end up in that forest with him? Why else would I be meeting him now?

I couldn't stop thinking about how completely lost I was. I had no idea what it all meant and what I was supposed to do. Why had everything changed? First my visions went haywire and

I lost another soul, now this. It was all too coincidental. I learned long ago there weren't any coincidences in my life.

I needed to talk to my mom. Why hadn't she called back? I looked down at my phone, willing it to ring. I was going crazy. I needed my mom to tell me everything was all right again; that this was supposed to happen, and I'd work it all out, like I did when I found out I was a Guardian. But I had a terrible feeling this time was very different.

Hunter noticed my obsession with my phone. "Are you expecting a call?"

"Yes. My mom was supposed to call me back. I'm getting a little worried."

"You and your mom are close?" Caleb asked.

I welcomed the break from Hunter's gaze. Talking to Caleb seemed easier and much less dangerous for some reason. "Yes, very. She's the only family I have left."

Caleb wiped down the bar around us. "Ahhh, that's nice. It's important to keep your loved ones close. Never know when they won't be in your life anymore. Just look at that poor guy from the accident tonight. Bet he never thought today would be his last."

What an odd thing to say. He couldn't have known how horrible it was to hear in light of the circumstances. His statement made me even more edgy.

"I'm sure your mother is fine, Cassandra," Hunter assured me, putting his hand on my thigh. My jeans didn't hold enough of a barrier from the heat of his touch. It spread throughout my body; resting in places I hadn't felt alive in a very long time.

He pulled his hand back, watching my reaction. The energy between us was palpable. I'd never experienced anything like it. Was it possible he felt it too? I suspected anyone within a hundred mile radius could have felt its effects.

I had to get out of there. I needed to talk to my mom. Like now, before I had a breakdown. I downed the rest of my beer and set it on the bar. Caleb grabbed the glass and moved to refill it.

"No, thanks, Caleb. I really should get going." I stood and grabbed my purse. "I think I'll try to track my mom down. Thanks so much for the beer. It was nice meeting you both." I regarded each of them before walking to the door.

"Hey, Cassie," Caleb called me back. When I reached the bar, he leaned over and motioned me closer. "I was wondering if you'd like to go out sometime?" His question was asked barely above a whisper, as if he didn't want Hunter to overhear. "You never told me about that crazy night you had."

I'd been asked out plenty of times before, but I usually made it a habit of turning men down. With my lifestyle, friends had been difficult to keep; boyfriends even more so. Neither really got used to being stood up at any given time. I got tired of trying to explain my actions, so eventually I gave up on the social life. Not much time for it anyway. My life consisted of school, working at the hospital, my mom, occasional nights out with Nora, and, of course, saving people from an early death by demon.

I glanced at Hunter. He was intent on swirling the remainder of his whiskey in his glass, seemingly uninterested in the conversation Caleb and I were having. I wondered how much he'd heard.

"Oh, Caleb, I'm flattered. Really. But I don't think right now is a good time for me. I have so much going on in my life." I smiled at him, hoping I hadn't hurt his feelings. I'd turned down guys before, but I actually kind of liked this one. He seemed easy to talk to, even though I hadn't really gotten the chance. It was merely a vibe I had about him.

He grabbed a napkin and pen from behind the bar and wrote something on it. After folding it once, he handed it to me. "You can't be busy all of the time, Cassie. Everyone needs a little down time. When you have that break, give me a call. I promise to keep it on the non-crazy level," he said with a smirk.

I reached for the napkin. He held on to it long enough to brush his finger across my knuckles, sending a tingling sensation up my arm and through my body. What was it with these guys? Were they both made from the same electrical current? Or was it because I hadn't been with someone in so long that any whisper of a touch sent me into a hormonal outrage?

I noticed Hunter watching our hands. I got the feeling he hadn't missed a bit of what was happening between Caleb and me. As stupid as it sounds, I got the impression he didn't like any of it.

"I definitely will, Caleb. Thanks." I smiled at him. I meant it too. As soon as I got my life back in control, I was going to call him.

"Good. I look forward to it," he said. There was a glimmer in his eyes I hadn't noticed when I first met him, making the blue hue appear closer to gray. They were almost as hypnotizing as Hunter's. "Good luck with your mom." He released the napkin.

I pocketed the scrap, thanked him again, and walked toward the door. As I passed Hunter, I wished him a good night, but he didn't seem to hear me. All of his attention was focused on Caleb. If his eyes could shoot daggers, Caleb wouldn't stand a chance. Why? What had happened between them?

I didn't understand any of it. The whole situation seemed ridiculous. These men were strangers, but I got the feeling they were trying to mark their territory with me. Maybe I just didn't understand testosterone and how it worked. Maybe when you put two men in the same room with one woman, they automatically had to prove their conquests over each other.

I didn't have the patience to deal with the male hormonal displays. I had enough of my own problems. They could puff their chests to each other as much as they wanted. I was out of there.

As I walked out, the memory of my vision reminded me one of those problems had everything to do with the man sitting at the bar puffing out his chest. So much for not dealing with male hormones. I was hoping Mom would have answers for me and I could avoid Hunter altogether after tonight. Even though he was quite possibly the most beautiful man I'd ever laid eyes on, the attraction I felt for him scared the shit out of me. Dealing with the tug of his magnetism in my visions was one thing; fighting that pull in the flesh was something I wasn't sure I had the strength to handle. With my visions, came death. I needed to heed my own warnings, so my plan was to get as far away as possible.

CHAPTER FOUR

I tried my mom again when I got back into my car. Voicemail picked up and my heart fell. Where was she?

"Mom, I need you, please call me back."

I wanted to spill my guts. Maybe letting it all out would help make sense of the jumbled mess addling my brain, but the only person who could provide the therapy I needed wasn't available.

I dropped the phone into the middle console of my car. Loneliness and confusion overwhelmed me. My tears fell fast, a river of burden seeping through my lids. I would have given anything to escape the prison of responsibility thrust upon me as a Guardian. The heaviness I felt when I was sixteen seemed to have lightened up over the years, only to now become a mass so big, I feared it would crush me. Who was going to save *me* now?

With my arms crossed over the steering wheel, my head resting on them, I cried in my car. I had no idea how much time went by. I didn't care. I had nowhere to go, and I sure as hell couldn't go back to my apartment in the state I was in. Nora was too sensitive to my emotions, and as much as I wanted to confide in her, I just couldn't bring her into everything. Not now. I had to figure it out first.

As I sat there feeling sorry for myself, my car door opened, making me jump in my seat. Shocked, I could only stare as Hunter crouched in the open door, his beautiful face filled with concern. My defensive reflexes set in, and I moved as far back from him as the seat would allow, the console digging in my back as I leaned into it.

"Cassandra, I'm not going to hurt you. I came out of the bar and saw you were still in your car. Is everything all right? Is it your mom?" His eyes roamed my face searching for answers.

Embarrassed, I made a feeble attempt to wipe away the remaining tears from my face, but I was sure my eyes were red-rimmed and puffy.

"Oh, um...no, I haven't gotten a hold of her yet. I'm going to drive to her house now to make sure she's all right. Thanks for checking on me, Hunter," I sniffled, "but I'm fine."

He reached his arm across my body, and I trembled from the mere breeze of his action. Holding my breath, I froze. My eyes were the only body part capable of motion, as I watched him open up the console and grab a tissue. I was so hypnotized by him I couldn't even form the words to ask him how he knew they were there.

He offered the tissue to me, and I took it slowly. As I wiped my nose, he continued to watch me, his body still too close to mine. Even after I was finished, I remained frozen in my awkward position, afraid to move. Emotions warred within me. My mind told me I should be terrified of this big, powerful man, whom I just met. Crouching in front of me, he was close enough I wouldn't stand a chance of escape if he chose to attack me, but something deep inside made me feel safe with him. Maybe it was because I felt I knew him from all the years I'd dreamt of him. Maybe I simply had a death wish.

My emotions battled silently, and my pent-up breath rushed through my lips in a pant. As his eyes moved to my mouth, the air between us became so thick, I thought I might suffocate.

He moved back, but remained crouched next to the car.

"Are you okay now?" he asked.

"Yes."

He stood, and I was struck by an incredible urge to make him stay, if only for a second longer.

"Hunter, have we met before?" I blurted. It wasn't merely a question to keep him near me; I had to find out if he somehow knew me too.

He looked at me for a moment with his head tilted slightly to the side, as if a better angle might help him place me. Slowly, he crouched next to me again, causing me to lean back once more.

"No, we've never met."

Not willing to come to terms with the fact I was the only one who could feel this powerful connection between us, I asked, "Are you sure?"

"Cassandra, if we had met before," he said in a deep, almost seductive voice, "I assure you, it would have been memorable."

My body shook from the meaning of his words. I was sure he had me under some kind of spell, because I didn't realize he'd moved in closer. Wiping a stray tear from my cheek with his thumb, his fingers rested softly against the side of my head. His touch was so light, I would have considered it a mere caress, if not for the burning sensation it left when he pulled it away. My hand immediately flew to the spot he touched, and I stared at him in astonishment.

"I should apologize for being so forward as to touch you," he said, "but I'm afraid I'd do it again if given the opportunity." He stood. "I hope your mother is well. Maybe we'll see each other again."

I felt as if I were in some crazy trance I couldn't shake, so it took me a minute to process what he said. As he started to walk away, I stood and called out, "I thought you were just passing through?"

I heard him laugh, and then he stopped and turned. The smile was still on his face when he told me, "I was, but I'm starting to like what I see here, so maybe I'll stick around for a bit longer." The shocked expression I wore was starting to feel like a permanent facial feature tonight. It remained in place as I watched him turn back around and walk into the night.

***

I drove to my mom's house in a daze, somehow managing to pull into the driveway twenty minutes later without getting into an accident. Sitting in my car, I gazed at my childhood home and was comforted with the knowledge that despite everything different in my life, it had remained the same as when I was a little girl. The light, russet-colored Colonial sat regally at the end of the cul-de-sac amidst its quiet, suburban neighbors. The lawns were well manicured, some of the older owners having to resort to lawn care services that came on a weekly basis.

Mom's zinnias, hydrangeas, and shrub roses were still in full, multi-hued bloom. Summer weather in the Midwest was famous for starting pretty late, but it also lasted longer, sometimes even into October. Indian Summer was always a favorite time of mine with its warm, sunny days so close to the long, cold winter months. Mom needed no help with the maintenance of the yard, and she took great pleasure tending her flower garden. Growing up, she would spend hours at it. She had a flair for placement and color coordination, mingling flowers with lawn ornaments and lights, resulting in a beautifully inviting, as well as, pleasantly surprising landscape.

The porch lamp was on, lighting up The Cosgroves plaque, which hung below the address. There was only one Cosgrove left in our house, but to her, it would always be home to all of us: Mom, Dad, and me. Seeing the light on was a good indication she was home.

I had a key to the house, but since it was late, I didn't want to scare her by walking in, so I knocked on the door. I didn't have to wait long before she answered, dressed in her blue, satiny, pantsuit pajamas and matching robe. Seeing her ready for bed surprised me. I hadn't called too long ago, and I knew she slept with her cell charging on the nightstand next to her bed. She always kept it on in case of emergencies, namely from me, which is why I was confused. Why hadn't she answered, or at least called me back?

"Cassie, is everything all right?" she asked, opening the door wide.

"I was going to ask you the same thing, Mom. Where have you been? I tried calling you a couple of times and left you messages to call me back."

Her brows furrowed. "What are you talking about? My phone hasn't rung all night. I've been home reading. I didn't get any calls from you." She walked over to the coffee table in front of the sofa. On it was her phone, a book, her reading glasses, and a glass of red wine. She picked up her phone and opened the display. After pressing a few buttons, she offered me the phone, shaking her head. "Look, there's nothing. No missed calls, no voicemail. The last call I show from you was yesterday morning. Are you sure you got the right number?"

"Yes," I cried, perplexed. "I heard your message before I left the voicemail. I know it was yours. What the hell is going on?"

"Honey, calm down. Sit down and tell me what happened." We both sat on the sofa, and she reached for her wine glass. "Here, have some."

I took a small sip and set it back on the table. "I lost someone, Mom," I choked out. "Tonight. I had a vision. It was different...*way* different. I didn't know what to do...I...Were my visions supposed to change? Is this something you were waiting to tell me because it wasn't supposed to happen until I was older, or something?" I was searching. Searching for anything to make sense of what was happening to me. I wanted her to explain it like she had when I was sixteen. Even though I'd be mad as hell at her for keeping it from me, I'd at least have answers. But looking at her face, I knew she had none. She looked as confused as I did.

"I don't understand, Cassie. How did it change? What was different about it?"

I told her everything—the vision of the woman, the car, the two men, and the feelings I got about the man with the strange eyes. I told her about the crash, and how I watched the car steamroll into the pole. After I explained to her how helpless I felt seeing the poor man dead in his car, wondering if I could have somehow saved him, I cried. The weight on my heart unleashed its mass. My mom took me into her arms and held me. I was a little girl again, crying over something overwhelmingly horrible. Just like then, she was the only one who could help me fix things.

She said nothing while I released all of the guilt inside my head. Tiffany's death found its way back to commingle with this latest fatality. Mom knew I needed to let it all out before we could attempt to piece everything together, as if emptying all of my tears could clean up the chaos inside my head and allow me to see things more clearly. If only it were that easy.

As my cries turned to whimpers, she pulled me from her embrace. "It's going to be all right. We're going to get to the bottom of this, okay?" She tilted my chin until I was gazing into her eyes. "Okay, Cassie? We'll figure this out together."

I nodded and wiped the last of my tears from my face. Mom stood and patted me on the shoulder. Picking up her glass of wine, she went to the dining room table, where the rest of the bottle was sitting. "All right, so, you didn't mention where the Shadows were. Since there seemed to be three different people in this vision, we need to start with where the Shadows were located." She grabbed another glass from the china cabinet and filled both glasses.

"That's just it, Mom. There were no Shadows this time. That's why I didn't know what to do."

She stopped midstride on her way back to the sofa and stared at me. I got up and took the glasses from her. My revelation seemed to hit a nerve. Maybe it was the starting point, the key to unlocking it all.

"What is it, Mom?"

Sitting down next to me, she grabbed my hands. "Are you sure there were no Shadows, Cassie? Maybe you missed them. Think hard. They could have been near any of the people in the vision, but they had to have been there." As much as I knew she wanted to comfort me, she couldn't hide the apprehension in her eyes.

"No, there were none. I looked for them, but they weren't in that vision." Her concern over the lack of Shadows scared me. It was one of the blatant differences the vision had from any others. But it was nothing compared to the man who seemed to have vanished from the...*wait. That was it.* The Shadows were missing, but there was something near the victim in its place.

I grabbed my mom's shoulder and nearly shouted, "Oh my God, Mom. I can't believe I forgot to tell you the most important thing. The guy...the one with the crazy blue eyes...he was...he wasn't..." I stumbled over my words trying to get them out faster. After taking a deep breath, I tried again. "The guy I told you about with the strange eyes, he wasn't there after the vision."

"What do you mean he wasn't there?" she asked, her forehead creasing. "Where'd he go? He survived the...I don't understand."

"I mean he was never in the car. Everyone I talked to after the crash never saw a passenger. It's almost like he was the human form of a Shadow." I told her how I went to look at the passenger seat and could find no evidence of anyone sitting there during the crash.

"Maybe he was able to jump out of the car before it hit the pole."

"No way. Trust me on this. I may be completely lost as to why this is all happening, but I know there was something totally off about this guy." I was pacing now, my fingers running through and pulling at my hair as I walked back and forth. "His eyes were so...I don't even know how to describe it...almost magnetic, like he was pulling me into something."

My mom had been sitting on the sofa, her head down, finger in her mouth, deep in thought. At the mention of the man's charm over me, her head snapped up, and she was instantly in front of me.

"What did you say his eyes looked like again? Didn't you say they were blue?"

"Not just blue. These eyes were almost silver, and shimmered when he smiled. They were hypnotic. It's like nothing I've ever experienced before."

My mom shook her head. Something told me she knew exactly what I was talking about. Both recognition and disbelief crossed her features when I explained the man and the feelings he had evoked in me. Did she have a similar encounter in a vision she'd forgotten about? Or just didn't want to tell me?

"What is it, Mom? Do you know this guy? Have you seen him before?"

She hesitated, looked me in the eyes, and said, "No, Cassie, I've never had visions without Shadows. It's always been the Shadows. I don't know why your vision was so different. I need to check into some things. There are places I can go to try to get some answers."

"I'll go with you—"

"No, you can't. I have to go alone. I promise it will only take me a few days, and I'll fill you in as soon as I find anything out."

"But where are you going?"

She sighed, and I could tell she wasn't looking forward to what she felt she needed to do. "The people I'm going to see know a lot about the Guardians of Fate. They helped me sort out some things a long time ago, and I'm hoping they can help clear this up too."

I argued with her, wanting her to take me with her, but she raised a hand to stop me. "Cassie, you need to trust me. I'll be fine. There is no more to say about this because you are not coming with me. It can only be me. I want you to calm down and go about things like you normally would until I get back. Okay? Can you please do that so I can help you?" It wasn't really a question. She wasn't going to give in. I knew my mom. She could be as stubborn as I if it were something she felt strongly about, and obviously, she felt very strong about not wanting me to go.

It made me angry. How ironic that while I was responsible for so many others' fates, I was never allowed to have a say in mine. I wanted to argue and tell her this was my life, and I had every right to know what was going on with it, that I was sick and tired of having no control. But I couldn't. It wasn't like she was an overprotective, domineering mother who needed to manage her child's life as if it were her own. The things she did were only to help me cope with a destiny I didn't ask for, because she'd been through it too. What scared me was that I was now experiencing things she had never been through. It was new territory even she didn't know how to handle. My mom wouldn't stop looking until she had answers.

Still compelled to voice my frustrations, I muttered, "As if my life could ever be normal." I lowered my head in defeat.

Mom recognized my surrender and put her arms around me. "Everything is going to be okay, Cassie. I promise. We'll get to the bottom of this, and you'll move on to what's *normal* for us." She held my shoulders at arms' length. "I know you're frustrated by everything right now, and you feel like your world is filled with events over which you have no control. But never forget how special you are. This world needs you. People need you. You are their Guardian, and without you, their souls would suffer. Always remember that for me, okay?"

"Okay." I was so tired of fighting and trying to figure out my chaotic life. Add on the fact I would now worry relentlessly about my mom until she returned, and I expected to pass out from sheer exhaustion soon.

I hugged her to me. "Make sure you call me the minute you can. I don't care what time it is. I'm going to be so worried about you."

"I will, baby. I will. Don't worry. I'll be back soon, and everything will be okay."

I made my way to the front door and Mom followed. Turning, I gazed back at my mom with loving eyes. "Thank you, Mom."

She brought her hand to my face and brushed my cheek. The motion triggered the memory of Hunter wiping away my tears. Their difference in touch was so extreme. My mom's was soft and feathery, emanating from love and compassion. His was as soft on my cheek, but the energy that came from it was full of power and intensity.

"I love you, Cassie," my mom said, breaking me from my reverie.

"I love you too."

I went back to my car. Anxiety over my mom's mysterious trip should have overwhelmed my thoughts, but the memory of Hunter's touch seemed to push all other concerns out of my head. I drove home, reliving the intense pull his touch had on my body and soul, all the while berating myself for having such reactions to someone I didn't even know...at least, not in the flesh.

CHAPTER FIVE

By the time I got home, it was almost midnight. All of the lights in the apartment were off except for the small light we left on above the sink at night. Nora was home. Her car was in the parking garage. She must have been sleeping, which I was thankful for since I wouldn't have to make up some story for my being out later than usual.

I went straight to my room and into bed, not bothering with the usual bedtime rituals. I was too exhausted, and I fell into a deep sleep almost immediately. The day had been full of twists and turns, which had me spinning, as if being consumed by the powerful winds of a relentless tornado, struggling to reach ground, only to be thrown back up by another force of coiling air. Sleep should have been a sweet repose after the storm I'd been through, but it too, threw me into a whirlwind of unpredictability.

I was being chased in the woods by the same man as usual, which I knew now to be Hunter. I ran into him, but when he leaned in to kiss me, our surroundings changed from the woods to my car. These scenes flickered continuously back and forth with our bodies being the only constant, until finally, we were back in the woods. Just as his lips touched mine, someone took hold of my right wrist and yanked my body away from him.

I stumbled, but the hand wrapped around my wrist steadied me. Slowly, I lifted my head to face my captor…or was it savior? I wasn't sure anymore. Caleb tugged my wrist, bringing me closer to him and away from Hunter. I watched them stare each other down, as if their eyes held a magical power that would force the other to surrender.

"You're too late, brother," Caleb spit out. "You should have done what you were told. She belongs to me now." With

that, he grabbed my hair, pulled my head back, and crushed his
mouth over mine.

I woke up from the sound of Hunter's screams.

***

I sat up in my bed and ran my hand through my hair. It
was drenched in sweat. Whenever I woke from the dream, I was
hot and exhausted, as if I were physically running through those
woods. The new twist left me with the same emotions, with the
added benefit of utter confusion.

I was sure now the man haunting my dreams was the same
man I'd met at Luke's. For some reason, I'd been warned years
ago Hunter would enter my life. But why? What role did he play?
My body and soul were drawn to him. But I also feared him.
Why? Was I in danger?

As if I weren't confused enough, Caleb had been added to
the mystery. Had I merely dreamed of him because of the
encounter at Luke's? Was my subconscious picking up on all of
the testosterone I sensed in the air? Or did he play a bigger part
in all of it? *"She belongs to me,"* he'd said. His kiss was so
violent and possessive; it was as if he were leaving his mark on
me. I could *still* feel the pressure of his lips lingering on mine.

The clock on the nightstand next to my bed showed seven
o'clock. I had class at nine, but I wanted to check in with Nora
before I left. We were supposed to study together after work last
night, but things had gotten so crazy, I never had the chance to
call her and apologize for not making it. She was used to my
unplanned absences, but normally, I'd call and give her some
excuse. I definitely had to come up with something good this
time. She'd be working at the health clinic today, but she didn't
start until ten o'clock, so I had time before we both had to get
going.

I grabbed a pair of shorts from the floor of my cluttered
room. Clothing was scattered everywhere due to an overdue trip
to the laundry. Peering down the short hallway, I noticed Nora's

door was open. The light was out, and I went and peeked in to find the room empty. Her bed was neatly made, which was a clear sign she had left. It was a pet peeve of hers not to leave the apartment without tidying up. Luckily, she didn't push her vexation with unmade beds onto me. It probably helped I kept my door closed, whether I was in or not. Since I could see from the hallway she wasn't in the living room or kitchen, I checked the bathroom quickly as a last resort, but she was already gone.

Disappointed I hadn't caught her before she left the apartment, I went into the kitchen to grab something to drink. When I sat down at the breakfast bar, I noticed a note.

Hey Stranger,

What have you been up to? I'm starting to worry. Tried calling you twice last night, and you never called me back. What's up with that? Gotta get with the peeps today for study group. Prof. Geiger is running us ragged with his essay exams. Plus side: I'm off work today. How 'bout dinner if you're not busy? Call me later. You do still have your phone, right?

Love n stuff,

Nora

Dinner with Nora sounded great. A nice, ordinary activity was just what I needed to get my mind off everything. I only had two morning classes at school, and then a short shift at the hospital, so I'd be home at a fairly decent time. I decided to call her later to suggest we order a pizza in and watch some movies. If Professor Geiger were on a rampage, I was sure she could use a night of mindless tube watching. I jotted down a quick reply that dinner was on, and I'd call her later about the details.

Getting ready for school, I showered and threw on a pair of comfortable cargo-style capris and my favorite Waitling U Psych Dept T-shirt. After drying my hair, I haphazardly tossed it up in a knot to keep it out of my way. The humidity had mostly subsided for the season, but there was enough in the air to play havoc on my wavy locks, and I wasn't in the mood to deal with it.

Not only that, but the way campus was set up, there were countless wind tunnel areas that rendered me blinded by my own hair if it weren't pulled back.

Our apartment was only a few blocks from campus, so I walked. Waitling was a fairly good-sized University, with most of the housing within a ten-block radius rented by university students. I made it to class early and used the spare time to check my phone for Nora's messages. But when I checked my voicemail, I had none. I made a mental note to take my phone in to have it looked at, since this was the second time in the last twenty-four hours something strange had happened with it.

The two classes went fairly fast and helped to take my mind off things. It was amazing how learning something I liked consumed my attention. That's what psychology did for me. Call me a total nerd, but I couldn't get enough of learning about the human mind and how it worked. It made me wish my dad were around so we could talk about it together. I imagined us staying up late into the night as he told me stories of patients he'd had, theories he applied, and how he came up with particular diagnoses. As it was, I settled for knowing we shared a love of science and the human mind.

After my last class, I was on my way to the Union Hall to grab a quick sandwich, when some guy collided into me, his book bag sliding from his shoulder and smacking into mine. The crash wasn't powerful enough to knock me down, but I did lose my balance slightly. The student lifted his book bag back onto his shoulder and grabbed my upper arm, trying to steady me. After offering a quick apology, he continued on his way.

I said a quick, "No problem," to his back, and I realized he wasn't alone. Directly behind the student another man followed. He was extremely close behind him and matched him, step for step, almost as if he were his...*shadow*. As I processed the significance of the situation, the man turned to look straight at me, and I almost passed out. It was the passenger of the car in my vision, the man with the blue eyes. I'd never forget those eyes. He gave me an eerie smile as he continued to follow the student into the building.

I had myself almost convinced I'd imagined the passenger in the car. I even contemplated that notion my vision was wrong for once. Seeing him here now, I knew it wasn't. This guy had something to do with my visions, and I had to find out what it was. I ran after them.

As I entered the building, I quickly scanned the area. It was spacious and bright inside, so it was not hard to spot the student, but the man was no longer trailing behind him. I frantically searched for him, scrutinizing the eyes of every person I saw. He was gone. I didn't know whether I was relieved or terrified I could no longer see him.

The student zigzagged through the crowd and reached a staircase, which led down to a lower level. As he stepped to the top of the staircase, I saw him waver as if he were losing his balance. His body lurched forward and his arms flailed about, as if searching for something to grab a hold of. But the staircase was wide and he was too near the center, too far from either railing to reach them. There was no way I could bridge the distance between us before he fell.

If I hadn't seen the man from the crash hanging around this guy, I may have assumed this would end as no more than a few broken bones. Somehow, this man, this devil with hypnotic blue eyes, had replaced the haunting Shadows in my visions. And for some reason, I was no longer dealing with premonitory visions, I was dealing with the here and now. By the looks of this particular here and now, I was going to have another death on my conscience.

His fall appeared inevitable, but I had to do something. It was hard enough knowing he was about to die, but to do nothing seemed inhumane. I was a Guardian. It was in my nature to do everything I could to save people's lives, regardless of how hopeless it appeared.

Running toward him, I yelled incoherently, trying to get his attention. I closed about half the distance between us, when his body jerked backward onto the top step where it steadied. I pulled up short, confused. I was so sure I had lost him that it took me a moment to comprehend he had been saved without my help. It was as if some invisible force had pushed him back up before he'd completely lost his footing. I actually might have believed that, after what had transpired lately, but then he took another step back, and I saw hands letting go of his forearms.

I froze as Caleb appeared from the step below.

What in the hell was he doing here?

Caleb joined the student on the top step as they shook hands, the man thanking Caleb for his rescue. The student took off down the stairway, and Caleb turned toward me. Recognition registered on his face, and he walked over with a friendly smile. I was rooted to the floor, dazed by what had taken place. In the last twenty-four hours, I was swimming in a world of crazy coincidences. Since I'd learned not to believe in them, I was having a hard time coming to terms with reality even when it slapped me in my face.

My eyes came back into focus. Caleb stood directly in front of me, concern replacing his smile. I must have looked like a complete psycho standing there, stunned and lifeless, caught up in my own thoughts.

He touched my forearm. "Cassie? Cassie, are you okay?"

"Uh...yeah." I put my hands over my face, fanning my fingers across my temples, symbolically wiping away the haze. "Geez, I'm sorry, I was completely out of it for a minute there. I'm fine, really. I saw that guy by the stairs and thought he was going down for sure. I was running to help him, but didn't think I had time, and then you were there, only I didn't see it was you." I was rambling. Heat spread over my cheeks.

"Yeah, great timing on my part, I guess. You sure you're okay though? You're breathing kind of heavy." His eyes moved to my chest, and I got the feeling my pulse wasn't all he was concerned with. I wasn't blessed with the kind of breasts some women paid money for, but I did okay for my smaller frame. Apparently, Caleb thought so too.

I placed my hand over my chest, a mock attempt to slow my breathing, but more so to avert his eyes back where they belonged. It worked, but it was a slow victory as his gaze crawled back up to meet mine.

"Yeah, yeah, I'm fine," I said. "What in the world are you doing here, Caleb?"

He chuckled as he pulled at the strap of a backpack hanging over his shoulder, clearly noticeable to everyone but me, apparently. I was sure he would ask for his number back any second now. "I just got out of class. Happened to be walking up the steps when I saw the guy lose his balance. Lucky for him, I stayed after to talk to my professor or I'd have missed him. I didn't know you went here. What are you going for?"

"Psych. I'm on my second year of the PsyD program. What about you? I can't believe I've never seen you around here."

I got bumped from behind and stumbled into Caleb. He reflexively put his arms around me, and I sank into his chest. I heard him say something like "Watch it," to the person who knocked into me. I knew I should pull away. It wasn't like I was in any danger, but his arms felt good. They were strong, even stronger than his appearance portrayed. The memory of his kiss in my dream flashed through my head, and I jerked away, feeling too hot and close all of a sudden.

"I...I'm sorry. I don't know what it is today. I must be invisible or something. That is the second person who's run in to me in the last hour."

"Cassie, you are *definitely* not invisible. Trust me on that," he said with a sexy smile.

My cheeks heated.

"So do you have another class coming up?" he asked.

"No, I'm actually done for the day. Why?"

"How about we get you out of the line of fire and make good on that date? And if you're not good with the date part, how about we just call it getting a bite to eat?" I'm not sure if I even considered denying Caleb's request because his smile made me forget everything but saying, "*Yes*."

CHAPTER SIX

We ended up at Grubs, a local diner on campus known for its delicious burgers. The only problem with the place was that it wasn't big enough for the crowd it attracted during the lunch hour. I'd heard rumors of them relocating to a bigger building, but they had been circulating for almost two years now. People often joked the gossip was started by someone not willing to wait for one of their few cushiony booths. Most people ordered and took their food outside, especially in the spring and fall months. Midwestern winters posed more of a challenge to eating outside. It was hard to eat a greasy burger while wearing mittens, and don't even think about tackling the fries. It was more common to see students take their food into Waitling's Union Hall, which was less than a block away. It had a great TV room with many comfy sofas and chairs to relax in.

Taking advantage of the warm weather, Caleb and I decided to eat our burgers in a park near campus. Park benches were filled with people studying while enjoying their own lunches, their motions robotic, as if food was merely a mindless necessity of the body. No one glanced up to acknowledge anyone else, too absorbed in the books or papers on their laps.

We sat in the shade of a maple tree. It stood high and wide, providing ample room for us to sit comfortably in its protective shadow from the sun's rays. A life-sized bronze statue of the famous architect, Frank Lloyd Wright, sat on a raised cement pedestal, surrounded by a bed of colorful hibiscus and daisies. I remember learning about how *the greatest American Architect of all time* was born and raised in the Midwest.

Caleb stretched his legs out in front of him, and extended his arms behind to support the lounged position. Not wanting to get too close, I sat cross-legged near his knees, facing him. I handed out our burgers and placed the fries between us. Caleb took his burger and put it on the ground next to him. I dove into mine the second I got the wrapper off.

"Oh my God, this is so good," I said with a mouthful of cheeseburger, forgetting my manners completely.

Caleb laughed.

"What's so funny?" I asked him, swallowing the burger and grabbing a few fries.

He pushed himself to sit straighter and reached his hand toward my face. Before I could react, his thumb gently swiped the corner of my mouth, coming away with a dollop of ketchup. "Watching you eat that burger reminded me of the way you drank your beer at Luke's. You're completely engrossed in it."

"It's a great burger. Aren't you going to eat yours?"

"Nah. I'm not really hungry. I ate a little while ago."

I choked on the fry lodged in my throat. "What? But it was your idea to get lunch."

"I know, but it seemed the only way to get you to go out with me. You already blew me off at Luke's with the excuse you didn't have time. Figured you had to eat, right?"

I wanted to be angry with him for tricking me into this *date* that wasn't really a date. I should have gotten up and left him sitting there. But looking at him, so relaxed and sexy, in his faded jeans, black T-shirt, and sandals, made me think maybe this was just what I needed, something exciting, in a normal kind of way. Something that didn't involve death and mysterious men with haunting blue eyes.

Speaking of blue eyes, Caleb's were so light and inviting, they reminded me of the sky on a bright sunny, cloudless day. He had cute little creases that came out on the sides when he smiled. His blond hair, which seemed to wave despite its short length, accentuated their lightness.

"That's pretty low, Caleb. Tricking a hungry girl with a greasy burger. What's next? Faking a sore neck so I'll rub it for you?" *Please tell me those thoughts did not come through my lips. What in the hell made me say that?* I had been admiring the way his T-shirt emphasized his broad chest and shoulders. *Note to self: do not talk while wondering what Caleb looks like without his shirt. Scratch that, self. Quit wondering what any of his body parts look like, period.*

His eyes lit up. "Would it work?"

I avoided his gaze. Suddenly weeding the grass became of utmost importance. "So...um...yeah...what are you going to school for?"

He seemed to find humor in my escape, but answered. "I'm in the law school, educating myself on being a more persuasive person. Apparently, I need to study harder."

I laughed. "What year are you?"

"First year law student and first year at Waitling. I did my undergrad back home in Lubbock, Texas."

"Wow, Texas. I'm sure there are plenty of law schools in Texas. What brought you up to the Midwest?"

"None came with a huge discount. My uncle and I have always been pretty close since my dad passed, even though we live thousands of miles away. He offered to let me stay in an apartment above his garage for free. And he also pays for part of my tuition in return for working at his bar. I couldn't beat his offer. I'd be in debt for life going anywhere else. You done with that?" He pointed to the bag of fries and my empty burger wrapper.

"Yeah, I wouldn't want to embarrass myself anymore eating in front of you." I giggled.

He grabbed the wrappers and went toward a garbage bin a few feet away.

"So your uncle owns Luke's?" I asked.

Caleb threw the wrappers out and sauntered over to the statue of Wright. "Yep. And before him, my grandfather owned it." He crouched down in front of the flowerbed, picked one of the red roses, and held it to his nose. Seemingly satisfied with its scent, he walked back. "For the beautiful lady." He smiled, handing me the flower.

I stood, taking the rose and inhaling its sweet scent. The aroma was much stronger than I anticipated. It saturated my senses like a drug. I was drawn in, not completely sure if it was the flower or Caleb. "Thanks for stealing me a flower, Caleb. That was sweet."

He grabbed my hands, and a small jolt of electricity hit me. I wanted to pull away, but his grasp was firm.

"So what do you say to that date now?" he asked.

"Now? I...I can't now, Caleb. I'm sorry, but I promised my roommate I'd be home after classes today."

"Not *now*, Cassie. I meant now that we've shared your love of greasy burgers, and you know I'm not a serial killer planning to do crazy things to your body."

The blood rushed to my face at the mention of him doing anything to my body, but his eyes never strayed from mine. It was how I measured honesty and trust in someone. Not that I judged completely on this trait, but it helped me get an idea of them. His eyes were so clear; it was as if I could see straight to the truth of his words. He wasn't a serial killer, I trusted that, but he held a lot of power with those eyes. And even though I really didn't know Caleb, I did know the power was hard to resist.

"I *still* don't know if you're a serial killer. In fact, I hardly know anything about you, other than you're from Texas, you came to Waitling for law school, and you live above your uncle's garage. That's hardly enough for me to compare with serial killer profiles. I mean, did you set any fires when you were a kid?"

His grin widened. "Oh, more than you know, just not the kind of fires you're thinking of. How about I tell you all about them over dinner? No greasy burgers this time, somewhere nice."

I knew I shouldn't even consider bringing someone else into my unstable life at the moment, but I really wanted to see him again. I felt a connection to him that was indescribable, but it was definitely there. I wanted to know more about him. Was I being too reckless going out with a man I just met?

"I would really love to go out with you tonight, but I promised my roommate we'd do something together. As a matter of fact, I have to get going. I told her I'd be home about an hour ago. How about I call you?" I shot him a playful grin. "I haven't thrown your number away yet."

"How about I walk you home, and we can pick a date on the way?"

"You don't like to take no for an answer, do you?"

"No I don't," he said with a squeeze of my hands.

"Well, I guess I don't have a choice then, do I?" I pulled my hands from his and turned to walk down the block toward my apartment.

We walked side-by-side the entire way back. He didn't try to hold my hand, or anything else, which I appreciated. We decided on meeting for dinner the following night. I had to work at the hospital until five. The plan was for me to go straight to Luke's. Caleb was working until seven, but he was certain his uncle would give him a break.

My apartment building was a multi-unit complex divided into several two-level buildings, each with its own parking garage and several entrances for easy access to everyone who lived there. I lived on the second floor, half the distance between the entrance and the end of the building, so we had neighbors on two sides. It wasn't a bad location except for the fact that our apartment overlooked the parking lot instead of the woodsy view on the opposite side of the building.

When we reached the entrance door Caleb turned to face me. He took my hands in his, as he had done in the park. The stimulation from his touch was more familiar and not as shocking to my body this time. "I really had a great time with you today, Cassie. I'm so glad we ran into each other, although I'm sure you would have called me anyway." He winked. "Right?"

"Of course." I smiled. "And I'm really looking forward to dinner tomorrow night. I'm glad we—"

My words died as I watched Caleb's gaze shift over my shoulder. A scowl came over his face. I turned around just as Hunter came out of the other building's entrance door and walked through the parking lot toward a row of cars.

"Is that...Hunter?" I asked, squinting.

As if he'd heard me, Hunter twisted his neck gave a nod in our direction, before getting into a black Mustang.

"What is he doing here?" I asked quietly, more to myself than to Caleb.

"I was thinking the same thing," Caleb murmured.

Hunter rolled past us in the mustang. Caleb tensed next to me, his jaw tight and fists clenched, as he glared at the driver. I could practically feel the anger emanating from him like a wave of heat.

The car's taillights were eventually out of sight, but Caleb's tension did not wane. I touched his arm, afraid he may violently snap from his own body's rigidity, but it seemed to soften immediately from the light contact. He looked at me, eyes focusing on my face, as he clamped his hand over mine.

"Look," he said with a sigh. "I know you probably think I'm being overprotective of you, but I would feel a lot more comfortable if you'd let me walk you up to your apartment."

He appeared uneasy. About what, I had no idea. But it seemed to have something to do with Hunter.

I scanned the street off the parking lot. There was no sign of Hunter's Mustang. But the tingling sensation I had on the back of my neck was giving me the willies. My independence argued with me, but my nerves won out. "That's fine. If it will make you feel better."

After unlocking the door, Caleb followed me up the flight of stairs and down the hall to my apartment. "This is it," I said, turning toward him. "Thanks for walking me up."

"Is your roommate home?" he asked.

"Yes, her car was in the lot. She should be here."

Caleb nodded. An awkward silence came over us, and I noticed how close he was to me. My breathing became heavier as he took another step toward me, putting us mere inches apart.

"Okay then, Cassie. Goodbye."

His face moved in. The air between us was fully charged, and I held my breath as his lips hovered over mine.

The door to my apartment sprang open, and I nearly fell inside, but Nora broke my fall as I crashed into her. Dazed, it took me a few minutes to realize what happened. I was both furious and grateful for the interruption of the potential kiss with Caleb.

"Oh my God. Cassie, what are you doing lurking at our door?" Nora ran a hand over her shirt, as if brushing out any wrinkles our collision may have caused. Since she was wearing a cotton tank top and a pair of boxer shorts, so wrinkles were highly unlikely. When her eyes fell on Caleb, she said, "Oh, I didn't realize you were with someone. Hi, I'm Nora." She extended a hand out to him.

Caleb studied Nora. There was nothing sexual about his examination, more like he was trying to figure out if he knew her. The same look a person got when they ran into someone they knew from long ago and couldn't remember their name.

"Caleb." He took her hand and shook it. "Nice to meet you, Nora."

"Now I understand why you were lurking, Cassie," Nora said with a smirk.

"Shut up, Nora. Caleb and I met at school. Well, actually we met at Luke's last night and then ran into each other at school today. We got to talking, and he was nice enough to walk me home. What were you doing?"

"I was checking to see if our paper came. I thought I heard the delivery guy at the door."

"Uh huh," I said, before facing Caleb. "Well, I guess I'll see you tomorrow night then." I stuck my hand, not willing to pick up where we left off with Nora around.

He grabbed my hand, pulled it up to his lips, and lightly kissed my fingers. "I'm really looking forward to it, Cassie. Goodnight."

Enchanted, my hand slowly drifted back to my side as I whispered, "Goodnight."

He shot Nora a smile. "It was a pleasure to meet you, Nora. Have a good night."

"Good to meet you too, Caleb. Bye."

I stayed in the hallway listening for the front entrance door to shut with its familiar clunk. When I knew Caleb was gone, I squared up with Nora, hands on my hips.

"Okay, what gives?"

CHAPTER SEVEN

"What?" Nora made a feeble attempt at claiming innocence.

"What were you doing out here, Nora Hawthorne?"

"I told you, I was checking to see if our paper had come."

"Nora, I live here. We don't get a paper. Now 'fess up." I pushed her back into the apartment and closed the door.

Avoiding me, Nora went to the cupboard and grabbed a wine glass. She held it up, raising her eyebrows, her tacit invitation for me to join her. I nodded, and she grabbed another glass, along with a bottle of wine from the cabinet. She filled the glasses without a word.

"Well? Spill, Nora. Were you spying on me?"

"What? No, of course, not. I was just as surprised to see you guys at the door as you were to see me."

"C'mon, Nora. I've lived with you for two years now. I know all about your nosey neighbor habits."

I met Nora in one of my undergrad classes when we were paired up for a psych project. We hit it off from the start. She asked me soon after we met why I disappeared so much, and I told her it was a long, complicated story that I'd tell her about someday. She never asked again, accepting me with all of my absences and stand-ups without questions or complaints. I often thought about telling her, but was too afraid of losing the only other person in my life, who accepted me for who I was, or at least, whom she thought I was. People had a tendency of shying away from what they didn't understand. We knew everything about each other, aside from that.

"Okay, you got me," she said, laughing. "I *was* being a nosey neighbor, but not to spy on you. I heard voices earlier coming from the empty apartment next door, so I decided to see what was up. When I got out into the hallway, the property manager was out there with this gorgeous hunk of maleness. Of course, I stuck my tail between my legs and ran back inside before they could even say, *Hey, Nosey Neighbor.*"

As talkative and outgoing as Nora usually was, she seemed to lose all sense of formative words when it came to good-looking men. Unless she was all dolled up, she lacked the confidence to initiate anything. Her shoulder-length, blond hair was piled on her head and there were no signs of makeup. She was never less than beautiful, but it was definitely not a look that would have given her the confidence to strike up a conversation with the hunk she claimed was next door.

Hunk next door looking at the empty apartment? Could it have been Hunter? It would explain why he was at the complex. There were only two apartments open, one next door, and the other in the building next to ours...the building he'd come out of.

"So when I heard voices again," Nora continued, "I planned to go out and apologize for being such a rude potential neighbor. I didn't want to scare this one—"

"Nora, what did he look like?"

She flinched at my sudden change in demeanor. I was sure she could see how tense I'd become.

"I only saw him for a minute, but he was tall and muscular, not bulky muscle though, you know? Um...short dark hair, a little messy on top. Oh, and his eyes...they were the bluest I've ever seen in my life. When he turned to look at me, I nearly lost my breath."

No doubt about it, Hunter had been next door with the property manager. He was looking for an apartment? And it just happened to be in my complex? I was freaking out. Maybe Caleb was right, and I needed to be careful. Who was this guy? I made a mental note to talk with the property manager in the morning and see if she would give me any info on him.

"So what's the big deal?" Nora asked.

I wasn't ready to tell her about Hunter. I could see her going straight to the cops if I told her I'd met him, as well as Caleb, at Luke's yesterday, and they both mysteriously showed up in my life today. Nora didn't like to take chances. Not that I did, but I had a little more going on in my life to relate to these coincidences. I had to find out for myself first. It was better to keep her in the dark until I knew more. I hoped the info my mom was tracking down would shed some light on all of it.

"Oh, nothing." I waved it off, moving toward the couch with my wine in hand. "I just saw the same guy coming out of the other building while I was in the parking lot tonight. He must be looking at both apartments." Well, at least I hadn't lied completely. I sat down, placing my wine on the end table next to me and picked up the remote for the TV.

"Hold up there, sister." Nora came around and sat next to me, putting her hand over mine on the remote before I could turn it on. "Are you sure that's it? You looked pretty freaked out when you asked me about him. You sure you don't know him?"

Nora was good at reading me...too good. I had to tread carefully unless I wanted to tell her everything. If I told her even an ounce of it, she wouldn't be satisfied until she knew the whole thing. I hated lying to her, but as usual, when it came to my secret life, I had no choice. I wasn't proud of it, but I was pretty good at it.

"No, at least, not that I know of. I only saw him from across the parking lot, so I can't be positive. He didn't look familiar. I was a little weirded out about seeing some guy in the complex I'd never seen before, that's all."

Nora searched my face. "Okay, if you're sure there's nothing you want to tell me then." She left the statement as more of a question.

How I longed to answer her with the truth and spill my guts, ask her to take everything on with me. I was so close to doing it, knowing her willingness to accept anything I confided in her. I just couldn't.

"There's nothing to tell, Nora. Really. That was it."

"Okay, then." She removed her hand from mine and took a sip of her wine. I did the same, not out of thirst, but to hide my shame about lying to my best friend.

"Well, I *did* see this guy, and I sure wouldn't mind that eye candy living next door to us. Speaking of eye candy, what's the skinny on Caleb?" she asked with excited anticipation. "Did I hear you are actually going out on a date?"

I gave a little laugh at her high school antics. "Yeah, we're going out to dinner tomorrow night after I get done with my shift at the hospital. It's no big deal really."

"No big deal, huh? When's the last time you were on a date, Cassie? Seriously, this guy must have *really* charmed you. I've seen you turn down the *hottest* guys. So, give it up. What's this guy got?"

I knew it was coming. There was no way she was going to let me get away with being so blasé about a date I had finally agreed to, after not doing so for eons. But to make her squirm, I said, "So pizza and a movie tonight? I think the new *Saw* movie is available. What number are they on again? Fifty-five?"

Nora and I loved to turn out all the lights in the apartment and watch slasher movies that scared the crap out of us. Although, after the things I'd seen lately, I wasn't sure men in masks were as frightening as they used to be.

"You will get *nothing* until you bare your soul on Caleb, Cassandra Cosgrove."

Hearing her call me Cassandra made me think of the way Hunter said my name at Luke's. It had been so sensual coming from his lips, creating waves of pleasure throughout my body. How could mere words spark such a reaction within me?

"Heellooo." Nora snapped her fingers in front of my face.

I came out of my trance, and put my knee up on the couch, facing Nora. "Okay, okay," I said with a sigh. "What is it with people and their bribery today?"

"Huh?"

"That's how Caleb got me to go for lunch today, but I'll get to that." I proceeded to tell her how I met Caleb at Luke's last night, and worked my way through the story until she found us at the door. The only parts I left out were the ones that had to do with my dreams and Hunter.

She appeared satisfied, and even happy, with my confessions. "So, is he taking you somewhere nice?"

"I think he mentioned something like that."

"Uh oh. That means you have to get dressed up for this little shindig. I'm all over that. God knows what you'd come up with."

"Whatever." I gave her a nudge, blushing because I knew she was right. It had been a long time since I'd needed to dress up for anything. I didn't have a clue as to what to wear. Nora could transform even the plainest caterpillar into a beautiful butterfly. I had no doubt she'd have me looking no less than perfect for my date with Caleb.

After ordering pizza, we talked about school and our jobs, simple, normal things between friends. Nora joked more with me about my date with Caleb. I didn't mind; she had a way of making me forget all about the abnormal things center stage in my life. We got more serious when it came to my concerns over getting involved with someone at a time when I felt I couldn't fit anything else in my life. I told her I only wanted to concentrate on school and my career, without interference. She eased my concerns, advising me to simply have fun on the date and stop thinking so much about where anything would need to fit in.

"If fate would have it this guy belongs in your life, there is nothing you can do about it," she told me.

Fate. I thought about the irony of it. I controlled the fates of others, but what was my fate? Would there be someone to help me if I were to take a wrong step? Was it possible for me to be a Guardian of my own fate? I would never know any of the answers unless I took a chance.

"I guess you're right," I told her.

"Of course I am." She laughed. "Hey, I finally got my painting back from being framed. I want you to check it out and see if you think it would look good in here. Be right back." She ran to her room.

Nora was a true artist. Her paintings amazed me. Every one she created was ten times more beautiful than the last. We already had several of them hanging on the walls throughout the apartment.

While she was gone, the apartment buzzer rang. Assuming it was the pizza man at the door, I yelled to Nora that I was going to run down and get it. We never buzzed anyone in, not with all the crazies in the world. A few minutes later, I was setting the pizza on the breakfast bar, when I realized Nora still hadn't come out from her bedroom, unless she had during the few minutes it took to get the pizza. Either way, she wasn't in the living room and neither was the painting. Just as I was going to call out to her, she stepped out of the bedroom, her jacket on and purse and keys in hand.

"Where are you going?" I asked.

"I'm so sorry, but I got a call from one of my project partners and she's freaking out. Our project is due tomorrow, and she forgot to get my notes, which directly correlate with her section of it. I'm so pissed. I hate people who wait until the last minute."

"Do you want me to put the pizza in the oven and wait until you get back?"

Nora groaned. "I hate to do this, but we are going to have to reschedule our night, hon. I'm so sorry. She lives like halfway across town, and I'm going to have to explain some things to her. She's not the brightest crayon in the box, so this could be awhile."

"That's okay. Not your fault. We'll do it another night. Go do what you need to do."

She was already halfway out the door as she said, "I'm really sorry, Cassie. But at least I got to meet your new man. And we can talk more when I'm helping you get ready tomorrow, right?"

"Absolutely. Now get out of here and do your Good Samaritan deed for the night." I waved her out the door and shut it behind her as we said goodbye.

Not knowing what to do with myself now that the night we'd planned was cancelled, I grabbed a slice of pizza. Then I took a seat on the couch and turned on the TV. I found a channel showing *Silence of the Lambs*, but it wasn't on for another half an hour. I decided to pass the time until the movie started by reading a magazine. As I got up to get one, my phone rang.

Praying it was my mom finally calling to let me know she was all right, I grabbed the phone from the breakfast bar and read my mom's name on the display.

"Mom, where are you? Are you okay? I've been trying to call you. Why haven't you answered?"

"Cassie, calm down. I'm fine. Sorry, I haven't called before now, but I've been in areas without reception. I should only be a few more days. I'm meeting with someone tomorrow who should have some answers for us, and then I'll be home. Everything okay there?

"I saw another one of those men, or whatever it is, again."

"You mean like the passenger of the car?" she asked, fear in her voice. "With the eyes? Where?"

I didn't like hearing my mom scared, but the more information she had, the more helpful it might be in getting answers.

"He...it...was at school, following some guy. It stared me dead in the eyes. The guy almost fell down the steps in one of the buildings. Luckily, someone caught him before he went down. There was no way I could get to him in time. Just like the last time, the thing was gone before it all went down."

There was silence on the other line for so long, I thought I lost the connection.

"Mom?"

"I'm here, Cassie. So this guy was saved then?"

"Yeah, by this other guy I know. He happened to be walking up the stairs at the time." I didn't want to bother my mom about Caleb. I'd tell her about him once she got back and we got everything sorted out, if there was even anything to tell. Dinner with Caleb could end up being a complete bust.

"That's odd. You've never had one saved by someone else before. You said you knew him?"

I guess I wasn't going to get away with keeping Caleb out of it after all.

"His name is Caleb, and I met him the other night. He goes to the law school at Waitling. We had lunch today. He seems pretty cool. Nora met him tonight and agrees."

"Nora met him?" she asked.

"Yeah, briefly when he walked me to the door tonight. Why?"

"Oh, nothing. I just think Nora is a good judge of character. I value her opinion. Is that it then, Cassie? Did anything else happen? I need to get going, the call is going to cut off soon."

"But you haven't told me anything yet. Where are you? Who are you meeting?"

"I'll tell you everything when I get back, I promise. Now, I have to go. Be careful, baby. Try to stay low until I get back, okay?"

"Yeah, Mom. I will," I murmured, disappointment clear in my voice.

I listened to silence for a while after my mom hung up. I hated that she kept things from me. Waiting for answers was the worst.

Not much in the mood for the movie anymore, I decided to take a quick shower and go to bed. The day's confusion exhausted my mind more than my body. I wished for a peaceful night of sleep before drifting off.

CHAPTER EIGHT

I woke up the next morning feeling refreshed. Glancing at the clock, I realized why. I'd slept almost a full eight hours without any dreams to wake me. It was something that hadn't happened in a while. It was still fairly early, and I had a few hours before I had to be at the hospital for my shift, so I went for a run.

Near the apartment complex, there was a trail bikers and runners frequented in the warmer climates. Only the die-hard runners could be seen on it in the winter months. It ran alongside a small creek for about a mile, ending in a park, with a loop-around to bring you back onto the path. It was a great two-mile jog that I used to run daily, but lately, school and work had become my excuses not to go.

Feeling the euphoria of the run about a half-mile into it, I vowed to make sure I squeezed it back into my daily routine. With music in my ears, I reveled in the smell of morning, which always seemed to be so fresh, as if not yet tainted by the day. The trees off the path were hinting of fall, their colors promising bright reds and yellows before the world turned white. My mood easily blended in with my bright surroundings, reminding me of the pleasant things in my life, instead of the doom and gloom that had monopolized my thoughts lately. I wanted to make the most of the nostalgia.

My mind wandered to Caleb. The familiar settings reminded me of our lunch in the park and sparked fresh feelings of my newfound interest in a man. I thought of the way he made me feel when he directed his gorgeous smile at me, and the flirtatious innuendoes. Coming from some men, it would have had me launching a physical attack, but coming from him, it sent little wings fluttering in my belly. I smiled to myself over the reaction I had to the flower he gave me; how its scent smelled so much stronger than any other flower I could remember.

I was coming up on the loop in the park, still wrapped up tight in my own reverie, when my mind went blank, as if all thoughts had been swiped from my mind, and my focus forced back to reality. Had I not been thrust from my daydream, I would have collided right into Hunter.

Stopping abruptly in front of him, I could barely catch my breath. His calm demeanor seemed a complete contrast to my pounding heart. I got the impression Hunter didn't wear his reactions for everyone to see. He appeared to be the kind of man who kept his emotions completely under control.

"Cassandra, what a pleasure to see you here this morning," he said, as if he were in the park every morning, and I merely happened to show up one day.

A smile brightened his face as his eyes roamed over my body. The heat had not yet set in on the day, but my body felt as if the sun were high in the sky, shining its thermal rays directly on me. The running shorts and tank top I wore clung to me, burning my skin and highlighting every curve. In a self-conscious gesture, I pulled the tank away from my chest, only to have it land right back. All I managed to do was draw his attention directly at my breasts, which he shamelessly observed.

If I would have been able to catch my breath, I might have said something about how rude he was, but my breathing only seemed to accelerate with his attention. He, on the other hand, appeared to be perfectly content standing there in the worn blue jeans that hung casually from his waist and hugged his hips. The lightweight, black T-shirt did little to cover the muscles of his chest and biceps underneath.

"Cassandra, you look like you need to sit down. Are you okay?" One hand gently grabbed my elbow as his other arm wrapped around my waist. I flinched from his touch, and he withdrew his hand from around my waist, but kept his hand at my elbow.

Finally finding my voice, but still a little breathless, I said, "Oh…no…Hunter, I'm fine, thanks. You surprised me. I was in a zone. What are you doing here?" I pulled my arm down, releasing his hold of my elbow.

"I was checking out the area. I'm contemplating getting an apartment in the complex I saw you and Caleb at yesterday, and I wanted to see what the neighborhood was like. Here, come and sit for a second." He pulled at my wrist, leading me toward a bench off the path.

I tried to pull back. "No, Hunter, I'm fine. Really. I have to get to—"

"Cassandra, your heart is racing and you still can't seem to take a full breath. Sit." He pulled harder at my wrist, forcing me to sit next to him. I didn't notice my heart was beating as hard as it was until I looked down at my chest and saw it rapidly rising and falling. Our knees were inches apart as our bodies angled in, slightly facing one another. The closeness, and the fact that I was half naked, did little to dispel my anxiety.

"I'm better now, thank you." I tried to ease back on the bench, but there was little room left on my end. "You know, I was really surprised to see you at the apartment yesterday. What's with the change of heart? When we met, you said you were only passing through. Now you're going to rent an apartment?" *And in my complex, no less.*

He laughed. "I told you, Cassandra, I like what I see here."

I didn't want to look him in the eyes, but I did. His penetrating gaze hinted that location wasn't the real topic of our conversation.

"Yeah, but I thought you were merely—"

"Hitting on you?"

"No, I was going to say kidd—"

"I was."

"You were kidding? Then why are you looking at—"

"I was hitting on you."

It took me a moment before my brain processed his quick response, and when it did, I was still at a loss for words. I must have looked like an idiot with my mouth hanging open, which I only realized after I noticed where his eyes had fallen.

Well, this was awkward. I was looking my worst, sweat dripping down my face (and other unmentionable areas), sitting with *the* most gorgeous man I had ever met, and he just told me he'd been hitting on me. Someone had to be playing a cruel joke on me, or some higher authority was testing my willpower. There was no other explanation. My life was a wreck, and all of a sudden, two hot guys were either asking me out or hitting on me. What were the odds of that? None to one, because I didn't believe in happenstance. Something was going on.

"Look, I'm flattered, Hunter. I really am. But I don't have time for someone in my life right now."

His features revealed nothing—no disappointment, surprise, or even comprehension. I only received a cold, hard stare. "So where does Caleb fit in?"

"Caleb?" I had no idea what was going on between us, and even if I did, there was no way in hell I was sharing it with Hunter.

"Yes, Caleb. I saw you two at the apartment, remember? What were you doing with him?"

His penetrating eyes stayed riveted on mine. I felt the urge to squirm from them, but I stayed my ground and stared right back.

"We ran into each other at school, and he walked me home. It was nothing." Why did this guy make me feel so defensive? And why was I telling him *anything*?

"Did you kiss him?"

"What?" I couldn't believe his candor. Unfortunately, my brain reacted to his question, and I pictured the near kiss between Caleb and me, broken up only by Nora's interference. I could feel my cheeks heating from the memory, and I hated the effect Hunter seemed to have over me. I don't know why I cared what he thought of my reaction, or the near kiss with Caleb, for that matter, but I let out a resounding, "No."

"Good."

Hunter's lips were on mine so fast my brain refused to process how wrong it was. My first reaction was to gasp, which his tongue took complete advantage of. Each caress sent shock waves through my body as his tongue sensually mated with mine. My mouth had a life of its own, seeking pleasure in the dance. I breathed in through my nose and his powerful scent, a mix of lavender and musk, intoxicated me. His hand plunged through my hair and grasped the back of my head, keeping me locked in his hedonistic torture.

He groaned inside my mouth, a deep, vibrato tone that pulsated through my body. I opened my eyes to find him watching me intently; so much so, he might have been able to read my forbidden thoughts. When he smiled against my lips, I came my senses.

I pushed against his hand at my head, but it wouldn't budge. Bringing my hands up to his chest, I pressed against the hardness beneath my palms, but I was no match for his strength. Finally, he released his hold of me, and allowed me to pull away.

"What the hell do you think you're doing?" I yelled, standing and backing away from the bench.

He continued to sit, a smirk on his face, as composed as before he kissed me. How could he be so damn calm? Did nothing affect him?

Hunter's smile faded, his features tightening into a humorless expression. "Setting the bar."

Clenched fists against my thighs, I restrained myself from battering them at his face. "What bar? This isn't a competition. I barely know either of you."

Hunter stood and moved toward me. I stood my ground and faced him, proving I wasn't some weak-kneed girl. If he only knew how contrary to that kind of person I really was. I've seen and dealt with much more than a lot of women...*no*...*people*, have in an entire lifetime. I wasn't going to back down from some cocky male who thought a kiss could make me melt like a schoolgirl with a crush. Granted, it was the most electrifying kiss I'd ever felt in my entire life, but how dare he think he could oblige himself on me that way.

He was inches away from me, forcing my gaze up to see his face. Being so close, the strength of his compelling scent anesthetized my resistance. I opened my mouth, forcing myself to block out the seductive fragrance. His eyes fell back to my mouth, and he slowly leaned closer. I closed my mouth and tensed, but did not move. I was determined to remain in place and show him that, although he took me by surprise before, I could withstand his attempt at seduction.

His face stopped so close to mine I felt the wind of his breath when he said, "Do you want to know me, Cassandra?" Even the sound of my name came out as a caress. I had to get out of there.

"You know what, Hunter? I think I do know you. I know your type, and it's usually the kind I try to stay away from." I turned to go, but he grabbed my arm and spun me back around. Colliding with his chest, his hand pressed into my back as his other grabbed underneath my chin, forcing me to look up at him.

"I guarantee you won't be able to stay away from me. And I'm definitely not the type of man you've ever met. I will take great pleasure in teaching you all about my kind, and I promise you, Cassandra, you'll take great pleasure in learning it."

Once again, his lips were on mine, but I was quicker to block his tongue from my mouth. He quietly laughed into my lips right before his tongue taunted them, promising them great things if they were to open. After several failed attempts, he pulled away.

"We'll start our lessons soon. But I think I'll wait until you ask me to teach you."

"You conceited ass," I spat. "What makes you think I'll ever ask?"

"You *will* ask. Of that I'm sure. You've had a taste, and you'll crave more." His head moved quickly to my ear. "Until your next lesson..." His lips suckled my neck, right below my earlobe. He seemed to know exactly the right spot to kiss, sending goose bumps down the left side of my body. Closing my eyes, my head tilted to the right, giving him more access. But instead of feeling the pressure of his lips on my tender skin, cool air passed over the area still moist from his tongue's wet trail.

I opened my eyes from the sudden withdrawal to see him regarding my features, which I was certain revealed the pure ecstasy he had me in. I expected a smug response, lapping up my weakness, but instead, I saw the same look of desire mirrored on his face, along with a hint of surprise. It only took a moment for the self-satisfied grin to take over his expression, though. He let go of me, and I stood limp, my composure not ready to take control yet.

"Goodbye, Cassandra," he whispered. "I look forward to your next lesson."

I opened my mouth to speak, not really knowing what to say, but it didn't matter, because he walked away without giving me the chance.

I didn't remember seeing another soul throughout the entire scene with Hunter, so luckily, there was no one around to witness me stumbling back and melting into the bench. My energy was drained. It could have been because my heart rate had been on overload the whole time I was with him. Or maybe he was so powerful he'd sucked it right out of me. With everything else going crazy in my life, it wouldn't have surprised me. I certainly *felt* powerless against him.

As I sat there, lifeless, on the bench, I thought about how relieved I was Hunter was gone. But in the next instant, I sat wondering what the next lesson entailed.

CHAPTER NINE

I don't know how long I sat on that bench in the park, or how I even got home, for that matter. My thoughts were consumed by Hunter's lips on mine, his tongue taking complete control of my mouth and my senses, his hard, powerful body pressed against me, and his promises of more to come.

Still in a daze when I got home, I checked the clock and realized how much time had passed. I wanted to take a long, hot shower and rub away the effects of Hunter's touch from my skin before I had to be at work, but as luck would have it, there was no time. I was in and out before the water even had the chance to heat up. Ten minutes later, I was out the door.

Park Hill Hospital was about a half hour ride from my apartment. It was a smaller community hospital, so it wasn't overwhelmingly busy, needing fewer personnel than the metropolitan hospitals in the bigger cities. Most of the staff, including the doctors and nurses, had grown up in town, so there was also a sense of hometown pride and camaraderie at work. That was one of the reasons I put in to intern there.

After high school, I realized that, like my dad, I was drawn to the science of psychology. I figured if I were going to be saving souls anyway, I might as well save their minds too. Attending the local university, I majored in psychology and found I was a natural at it. As part of the second year requirements for Waitling's PsyD program, I decided Park Hill's Behavioral Health ward would be perfect for my internship. In three years, I planned to be a doctor like my dad.

Most of my time was spent shadowing the psychologists and psychiatrists at Park Hill. I would go with them through their daily routines of seeing patients, researching, and diagnosing. Some days, I attended seminars or workshops as part of both my curriculum and the doctors' normal activities.

With five interns in the Behavioral Health ward, which corresponded with the number of doctors, we rotated week to week, in order to experience the different methods of practice in action. I had my favorites, but I got along with all of them. I didn't mind the seminars, workshops, or research either. Even though it was similar to being in school, the sessions were geared more toward advanced methods in the field. I loved working at the hospital—watching the way the doctors helped patients, seeing therapy sessions in a live setting. My dream career was so close. I was grateful for being able to get a taste of living it.

When I was at the hospital, I really put my mind to watching and learning. There wasn't a lot of room for daydreaming, so I counted on my shift to get my mind off the morning with Hunter. My brain had completely surrendered to the memory, and I needed to plow myself into my work-studies to bring me back to reality. Fate, however, had another plan.

When I checked in with my intern supervisor, Grace, she informed me that my clinical mentor had called in with a bad sinus infection. I was given filing duties for the day. With no choice but to perform the banal task, I went over to the administration desk where the files were kept. Kelly, the day shift administrator, was at the desk and smiled when she saw me coming.

I met Kelly my first day at the hospital. She was one of those bright and cheery women…every minute of the day. Somehow, she managed to find the good in any bad situation. My mood always lifted when I was around her.

As I got closer to the desk, Kelly became…brighter. A fluorescent purple headband separated her pale blond hair at the top of her head. The color pattern seemed to overflow to her uniform: a yellow smock shirt, patterned with big purple circles, and matching purple pants. As if that weren't enough to make me wish I'd brought my sunglasses, she accessorized with a matching set of bright yellow and purple parrots dangling from her ears, along with a charm-filled bracelet. Eccentricity was a trait that matched Kelly's personality.

"Hey, Cassie." Kelly waved at me, her bracelet tinkling with the movement. "I heard you got stuck with the files today. I'm sorry." Her face contorted into a silly frown.

"Yeah, lucky me." I came around to her side of the desk and glanced around. Three huge stacks of files sat on the end of the desk. "Are these the files?" I asked. "Hasn't anyone done them in the last year?"

"Sorry, hon. But think of it this way, you get to spend all your time with me." Kelly smiled wide. "It'll be great. Think of it as a sleepover party, only without the sleeping part. Oh, and the part about the files. I don't think I'd ever have a filing game at one of my parties, but who knows?"

I laughed. "How do you do it, Kelly?"

"Well, it's a secret, and I'm really not supposed to tell anyone"—she leaned in closer and whispered—"but all you do is pull your lips up and try to touch them to your cheeks. It's called a smile, and it's great at parties."

"Okay, I get it. Maybe I'll give it a try." I laughed again.

Kelly and I talked about everyday things in our lives, like school and family. My thoughts eventually drifted away from Hunter as we chatted, and the day went on. About halfway through my shift, Kelly went on break and left me alone to continue filing my last stack. As I reached into one of the rotating files, my mind went black, and I felt the familiar sensation of a vision.

My reoccurring dream was back; only this time, it wasn't me.

Nora ran through the forest, while branches reached out, tearing her dress and cutting her feet. I tried to yell as she turned to glance over her shoulder, but she couldn't hear me. I was strictly a spectator. The same emotions I felt, time and again in the dream, were evident in her features. And just as I'd hit that wall of a chest, so had she. I gasped when I saw Hunter slowly lower his head toward hers. My heartbeat quickened at the sight. Although I knew he couldn't hear me, I yelled at him to stop. To my surprise, he stopped right before his lips fell on hers. I stared at them…at him…holding Nora. He slowly raised his head, and I screamed as glowing blue eyes bored into mine.

Huddled in a corner underneath the desk station, I woke up to Kelly shaking me, calling my name. Realizing my eyes were open, she breathed a sigh of relief, but the concern on her face remained.

"Oh my God, Cassie. What happened to you?" she asked, grabbing a box of tissues from the desk.

I used one of them to wipe my tear-streaked face. There were no words to explain what happened, at least not without getting me locked up in one of the rooms on the ward, but I was too perplexed about what I saw to care about what she thought.

"I'm sorry, Kelly," I said, standing. She moved to put her arm around me, but I sidestepped and moved around the desk. "I…I have to go. I'm sorry. Could you…could you cover for me with Grace? I need to go take care of something."

"Why don't you let me call someone for you, Cassie? I don't think you should go anywhere by yourself right now."

"I'll be fine, just please cover for me, Kelly. I'll explain everything to you later, I promise. I'll be all right. I need to go."

Not waiting for an answer, I took off. Kelly would cover for me, but I felt horrible putting her in the position. I'd have to deal with her later, however, because making sure Nora was safe was my only priority.

***

I drove through the city, not bothering to check my speed. When I pulled into our parking lot, I spotted Hunter's Mustang. It was parked close to the building. The dread I felt earlier from the vision reinvested itself in my stomach.

After pulling up next to his car, I jumped out of mine. Wasting no time, I raced into the building, up the flight of stairs, and down the hallway to my apartment. All the way home, images of Nora lying on the floor with Hunter leaning over her lifeless body had flitted around in my head. Praying to God that wasn't the case, I held my breath and opened the door.

The scene I walked in on was far from the morbid segment I imagined, but it was just as shocking. Nora was sitting on the couch, a glass of wine in hand, and laughing...*no*, giggling. The dread transformed into complete disgust when I noticed Nora's eyes twinkling as she gazed at Hunter, like a mesmerized groupie backstage at her favorite rock concert. Tunnel vision had obviously blocked out everything around her, because she didn't notice I'd walked into the apartment.

But Hunter did. His back was to me as he sat on the opposite end of the sofa, but I sensed he acknowledged my arrival. I felt it in every tingle making its way through my body.

As he pushed up from the sofa and turned to me, Nora watched his every movement. His eyes met mine, and the tingles turned into laps of fire, igniting the memory of his lips on my neck. When his scent hit my nose, I reflexively took a deep breath, inhaling it into my body.

Nora stood, and I shook off the wave of sentiment, refusing to let him take over my senses again. I was about to launch a verbal attack on him, when Nora came toward me.

"Oh, Cassie, I wasn't expecting you home so soon. Um...this is Hunter." She stood directly in front of me, blocking my view of him, and mouthed *that's him*, with eyes wide and a smile on her face. As Hunter moved closer, Nora turned to face him. "Hunter, this is my friend, Cassie."

"Cassandra. I'd say we must quit meeting like this, but it's a pleasure to see you again." He smiled as he took my hand and brought it to his lips for a soft kiss.

"Wait, you two know each other?"

I snatched my hand back, and quickly glanced at Nora. She didn't appear to have noticed my reaction. I didn't want to cause a scene. Not here. Not now. I wanted to find out what Hunter was up to.

"We met at Luke's the other night," Hunter explained.

Please don't bring up the park. The mere mention of us meeting in the park would be enough to put me off balance.

"And we ran into each other in the park again today," he continued. I think I actually heard myself sigh. "Cassandra gave me great insight as to what to expect if I were to move into the area." The double entendre slammed into me, and the smile on his face proved he knew it.

"Oh yeah? So what'd you tell him?" Nora asked. *Was that suspicion in her voice?*

I wanted to tell Hunter to get the hell out and leave us both alone, but I was speechless.

Hunter laughed. "Actually, it was much the same as the conversation we just had, Nora."

His words sunk in, and I wondered if they could possibly mean what I thought they did. Had he really done the same things with Nora as he did with me in the park? Could he be playing both of us? I was irate at the thought of the possibility, and maybe even a tad jealous.

He hadn't taken his eyes off of me, and I could almost see the challenge in them.

"Well, now you have both our words on it," Nora said, breaking the silence that had ensued. "It really is a great area. I think it'd be perfect for you."

"I think you're right, Nora. If it truly is a quiet area, with plenty of friendly people, then I think it will be perfect. I like the fact it's not far from anything I might need."

It felt safe to assume they were only talking about the neighborhood. I didn't sense any sexual tension between them. I was relieved to think Hunter hadn't tried anything with Nora.

"That's great, Hunter. Let us know if we can do anything else to help. We'd be happy to. Right, Cassie?"

"Uh...yeah...right."

Nora gave me a secret *what's up with you* look. Hunter, on the other hand, appeared to fully enjoy my discomfort.

"Did you say you met at Luke's?" Nora asked Hunter before turning back to me. "Isn't that where you met Caleb?"

There was no getting out of it now. She knew, and there was nothing I could do about it.

"Yeah, we all kind of met that night." I said it as if it were nothing more than mere coincidence. I walked around Nora and Hunter and went to get a glass from the cupboard. I was hoping my nonchalance would help Nora believe it was no big deal. But when I turned around, her eyes were wide with surprise.

"Wow, really?" she asked Hunter more than me. He nodded. "That is *wild*. What are the odds of that? Cassie happens to be going out with Caleb tonight for dinner."

Obviously, she believed in chance a lot more than I did.

I was getting water when Hunter's voice made the hairs on my arms stand.

"Oh really?" he asked with too much interest. I hadn't realized how close he'd come to me while my back was turned.

"Hey, I have a great idea," Nora said, moving next to Hunter on the other side of the breakfast bar. "Why don't Hunter and I join you guys tonight? That way we can all show him around town. If Hunter wants to go, of course. Oh, and if you don't mind, Cassie."

"I...uh...I'd..."

"I'd enjoy that," Hunter said, the now familiar smug smile directed at me. "If it's not too much of an intrusion on you and Caleb, that is. I'd hate to spoil your night with him."

I didn't believe him for a second. The vibes I was getting told me he would enjoy every minute of spoiling an evening between Caleb and me. When I glanced over at Nora, she had the biggest smile on her face. I didn't want to let her down, but I also didn't feel comfortable spending an evening with Hunter.

"Well, I'd have to check with Caleb," I said.

"Oh, you're gold. He's got it bad for you. I'm sure he'll go along with anything you say." Nora laughed, nudging me playfully.

Hunter appeared no longer amused. His full lips flattened, anger replacing his self-satisfied expression.

"I just don't know if he planned something special for the two of us tonight. I don't want to ruin anything he may have set up already."

"Oh, I get it, Cassie," Nora said with a grin. "You want to be alone with him. Well in that case—"

"In that case," Hunter chimed in, giving me a pointed glare before turning back to Nora, "how about I treat *you* to—"

"It'll be fine, Hunter," I said quickly. "I'm sure Caleb will understand. Why don't you meet us at Luke's at five-thirty." Nora and Hunter regarded me, him with a smug smile, and her with curiosity. If I didn't bring them with Caleb and I, Nora would go out with Hunter alone, and I didn't trust him. After all, he'd already lied to her by keeping the true nature of our encounter in the park from her. If he were going to be around Nora, I wanted to be there. Maybe this would give me a chance to figure out what he was up to anyway.

"How about I pick you two lovely ladies up at five o'clock instead? We can all ride together."

I argued, but Nora won out, thinking it a great idea.

"Well thank you both very much for making me feel so welcome," Hunter said. "I've got some things to get done before tonight. I'll see you both later."

He extended a hand to Nora, but she put her arms around his neck and gave him a hug. "No need to be so formal with me, Hunter," she told him. He looked a bit surprised, but hugged her back. She wasn't exactly coming on to Hunter; she hugged everyone.

"Fine with me." He smiled.

When he came to me, I held my hand out, but he decided to use Nora's act of friendliness to embrace me instead. The stubble on his face tickled my cheek as he squeezed me tight.

Hunter left, and Nora let out a girlish squeak once the door closed. "This is going to be so much fun. Do you realize this will be the first time since we've gone out on a double date since we've known each other? Hell, neither of us has been on a date in forever." Her enthusiasm suddenly changed when she noticed I didn't share her enthusiasm. "Oh, hey, Cassie, I'm so sorry. Are you sure you're okay with this? Really, if we're raining on your parade, we can go somewhere else. I only thought it might be fun for all of us to go out together. I guess I didn't give you much—"

"Nora."

"...of a chance to—"

"Nora, it's fine, really. It'll be great."

"Are you sure? You looked upset there for a minute."

"Yeah...no, it's good. I was just thinking about what the hell I'm going to wear tonight." It wasn't my wardrobe that consumed my thoughts, it was Hunter's whispered words in my ear as he hugged me goodbye. *Lesson number one, Cassandra. I always get what I want.*

CHAPTER TEN

I stood in the living room, thinking of what Hunter's words meant to me. It made me uneasy to know he'd planned to weasel his way into going to dinner with Caleb and me tonight, *and* that he succeeded. If he always got his way, as he claimed, what was his ultimate plan? Would I be as helpless to stop it as I was tonight and in the park? Would I even want to?

He obviously intended to continue with his *lessons*, and I was afraid to think of what they could progress to. I hated myself for being both horrified and curious about them at the same time. But I couldn't ignore the way he set my body on fire with his touch, leaving me feeling like a drug addict, knowing the high was so wrong, but needing another fix.

"Did you call Caleb?" Nora asked, breaking me out of my internal banter. I searched around for my purse. Nora pointed at the breakfast bar, where I'd left it sitting when I came in. "Guess that's a no. You want me to call him?"

After grabbing my phone, I held it up. "Nope, taking care of it now."

Nora went into the bedroom, and I called Caleb.

"Do *not* tell me you are canceling on me or I'm coming over there right now to kidnap you," he said upon answering.

I giggled. "No, I'm looking forward to it. But look, Nora kind of begged me to let her tag along with a date." Nora peeked her head out of her bedroom and made a face at me. "I told her it wouldn't be a problem, but I wanted to check with you."

I held my breath waiting for the ball to drop, expecting him to tell me the whole deal was off and that would be the end of things. I heard nothing for a minute or two, and I could almost feel the hesitation in his silence.

"You know what, that's fine, Cassie. As long as I get to be with you tonight, that's all that matters. I'll just call Celestino's—"

"*Celestino's*. Wow, Caleb."

"I told you I wanted to see you in a dress."

Celestino's was one of the finer Italian restaurants in the area. A couple of years ago, some famous food critic came in and gave it rave reviews. Apparently, this critic didn't hand them out lightly. Ever since then, reservations were hard to get, especially on the weekends. Sometimes you had to book almost two weeks in advance to get a table.

"What time is the reservation for?" I asked.

"Six o'clock. I'll call and change the reservation to four people. How about we meet there, though? I may be a little late. It's pretty crowded here this afternoon, and I don't want to leave my uncle to tend to this himself. The reservation is in my name."

My heart swelled at his desire to be with me even though I'd changed our plans at the last minute. I checked off understanding and easy going on my *reasons to date Caleb* list. But it also made me feel like scum knowing I was leaving out the huge detail of Hunter being one of the people coming to dinner. Hopefully, he would find a way to get over it and enjoy the evening with me anyway.

"Okay. Thanks for understanding, Caleb. We'll see you at six. Can't wait."

"Same here, Cassie. I'll see you soon."

"Oh, wait, Caleb, you never told me your last name. I assume I'll need it for the reservation if you're not there."

"It's Walker."

"Caleb Walker. Got it. See you then."

After hanging up, I went to Nora's room. She was knee-deep in clothes inside her closet.

"Nora, just pick something. You look good in anything you wear anyway, so what does it matter?" I laughed at her as she continued to fan through the remaining dresses hanging on the rod.

"Oh, I already know what I'm wearing. I'm looking for *you*." Holding a dress in her hand, she grabbed at another and turned. "Okay. Red…"—she held up a skimpy, spaghetti-strapped contraption I wouldn't be caught dead in—"or black?"

Since the black one was much less scanty, I pointed at it.

The dress was made of a flirty chiffon material that seemed to sway in a breeze of its own. Its sleeveless, halter-style straps met in light folds of material at the cleavage. A beautifully detailed, satin and jeweled belt banded around the middle, cinching the waist to reveal hourglass curves on the right frame, before ending in wavy fabric right above the knees.

"Chicken," Nora taunted for my conservative choice. "Well, if that's the case, then you have to wear those shoes I bought you last year with it."

My smile faded as I pictured myself attempting to decipher the strappy puzzle that made up those shoes. "Only for Celestino's will I endure that kind of suffering."

"Caleb made reservations for Celestino's? Ohhh, I like this guy, Cassie. If you don't take to him, can I have a shot?"

I threw a shoe at her that found its way across the room, where she was working on some kind of de-cluttering system.

"So he's cool with me and Hunter coming?"

"He's okay with you and a date. I didn't tell him Hunter was coming. They didn't seem to hit it off very well at the bar the other night. There was tension between them for some reason."

"They know each other?" She threw a dress on the bed.

"They both say no." I shrugged. "I don't know, must be a man thing."

"Well they'll have to check their attitudes at the door if I'm going to Celestino's tonight. Nothing can spoil my mood there." Nora stood with her hands on her hips. "You ready?"

"Is it going to hurt?"

With a roll of her eyes, she shook her head.

Nora turned out to be a pro at transforming me into what she termed, *her masterpiece*. In a matter of minutes, she managed to put my hair up in a stylish twist of waves, with a few pieces left to dangle around my face. While she went to get ready herself, I put on my makeup.

While finishing up in my room, Nora rushed in. Taking her breathlessness for excitement, I admired her ruche, form fitting, purple dress, which fell to right above her knees. The criss-cross style of the bodice accentuated her full breasts, before the thick, jeweled straps pulled up and tied at the back. Her stylish honey blond hair hung just short of skimming her shoulders. Her green eyes seemed brighter than usual, probably from the purple hue of the dress. I was about to tell her how stunning she looked when I realized the look on her face was not excitement. She looked terrified.

"Hey, what's up? What's wrong?" I stood and went to her.

She held up her hand. "I'm sorry, Cassie, but I have to go. Something's come up, and I have to leave right now. I don't have time to explain. If I can, I'll meet you guys at the restaurant." She quickly left the room, and I followed her.

"Wait...what? What the hell is going on, Nora? You're scaring me."

"I'm fine, I just...I have to go...I'll call you and let you know what's going on, I promise." She was out the door before I could say anything more.

I stood in the middle of the living room, one shoe in my hand, wondering what just happened. My heart was beating fast and hard in my chest. What made her leave so unexpectedly? Sitting on the couch in my dress, still holding onto the shoe, I tried to piece together a hint of reason for what just took place. Scenarios, both good and bad, played out in my head. I lost track of time and place, until the door buzzer jarred me out of my stupor.

Glancing up at the wall clock, I saw it was almost five. As I went to the door, I wondered if Caleb had gotten out early and decided to come pick me up. I didn't feel much in the mood for going anymore, being too worried about Nora, but she said she'd try to meet up at the restaurant, so I put thoughts of getting a rain check out of my head.

I pushed the speaker button on the wall.

"Hello?" I greeted.

"It's Hunter. You ladies ready?"

Oh, crap. Nora didn't call him to tell him about the change of plans.

"Actually, Hunter, Nora had to run out unexpectedly. She might not even make it. Sorry for the change of plans so late. I thought she would have called to tell you."

"I see." His tone was calm, as if he were unfazed by the news.

Just as I was about to say goodnight, he asked. "Are you and Caleb still going?"

"Uh...yes." I didn't want to tell him Nora might meet us up there. It was none of his business anyway. *If* Nora showed up, she could call him then. With no guarantee she was going to make it, I had an out.

"You said she *might* not make it. Does that mean she said she would try?"

Damn. "Well, yes, but she may not come at all. I'm sure you don't want to be a third wheel."

"But if she does make it, then *she* will be the third wheel. Cassandra, buzz me in. I won't talk to the door anymore."

I felt much safer with doors, walls, and stairwells between us, but I gave a sigh and buzzed him in anyway.

A minute later, he was at the door knocking. I opened it, but blocked his entrance. I didn't want to be alone with him in the apartment. After a long appraisal of my attire, and quite possibly what was underneath it from the way his eyes seared into me, he stepped toward me.

"Hello, Cassandra," he said, his voice deep and husky.

I stepped back to avoid being too close to him. He smiled and stepped around me.

Closing the door, I turned to him. "Hello, Hunter," I said with irritation. "So, like I said, Nora had to leave. She probably won't make it to the restaurant. Maybe we can do this some other time." I squirmed under his intense gaze. Why did he have to look at me as if he were trying to see to my very soul?

He shook his head, tsking me. "I'll go in case she shows up. I'd hate for her to be that third wheel you spoke of if she's able to make it. What happened, anyway?"

I moved to the couch, resigned to the fact he wasn't going to give up. After sitting, I grabbed one of the devilish sandals, which I was determined to conquer. "Not sure. She left so quickly she didn't have time to tell me. She said she'd fill me in later."

"Has she ever done that before?" he asked, standing next to the couch, looking down at me.

"What? Left when we had plans? Yeah, plenty of times, but I do it a lot too, so I don't get too upset when it happens. We're kind of the same like that." I paused for a minute as I thought about what I just said. *Could she be...no, that wasn't possible, was it?*

The couch stirred beneath me, and I realized Hunter had come around to sit near me. His eyes were on my chest, which I hadn't realized had become slightly exposed as I leaned over, struggling with the straps of my shoe. I sat up quickly, causing the shoe to fall off my foot.

With a hand to my chest, I made sure the dress was back where it should be. I could feel the quick rhythm of my heart beneath it, while my breath kept the same pace. I needed to gain my composure, but his presence was overwhelming me again.

"Yeah...so...the reservations are for six at Celestino's. It's one of *the* best rest...aur...ants..." My voice faded as I watched him reach forward and grab the shoe from the floor in front of me.

"Well, I guess we better get going then," he whispered as he held the shoe in his hand and reached for my leg with the other. I drew in a hard breath as his hand grazed down my calf, raising it, and then placing my foot in his lap. My calf burned from his touch, and the heat made its way up my thigh, before settling between my legs. He moved the shoe into his other hand, cupped the back of my ankle, and began to gently guide it onto my foot.

"What are you—"

"At the rate you're going with these, we'll never make it to dinner. Although, I'm not opposed to staying here all night and helping you with your accessories." He chuckled as he held my foot tighter when I tried to tug it free. A minute later, he had the straps expertly in place.

I snatched my leg from his lap and put it down on the floor, shocked at how quickly he had mastered the complicated straps.

"Uh...thanks." I reached for the other shoe.

He moved to do the same, but I held my hand up to ward him off. "I can manage this one, Hunter."

His smirk fueled my anger. All I wanted to do was get the hell out of my apartment. The walls seemed like were closing in on us, and apparently, my mind no longer controlled my body.

I fumbled with the shoe, but my fear of him taking over again made me determined, and I managed to work it out after a few minutes. I stood and moved to walk past him, but he jumped up in front of me and grabbed my wrist, swinging me around to face him. Caught up in his gaze, I braced myself for the magnetic pull, but it didn't come. I could sense he was fighting with himself. He was breathing harder, and his grip on my wrist tightened. I peered down when I felt a sting of pain, and he eased up, but didn't let go.

"Why do you fight your feelings, Cassandra?"

My chest heaved with the adrenaline pumping through it. It pissed me off that he assumed I had feelings for him at all. I snatched my wrist from his grasp.

"The only thing I'm fighting is the urge to slap you. What makes you think you can put your hands on me?"

He didn't even twitch from the anger pouring out of me.

"I apologize, Cassandra. I assumed you didn't mind. In fact, I thought you enjoyed it, just as you did in the park."

"I didn't—"

His cocky expression challenged me to finish my lie.

"*Ugh*. Let's just go, okay?" I stomped away, grabbing my purse off the counter and yanking the door open.

"As you wish." He walked past me and into the hallway, smiling the entire way.

The car ride was silent, aside from my blunt directions to Celestino's. I was fuming from our argument, if you could call it that. Sure, I was mad at him for being so damn smug and taking liberties he shouldn't, but I was angrier with myself for allowing any of it to happen without protest, which came after it was too late.

I tried to push all my anger aside in order to enjoy the night with Caleb, but my mind kept sneaking back to Hunter's expertise with my shoe.

"Hunter, how is it you can handle a pair of women's strappy sandals better than I can?"

He laughed. "Ahhh. Therein, lies another lesson, Cassandra. There are a lot of things I am an expert at with women. I'd be happy to show you all of them."

Blushing from his candor, I dropped my gaze to my lap.

Hunter placed his hand on my thigh, and I quickly shoved it off me. When I saw the smile on his face from my reaction, it reignited the fire of my anger.

"How about I give *you* a little lesson about *me*? Maybe all of the women you know, or have known, like it when you molest them. But you touch me again without my permission, and I'll make sure I wipe that shit-ass grin off your face. And that goes for Nora too." I sat straighter in my seat, feeling my backbone growing stronger. It felt good and was long overdue.

"Understood, but know this," he said, his voice confident. "You *will* give me your permission, and I promise you'll be the one with the smile on your face."

I threw my head back, closed my eyes, and breathed an exasperated sigh. "This is hopeless," I whispered. "*You're* hopeless."

CHAPTER ELEVEN

The atmosphere at Celestino's was exactly what I imagined it to be. I forgot all about Hunter lingering beside me as I looked around the spacious, but cozy room. Guests sat at candlelit tables, eating, talking, and laughing amongst themselves. Those that weren't, simply gazed across the table at one another, their eyes communicating everything that needed to be said, while their fingers grazed each other's to keep the physical connection.

The smooth brick wall at the back of the room stood out against the other three rich, mahogany ones, but only in texture, as they all harmonized in their deep brown tones. Scenic Italian decorative plates hung stylishly around the room. The only lighting came from pendant fixtures hanging randomly from the ceiling. Their soft, brushed glass created more of a radiant glow than stark illumination. There were a few windows lining the north wall, allowing only slivers of the outside into the restaurant. Linen curtains were pulled back, revealing old wine bottles placed strategically on their sills.

It was a dim, romantic ambiance that welcomed us immediately. Unfortunately, the lighting also made it difficult to tell if Caleb was seated at any of the tables. I squinted to get a better look, but as far as I could tell, he wasn't there.

As I approached the hostess' podium, I noticed the young woman behind it was having a hard time keeping her eyes off Hunter. In fact, she was blatantly ogling. I looked behind me to see if he'd noticed, and immediately realized the allure he held over her. How I missed how breathtaking he was, I'd never know. Maybe I was too keyed up in my apartment, or maybe it was the lighting in the restaurant, but there was a glamour about him that was undeniably sexy and magnetic.

The dim lighting caused the slight stubble on his face to appear as shadows defining his chiseled jaw, indicating his strength and power. His dark hair, in combination with the shadows, made his eyes look like glowing spheres of blue, possessing magical qualities of being able to see straight to your inner thoughts. He was dressed in a black suit with a crisp, white shirt, unbuttoned to reveal the tip of a white undershirt, while emphasizing the tan skin of his neck and face. The suit sculpted his body as if it were tailored only for him, inviting a woman's eyes to slide slowly over the length of him and appreciate every moment of it.

The smile he wore proved he knew more than one female in the restaurant was admiring him, including me. His confidence was natural, but held a mysticism that pulled at your inner spirit to be near him. He had the features of a movie star and the dark power of the bad boys your mother warned you about but you couldn't help yearning to have. In one word, he was delicious. It took sheer willpower for me to turn away from him. When I finally did, the hostess appeared content to pursue her admiration of Hunter. I cleared my throat to get her attention.

"Welcome to Celestino's." She greeted us with what was probably her biggest smile of the night, presumably more for Hunter's sake than mine.

After confirming with Natalie, as her nametag read, that Caleb had not arrived yet, she seated us at a table in the middle of the room. It was elegantly decorated in white, from the plates to the candle sitting in the center, as well as the tablecloth they all rested upon. Off the center, a vase sat, holding a beautiful spray of flowers and splashing vivid colors of reds, pinks, oranges, and yellows onto the bright white setting.

I moved to the chair furthest from the front of the room, in order to watch the door for Caleb. When he came in, I wanted to be the first person he saw at the table, hoping to start him off in a good mood before seeing Hunter. Hunter quickly moved in behind me, and I stiffened until I watched him pull the chair out for me. I relaxed as I sat; embarrassed I had assumed he was up to no good.

He pulled out a chair next to me. I would have preferred he sat across the table, but being the only two there, it made it easier for us to talk. By the time we were situated, a waiter came by to ask what we wanted to drink. Hunter took it upon himself to order an expensive red wine, and then the waiter left us alone.

An awkward silence fell over us, the kind that happens when two people are thrown together who have no idea what to say to one another. I couldn't stand it, so I picked a safe subject that wouldn't encourage anything that might make me more uncomfortable than I already was.

"So, what did you think of the apartments, Hunter?"

He placed his elbows on the table and leaned his chin forward to rest on his hands.

"I've already signed the lease. I move in this weekend."

The surprise on my face couldn't have been more shameless if he had told me he was a woman and eight months pregnant.

"What?"

The waiter, oblivious to the conversation he was walking in on, brought over our bottle of wine. Hunter nodded to him when presented with the bottle and continued to go through the ministrations of properly tasting the wine for approval. He refused to look in my direction until after the waiter had poured us each a glass, promising to return soon for our orders.

"I'm sorry, Cassandra. Now, what was your question?"

"When...uh...how did you manage to get in so quickly? I mean, moving usually takes weeks."

"The apartment was empty. The landlord was eager to start getting rent. And I'm a quick mover."

"I'm sorry. That was rude of me."

He gave me a friendly smile. "No problem. I can see how it would seem rather sudden, but I don't have a lot of personal relations with whom I have to contend."

"Oh? What about family? Friends?"

Hunter's head turned as the waiter walked up again. Why was it that when I *wanted* an interruption I couldn't find a soul in sight? The waiter asked to take our orders, but I explained we were still waiting on one, maybe two more people. He agreed to come back when he saw one or both had arrived.

"Where is Caleb, anyway?" Hunter asked. "It's a half hour past the reservation. That's not very good manners for a first date. Maybe you need to start considering other options." He sipped his wine, as if his bold statement was a simple matter of fact.

"He told me he might be late, Hunter." I took a sip of my own wine. "And if having one point against him was cause for dismissal, you'd be a distant memory already." I almost tipped my glass over, realizing what I'd said.

"Does that mean you consider me an option? I'm flattered, and I accept."

And then there was the smirk, which I deserved for my stupidity. I decided the best way to change the direction of the conversation was to avoid it all together. "He's working. They were really busy at Luke's and—"

"Hunter," Caleb's stern voice came from the front of the table. I hadn't even heard him walk up. "What the hell are you doing here?"

He was staring Hunter down, and now I felt the need to defend him as well. Caleb may not have liked Hunter, but there was no reason to be outright rude to him when he'd done nothing wrong. Yet anyway.

"Hello, Caleb," Hunter answered evenly. "It's nice to see you again too. I heard you were working. How was it?"

As Hunter and Caleb stared each other down, the air between them became so thick it settled under my skin. My eyes darted between them, trying to gauge what was really going on. Caleb stood ramrod straight, fists clenched at his sides, jaw working overtime as it clamped his teeth together. Hunter, however, never moved from his chair, still casually resting his chin on his fist. His eyes, on the other hand, defied his posture. They were liquid steel aimed at Caleb, silently challenging him.

"Work was hell," Caleb sneered.

Hunter stood quickly, barely knocking the chair over behind him. I followed suit in anticipation of breaking up whatever was going on between them. My heart was racing from the unexpected turn of events. I thought there might have been some animosity to overcome, but this was far beyond how I imagined it would play out.

"Cassandra, you need to call Nora right now," Hunter said, sounding lethal, his eyes still glued to Caleb's.

The tone of his voice scared the hell out of me. And the fact that neither of them had flinched from their stare-down was freaking me out. What did Nora have to do with any of this?

"Wait...what? Why? What the hell is going on, Hunter?"

"Damn it, Cassandra, call her now," he yelled.

"I'm not calling Nora until you tell me what is going on," I yelled back.

He growled, grabbing my purse from the floor.

"*Hey*. What the..."

Hunter rifled through my purse. After finding my phone, he punched at the buttons.

"Hunter, tell me what's going on. What do you want with Nora?"

He ignored me, listening to the phone before throwing it down with a curse.

It was then that I noticed Caleb watching the scene between Hunter and I with a sadistic smile on his face.

"Caleb?" I called out, hoping to get his attention.

The sweet, considerate, caring guy I'd been with the day before seemed to have transformed into an evil and devious looking man before my eyes.

"Caleb, look at me. Tell me what's happened. Why aren't you saying anything?"

When he finally faced me, I flinched. His eyes had taken on an otherworldly glow. I closed my eyes, attempting to clear them from the illusion I thought I'd witnessed, but Hunter pulled hard at my arm, forcing me to turn away from Caleb.

"Cassandra, I know you don't trust me, but I need you to go home right now and check on Nora." He shoved his keys into my hand. "Hurry. I'll be there soon to explain everything."

Weight bore down on my chest. Was Nora in trouble? How did Hunter know? And how did Caleb fit into all of it? I glanced over at Caleb again, hoping he'd tell me something.

Caleb came out of his mysterious spell and lunged at my arm. "Cassie, I told you not to trust this guy," he said, his features intense.

There was a whirl of movement around me. Caleb's hand was ripped from my arm. Before I knew what was happening, Hunter launched himself in front of me and faced Caleb. They were comparable in height, but somehow, Hunter appeared to tower over Caleb.

"Have you forgotten your rank, Caleb?" Hunter's voice was deadly. "If you touch her again, I'll make sure you remember."

"Consider this a rebellion," Caleb answered through clenched teeth.

Standing behind Hunter, I was blocked from seeing what was going on between them, but I felt the tension rise to the point of violence. I glanced around the room to see everyone in the restaurant focused on the scene playing out between us. Their faces were a mix of fascination and anxiety. The closer patrons had moved out of range, but no one said a word, and no one dared to approach. They all seemed willing to let this battle play out, no matter the consequences. I, on the other hand, was not so eager.

I held my breath and moved from behind Hunter, placing myself right next to their faced-off bodies, my small frame dwarfed by the two powerhouses in front of me. I planned to plant myself right in the middle of them, but they were standing too close to each other. There wasn't a breath of air that could squeeze between them. I put my hands on their arms, intending to pull them away from each other, but feeling the rigidity of their muscles, I knew there was no chance.

Voice low, but with steel conviction, I said, "Look, I don't know who the hell you guys are, and at this point, I don't even care. But this thing you have going on right now"—I wagged my fingers between them—"will not happen here with all of these people around. And if I have to—"

The air changed around me. It was like a surge of energy flowed right through me, and then there was complete silence. I glimpsed around the restaurant and screamed. Everyone had vanished. Not a single soul from the restaurant seconds ago was in sight. Chairs sat empty, in the same position they'd been when people were sitting on them.

"There," Caleb said, staring at me with a feral grin. "All fixed." He laughed.

"Damn you, Caleb," Hunter growled.

My head spun; forcing my mind in so many directions it was impossible to process a coherent thought. I became light-headed. Reality was fading fast. My eyes clouded over, and I knew I wasn't going to keep it together much longer when I heard a faint voice through the fog.

"Cassandra, get out of here, now. Go find Nora."

I wasn't sure who said it. I guessed it was Hunter, because Caleb's maniacal laughter was still ringing in my ears. The thought of Nora being in danger and wrapped up in the chaos before me was the only thing that seemed to clear my head enough to move. With Hunter's keys in hand, I ran and didn't look back.

CHAPTER TWELVE

The city was a blur as I raced through it, pushing Hunter's Mustang hard, but nowhere near its limits. I strained to still my trembling arms in order to steer. My adrenaline was on overdrive, trying to keep up with all of the emotions struggling for control. Nora was my main concern, but I couldn't stop the images of Hunter and Caleb from sneaking up on me. What I had witnessed was so far beyond unreal that I questioned my sanity, or at least, my reality. Was it possible the whole surreal scene had been some crazy vision, and I would be waking soon?

I told myself to sort it out later. I had no choice but to listen to Hunter and check on Nora, even though I had no reason to trust him. It felt like he'd been pushing himself into my life from the very first time I dreamt of him. Ever since, my life had slowly chipped away into pieces that didn't seem to fit together anymore. I was afraid if they ever came together, it would be far from the life I hoped it would be.

When I saw Nora's car in the lot, I breathed a sigh of relief. I raced up the stairs and shoved open our apartment door. The living room was empty, but there was an empty wine glass on the table by the couch.

Calling her name, I ran to her bedroom. The door was closed, and I heard her muffled sobbing beyond it. So as not to scare her, I swept open the door and called to her. She was lying on her bed, still in the dress she had on before she left the apartment. Her face was half-buried into the white pillow, which was now stained with patterns of color from the makeup running off her face with her tears.

"Oh, Nora." I sat on the bed next to her, rubbing her back with my hand. "Honey, what happened? Are you okay?"

She took a moment to gather herself, as I reached for the box of tissues by the nightstand and handed her a few. Sitting up, she wiped at her red, puffy eyes. As she peered back at me, her gaze revealed some kind of internal battle within. I was so afraid of what might have happened to her, especially after witnessing such unbelievable madness at the restaurant.

"It's okay, Nora, you can tell me anything."

"I shouldn't. I'm not supposed to tell anyone."

"Well, I'm not just *anyone*. There's nothing you can't tell me." I wondered what was so bad that she felt she couldn't talk to me about it. For the first time since I'd known her, she was scared. I waited while she debated with herself on whether or not to tell me.

"Cassie, I know what you are." She looked me straight in the eyes, gauging my reaction. Did she mean...*no*, she couldn't know I was a Guardian. Unless...

I had to hear her say it. "I'm not sure what you mean, Nora."

"I know what you are, Cassie, because I'm a Guardian too. I've known for a while."

My first reaction was complete surprise, hearing the words said out loud. In a small way, I was angry. Why didn't she tell me before? Things could have been so much different between us. We could have helped each other.

"But, how? Why didn't you say anything if you knew? I've never known any other Guardians, except for my mom. I...we wouldn't have had to feel so alone. We could have helped one another. Or, wait, do you know others?"

I always figured there were others, but never thought they'd be as close as living in the same apartment. Maybe there was a whole network of Guardians.

Nora put her head down and shook it slightly, as if in shame. "There are others, but I don't keep in contact with them, not regularly. I'm sorry, Cassie. I couldn't tell you. I was told never to tell anyone, and I never have, for any reason. Usually, it's easy to keep inside. I think of it as a job I do and continue on with my life. But tonight...tonight was different. Tonight someone died."

Nora appeared completely devastated, and I felt bad for unleashing my injured feelings onto her. I gave her a minute to let it all out again, being there for her. Once she settled down, I had to press her for more information. Putting her through anything more than what she'd been through killed me, but I had to find out how Caleb and Hunter fit in. There had to be something linking all of them together. "Can you tell me what happened?"

Her face grew distant as she relived the events that happened in the last few hours. "I had a vision while getting ready earlier. There was a guy walking on a pier down at the marina. He got pushed into the lake, hit his head on one of the docked boats, and drowned. When I got there, I spotted him walking down the pier, and I called out to him to try and get his attention. He wouldn't acknowledge me. Then I noticed he was wearing headphones, so I started running to him, but the gate was locked to get down to the piers." Nora started to get emotional again, talking faster, her voice rising. "I struggled with the lock and was about to jump the gate, when I saw him fall into the water. I couldn't get to him, Cassie." She covered her face with her hands and sobbed.

After handing her more tissues, I put my arms around her. "It's okay, sweetie. You couldn't have known there'd be a lock on the gate. It's not your fault."

I wondered then if this was the reason Hunter pushed me to find Nora. I couldn't see him caring if I was here to comfort her. How would he even know she needed comforting? He was with me the whole time. The only way I was going to figure anything out was to sit down and talk to him, no matter what torture he put me through. Remembering how he and Caleb faced off in the restaurant, I was terrified I might not ever have

the chance. And, for reasons I couldn't explain, I didn't want
Hunter out of my life.

"I haven't lost someone in a long time. I forgot how much
it hurts," Nora said into my shoulder.

"I know, Nora," I whispered. "It will always hurt, but you'll
move on and save so many more. All you can do is get some rest.
Unfortunately, the visions might not wait for you to get over this,
and you need to be ready."

She extricated herself from my arms and took the tissues I
offered her once again to clean up. Resting back against her
pillow, she said, "Thank you, Cassie. I know I wasn't supposed to
tell you, but I'm glad I did."

"I'm happy you told me. It's nice to know there is someone
else I can talk to about it. And now, I don't have to think of some
lame excuse every time I have to book out of here," I joked,
attempting to bring her spirits up.

I got a giggle from her, but then her expression turned
serious. "Oh my God, Cassie. What happened at Celestino's? You
still went right? Wait, it's only nine o'clock. What the hell are
you doing home already? Oh no, don't tell me Caleb turned out
to be some schmuck?"

I wanted to tell her everything, hoping to find some sanity
by spewing everything out to someone. But I couldn't share it
with her. Not tonight. Not when she was as vulnerable as she
was. She needed to rest and let her heavy heart ease before I
burdened her with any of it.

"Let's just say he's not the same person he led me to
believe he was," I told her, playing with the truth.

She sat up straighter, concerned. "Really? From everything
you told me, he seemed like such a sweetheart. What
happened?"

"We'll talk about it tomorrow. Right now, you need to rest.
You've had a really hard night, and I am not going to burden you

with my love life. No arguments..." I stood, pulling her comforter up. "Sleep."

"Yes, Mom," she said with a smile. "Hey, speaking of which, have you heard from your mom? Wasn't she supposed to be back from her trip soon?"

"You know, you're right. I haven't heard from her. I'm going to call her right now." I turned to leave.

"Oh, shit," Nora yelled. "I completely forgot about Hunter."

I stopped in my tracks at the mention of his name.

"I never called him," she continued. "Did he show up? He must think I'm a complete jerk-off."

I had no idea what to tell her about him. *I* didn't know what to think of Hunter. One minute I believed he was the Devil himself, and the next, he seemed to be guarding me from...*what? What was he protecting me from? Caleb? But what if I was wrong? What if it was Hunter whom I needed protection from?*

I needed answers, but I didn't know whom to trust to get them. I desperately wanted to talk to my mom. Maybe she'd have answers.

"Cassie?" Nora's voice broke through my thoughts.

I shrugged. "I figured you must have told him you weren't going to make it because he never showed up." I wasn't sure why I felt the need to lie to her about Hunter. Maybe I simply wanted her to forget about him; at least, until I found out what his real motives were with us...with me. I didn't want either of these men around her, or anyone close to me, until I figured everything out.

Nora's face dropped over what she thought was Hunter standing her up. I hated causing her to feel that way, but it was for her own good.

"Now sleep," I said. "That's an order. We'll talk about everything tomorrow. Promise."

I got to the door when I heard her say, "Thank you, Cassie. You don't know how much it means to have you here. You're...you're like a sister to me, and I love ya."

As I turned to face her, she put her head into the pillow. We never voiced our love for one another; we simply knew it was always there. But tonight was different.

Smiling at her head in the pillow, I said, "I love you too, Nora," and closed the door.

Out at the breakfast bar I went through my purse in search of my phone. Groping blindly, I couldn't find it, so I dumped everything out on the counter. No phone. I searched around, but it was nowhere. Hoping it fell out in Hunter's car on the way over, I ran to the door, yanked it open, and crashed into Hunter.

His strong arms wrapped around my body as he held me to his chest. My palms rested against him, and I could feel the solid muscle beneath the T-shirt he wore. I pulled back, but seemed unable to remove my hands. They slid down his chest of their own accord, as if making sure he was really there, while feeling every ripple on the way to his taut stomach.

The heavy pulsing of his torso caused my hands to follow along with its rhythmic beat, waking me up to the reality of what I was subconsciously doing. I tried to pull back, but his arms tightened around me. "Hunter." It came out more like a passionate sigh, than the scolding I'd intended.

I dared a look up only to find him gazing down at me with his now familiar smirk. His hips moved against me, forcing me to realize what my unconscious petting had done to him. He wasn't the only one reacting to our contact. Everything in my body was straining for him.

My eyes widened and so did his smile.

"Hello, Cassandra," he purred. "Miss me?"

CHAPTER THIRTEEN

Hunter's arrogance broke my erotic trance; however, my body defied my brain's commands by continuing to quiver from the residual sensations of lust. Blood rushed to my cheeks. Ashamed of my lack of self-discipline, I pushed against him with all my strength. He let go, chuckling.

"What the hell are you doing here?" I asked. I realized my mistake right after the words left my lips—I had his car. "I mean..."

"You left this at the restaurant." He held up my phone, his expression now devoid of any amusement. Then he put the phone in my hand and moved to come into the apartment. "We have to talk, Cassandra."

Sidestepping, I blocked him and pushed at his chest. "No, not here. Nora is trying to rest. I don't want her to hear you."

"She's okay?"

"She's shaken up, but she'll be okay with rest. It's been a very emotional night for her." I grabbed his arm, pulling him out in the hallway. "C'mon." Once out of the apartment with the door closed, a thought hit me—I never buzzed Hunter into the building. "How did you get up here?"

He reached into the pocket of his pants and produced a set of keys, jingling them at me.

"You stole the keys?" I asked.

"No. I have a set of keys because I'm moving in," he said, seemingly annoyed with my accusation. "As a matter of fact, let's go there to talk instead of entertaining the neighbors here in the hallway." He walked toward the apartment next to ours, but I froze with the reality that he would be living right next door.

"Cassandra, if you stand there any longer with your mouth hanging open, I may give the neighbors more of a show than they can handle."

I glared as I followed him to the door. "Why did I have to buzz you in earlier if you already had a set of keys?"

"I didn't want you to freak out before dinner."

"Guess that didn't work out too well," I mumbled, remembering the scene in the restaurant again.

Hunter unlocked the door and held it open. As I walked through, his hand rested on my back. "That, Cassandra, was your fault. You should never have let Caleb into your life," he said.

I spun to face him. "*Caleb*? What about *you*? You know what? Why don't we just have this out, once and for all? Why are you here? What do you want from me? And what the *hell* was that at the restaurant?"

Leaning against the breakfast bar, I folded my arms over my chest as I watched him close the door. I took the time to rein in my breath, along with my temper.

"Hell is exactly what that was at the restaurant."

"What are you talking about?"

He came over and stood next to me, leaning his elbow on the counter.

"All you need to know is that Caleb is not to be trusted."

I'd had enough of people holding out on me. Hunter had answers, and I'd be damned if he wasn't going to tell me every last one of them. Now.

Turning to face him, I got real close. "That is *not* all I need to know, Hunter. I'm sick to death of people keeping things from me. This is my life. Tonight, I saw things that had me thinking I was completely insane, and that is a hard thing to do, because I've seen a lot. So, *damn it*, start giving me some answers. You can start with why I should trust you? All I know about you is that you show up out of nowhere, tell me nothing but lies, manhandle me, and tell me not to trust the one person who seemed to be the most genuine guy I've—"

Before I could finish my rant, the counter was at my back and Hunter's hands gripped my arms. Breathing heavily, my breasts strained against my dress, drawing Hunter's eyes to the exposed skin above the bodice. As heat spread throughout my body, his gaze crawled up my neck and face until his icy blue orbs locked with mine.

"Caleb is *not* genuine, Cassandra. Do not let him fool you. If you don't believe anything I say to you tonight, at least, believe that. Promise me you'll stay away from him."

Hunter's fingers tightened around my arms as he drew me in to him. I winced from the pain, but refused to show any more sign of weakness. Stiffening my body as much as his grip allowed, I stuck my face close to his. "Tell me what Caleb is then, Hunter. *Make* me believe you. Because right now, you are no different to me than he is."

Yanking me forward, he put his lips against my ear. "The difference is," he whispered, his hot breath on my skin, "I have *you*, Cassandra." Then his lips were on my neck, suckling it, his tongue swirling over my sensitive areas. Shivers raced down my body.

Everything about it was wrong, I knew that, but the pleasure he evoked overwhelmed my sense of morality. My eyes closed with a languid flutter as I tilted my head back, giving him better access. He moaned against my skin, and my body responded, pushing against him. One of his hands slid down my arm, before it landed on my ass and molded it through my dress. His other hand was at the back of my neck, holding it in place as his mouth trailed succulent kisses along my collarbone and shoulders.

A soft cry of pleasure escaped my lips, and his kisses became more fervent on my skin. Angling my leg up, I tangled it around his hip, as his hand slid down the back of my thigh, stopping at the bend of my knee. He gently pulled at it, bringing our hips even closer together.

Cool air hit my shoulder when Hunter's lips moved back to my ear. His tongue teased my lobe for only a second, but long enough to send another shiver down my body. Once again, his breath was heavy in my ear, his words barely registering through the passionate haze he'd created. "Are you giving me your permission, Cassandra?" he murmured in my ear.

"What?" I asked on a breath.

"Tell me you want me." His hand slid up my thigh, underneath my dress.

His words finally penetrated my cloud of ecstasy, along with the realization of where his hand was headed. How did he distract me so easily? It was ridiculous the power he seemed to exude over me. I tried to move, but he held me firm, his hand tightening around my thigh, refusing to let me lower it. I pushed against his chest, but it was like pushing against a solid wall of concrete.

"Hunter, let me go."

"A deal's, a deal, my little temptress."

"I did not give you permission, *damn it*. Now get off me." I pushed him as hard as I could.

Locked in his gaze, I didn't realize he'd loosened his hold on my leg until his hand was once again underneath my dress and squeezing my ass. Glaring at the cocky smile on his face, I lowered my leg and shoved his hand away. With both feet planted on the floor, I was more stable and in control of my body. At least, I thought I was. I needed to get as far away from him as possible, but when I tried to move away, he placed his hands on the counter behind me, jailing me between his arms.

"Next time"—he grabbed my hand and placed it over the solid bulge in his pants—"you'll finish what you start, Cassandra."

I snatched my hand back and pushed at him. This time, he moved back, allowing me the space to step away from him.

"God, Hunter. I am not here to be mauled by you. I'm here to get answers. Now, are you going to give them to me or not? Because if you aren't, then I have no choice but to find Caleb and ask him to explain who, or *what*, both of you are and what you want from me." My adrenaline was pumping—from the sexual contact with Hunter, my emotions, my confusion. Unable to catch my breath, I was on the verge of tears. I'd already shown too much weakness by allowing him liberty over my body. I refused to let him see me cry.

Moving toward the door, I'd only gotten a few feet before I heard his command.

"Cassandra, do not walk out that door."

I stopped and spun to face him "Are you going to give me answers?"

Hunter leaned against the counter, folding his arms over his chest. "Yes."

I narrowed my eyes. "With words only?"

He laughed. "Sometimes our bodies tell us more than words could ever convey, but you already know that, don't you?"

"Words only, Hunter."

He gave a slow nod. "For now."

With a shake of my head, I went around to the other side of the breakfast bar to avoid any potential contact between us. Hunter moved to the refrigerator, pulled out a bottle of wine, and set it on the counter. I watched in awe as he moved to one of the cupboards behind me and pulled out two wine glasses. Strangely enough, they appeared to be the only things in there.

"You happened to have a bottle of wine and two wine glasses here?" I asked.

Hunter shot me a devious smile. "It's a rule of mine to have it available in case of special occasions. You know, like a beautiful woman in my apartment with a desire for...answers."

After opening the wine, he filled both glasses. I eagerly took the one he offered me, craving the chance to ease my nerves.

I gulped down a fair amount before realizing he wasn't going to offer up anything on his own, so I took the lead. "Why don't you start by telling me how you and Caleb know each other."

He eyed me, as if deliberating over what he was going to say. "You could say Caleb and I grew up together, but then grew apart. We still tend to cross paths through our work, however."

"What kind of work?"

With an impatient sigh, Hunter stared at me for a moment, and then nodded, as if he'd reached some kind of internal agreement. He balanced himself over the counter, leaning toward me, his shirt straining against his broad chest, defining every solid muscle. "Why don't we cut to the chase? I'm not sure how much time we have before Caleb decides to come after you again, and I need to make sure you know what side to be on when he does." His gaze was intense. "First and foremost, I am the only one you can trust, because I am the only one who can save your life."

His blunt words sent shivers down my spine. "Why would Caleb want to kill me? I'm nobody." My mind raced, searching through my life for any reason he would want me dead.

Hunter grabbed my hands, holding them across the counter. "You're wrong, Cassandra. You're special. You're a Guardian. And that's exactly why Caleb wants to take you back to Hell with him."

CHAPTER FOURTEEN

So, Caleb was from Hell and there was a price on my head. The mysteries of my life had been solved. *Wonderful*. And, of course, I had this guardian angel in front of me to thank. *Right*. Did he fail to remember he told me only moments ago he works with the hellish mercenary out to get me? Well, I sure as hell didn't.

Yanking my hands out of Hunter's grip, I knocked over my wine. The glass broke into several jagged pieces, and wine splashed out, creating a pool of red that stretched across the counter and dripped over the side. Attempting to catch the flow with my hand, I sliced my palm on one of the broken pieces. I yelped in pain, and Hunter flew up next to me. Despite my efforts to ward him off, he grabbed my hand and wrapped it with a towel.

"Are you all right?" he asked while forcing my hand upright.

"Well, other than the fact you just told me someone is trying to kill me, I'm great, Hunter. I guess a little cut is nothing to worry about when I'll be burning in Hell soon anyway, right?"

"If you stay with me, Cassandra, I'll make sure that doesn't happen. Now, sit here while I clean this up." He grabbed me around the waist and hoisted me up on the counter.

While Hunter cleaned the breakfast bar and floor, I unwrapped the towel to peek at the cut on my hand. It was worse than I thought. As I watched the blood pump out from the deep gash and drip down my arm, I became light-headed. My body swayed forward, but Hunter caught me, coming up between my legs and holding my shoulders back. Closing my eyes, I took several deep breaths.

"All right, that's it." Hunter wrapped my hand back up and lifted me from the counter. I attempted to open my eyes to see where he was taking me, but the room continued to spin wildly, forcing me to close them again. One of his arms was under my knees, the other supporting my back, as he carried me to some unknown destination. I relaxed and leaned into his body, placing my arm around his neck for support, allowing myself give in to him. When he gently put me down, it was on plushy cushioning with my head resting on a soft pillow.

Once the dizziness subsided, I opened my eyes to find Hunter kneeling next to me, offering me a glass of water. Not realizing how parched I was, I drank the entire glass. As I slowly sat up and glanced around, I realized I was lying on a lush, black sofa. A sofa that wasn't there moments ago.

I might have screamed, but the sudden brush of Hunter's fingers over mine as he grabbed the glass from my hand stopped me short.

He smiled. "Let's not do this again."

I released my grip on the glass, and he placed it on a table in front of the sofa.

"Hunter, tell me what's going on. I'm getting really freaked out here. I mean, where did this furniture come from?" My voice refused to stop trembling, as did my entire body. "What *are* you?" I whispered.

After pushing a hair from my face, he rested his hand on the curve of my shoulder. "It doesn't matter what I am, Cassandra. All you need to know is I'm here to protect you, and you must trust me if you want to survive this world."

I was so tired of not getting a straight answer. Well, technically, being told Caleb was trying to kill me was pretty direct, but I needed to know more. I needed to know why.

"I'm done with your cryptic messages. Tell me what you guys are doing here and why it involves me. Why would Caleb want to kill me? And, for that matter, why would you want to protect me?" My body felt stronger, along with my resolve, so I sat up straight.

Hunter sighed as he moved to sit next to me. Studying my face, he leaned back into the cushion, crossed his legs near mine, and put his arm on the back of the sofa near my shoulder.

"Hunter, please," I whispered, placing my good hand on his knee. "I need to know. I can't stand being left in the dark anymore." Maybe I could appeal to his sensitive side, that is, if he actually had one.

"All right," he said, looking at my hand on his knee. "I think you're much safer not knowing, but I'm finding it increasingly difficult to say no to you."

His hand covered mine and I forced myself to bear his touch. Not that the slight electrifying tingles it sent through my body were discomforting in any way. But by letting him touch me in the simplest of ways, he might see it as some sort of victory and give me the answers I needed.

"I will tell you everything you want to know, under one condition—you will not ask me how I know all of it."

Hunter's eyes were back on mine, waiting for me to acknowledge his stipulation. I nodded, prodding him to begin. His hand moved from the back of the couch to a lock of my hair, and he aimlessly wound his finger around it.

"Caleb comes from a realm called Sheol. It's a place people, such as yourself, would call Hell."

I flinched at the word. For some reason, it sounded more evil coming from Hunter's lips than it ever did in my head. "So, what, he's like a demon from Hell?"

"Yes, but he's a special kind of demon that deals only with special people. People like you, Cassandra."

"What do you mean, people like me? Because I'm a Guardian?"

His fingers continued to play with my hair. "Yes. Sheol wants to build armies of demons in order to battle the angels of Heaven for the Earth realm. Initially, they used what they call 'Core Demons' to steal people's souls. These souls were then forced to suffer eternity in Sheol as indentured servants, working to build it up and help it expand. But the angels fought back and gave mortals the ability to see these demons and save the souls they were taking."

"Guardians of Fate," I whispered, not even realizing I had voiced the name out loud.

"Guardians," he repeated. "And it worked. Sheol was at a standstill. The angels made sure there were enough Guardians to defend against the multitude of Cores. Nergal, the leader of Sheol, was so enraged that he came to Earth himself and found he could detect these Guardians. He realized it was because he was an angel. He captured one of the Guardians and tortured him, forcing him to do many things against his will, including drinking the blood of one of his Core Demons."

I drew in a breath as I pictured one of the demons I'd seen in my visions forcing his blood onto a helpless Guardian. The story terrified me. Being a Guardian, I felt a special kinship to others like me, regardless of whether we ever met. Hunter caught on to my tension and stopped playing with my hair. His fingers moved to my chin and forced it up until I met his gaze.

"Please, don't stop," I urged. "I'm okay. I need to hear this."

"You don't look okay, Cassandra." Moving his hand to my face, his fingers lightly rested behind my ear as his thumb brushed back and forth across my cheek. The tenderness of his touch felt so good that I couldn't help from leaning into his palm. Before I knew it, Hunter was urging my head toward his. We were only a breath away from each other's lips before I realized what was happening.

"No, Hunter," I pushed back on his chest. "I want answers. No touching until after I have them."

He laughed and sat back. "So that's the deal? Business before pleasure? It'll be hard, but you should know, I can hold out for a very long time."

"I didn't mean that, and you know it."

"The subconscious mind often speaks the truth. You should listen to it once in a while. Maybe then, your pleas would be for much more pleasant reasons." His fingers were back, this time lightly caressing my shoulder. I flung them away.

"Are you so sure of yourself? What makes you think I wouldn't run out of this apartment, as far away from you as I can get?"

"I'm quite certain of my abilities. If you'd only let me prove them to you, we could end this debate."

He inched his hand toward me again, and I grabbed it before he had the chance to touch me. Placing it firmly back where it came from, I glared at him. "Hunter, enough. Tell me what I want to know. Now. I won't play these games with you. Please, continue."

Laying his head back against the couch, he took a deep breath. I wasn't sure if he was preparing himself to tell me something big, or calming himself from the sexual tension that still hovered between us.

"The Guardian changed after being forced to take the blood of the Core. His soul became lost to Sheol, transforming him into one of them. But he was different. Special. The ability given to him from the angels allowed him to detect other Guardians, as previously only Nergal could do. They were able to spot other Guardians, whereas the Cores could not, and use their own blood to turn them. Nergal had created the perfect counter-attack to the angel's weapons—what he termed, a Seeker. Eventually, Nergal had enough Seekers to replenish what he lost of his army, but it's not enough. He continues to set his Seekers out to take out the Guardians, while the Cores are back to stealing the souls of the innocent. You, my lovely, are in the sights of one very powerful Seeker."

"Caleb," I whispered. Hunter silently affirmed my declaration. Shivers ran up my spine, as fear seeped into my body from a threat I never imagined was possible. I could almost feel Caleb in the room with us, focusing all of his energy into killing me. And it would be a death of the worst kind; becoming the very thing I hunted, or worse. It was far more terrifying than the end of life completely. I'd rather be gone from this world for all eternity than become a slave to Hell.

"You said Caleb is a very powerful Seeker. Does that mean he is more powerful than others?" I asked, unable to keep the fear from my voice.

Hunter leaned forward and grabbed my hands, being careful with the one still wrapped in a towel. I looked down at them, hoping to hide the fear in my eyes. I wanted to be stronger. Lately, I'd felt like a confused victim waiting for the next thing to happen to me. I wanted to take charge of my life. But how could I? How could I possibly stand up to something as powerful as Hell?

"Caleb is very high up on the hierarchy in Sheol. He is in charge of a large army of Cores, whom he directs to take out friends and family of the Guardian he has targeted. That is how he works. He makes sure the Guardian is alone and mourning the loved ones he's killed, and then he steps in to comfort them. Once he gets close enough, he turns them." The hatred Hunter felt for Caleb was evident in the black scowl on his face as he told me of his evil ways.

"So he tries seducing me, and then goes after Nora. *Oh, shit.* My mom...what if he's gotten to—"

"He hasn't, I've been looking out for your mom. She's on her way home and should be here tomorrow."

"But how—"

He squeezed my hands, avoiding the question I wasn't supposed to ask. "I won't let anything happen to you, Cassandra. As long as you stay with me, I can protect you from Caleb."

I searched Hunter's face in hopes of spotting something in his features that would tell me how he could know everything he'd explained. Or maybe, what the hell kind of entity he was. All that sat before me was the most beautiful man I'd ever seen. There were no horns sticking out of his head, or third eye in between his gorgeous blue ones. There were only the most kissable lips, set on a perfectly sculpted face, telling me he would do anything to protect me.

"But why, Hunter? Why are you protecting me? What's in it for you? Are you some kind of angel or something?"

His hand was back on my face, caressing my lips with the pad of his thumb. "Right now, I'm *your* angel. That's all you need to know."

Snatching his hand from my face, I forced it down into his lap and held it there. "No, I need to know more. I'm just supposed to trust you? You show up out of nowhere, same as Caleb, and have all these—" I waved my toweled hand around the room, gesturing to all of the mysteriously appearing furniture "—*powers*, same as him. You seduce me, *same as him*, and you won't tell me what the hell you are. No, I will *not* trust you."

He glanced down at my hand, still clamped over his in his lap. I seized it back and glowered.

"If I tell you why I'm protecting you, will you trust me then?" he asked, resting back into the couch.

"It'd be a start."

"All right, then." His eyes slid down my neck and came to rest on my chest. He reached out, and I instinctively brought my hand up to protect myself. It provided no barrier, however, as he easily pushed it aside and lifted the necklace from my skin. "Do you know what this is, Cassandra?" He fingered the ring from my dad.

"Yes. It's some kind of heirloom from my father. My mom gave it to me when he died."

Hunter's eyes fleeted away for a second before landing back on the ring.

"This ring is more than an heirloom. The jewel in this ring signifies the bloodline of a very powerful angel, and you happen to be the last descendent of this line, after your father. That makes you the most powerful Guardian...and also the hottest commodity to Sheol and the angels. You are a very popular woman, Cassandra."

Resting the ring back on my chest, his fingers lightly brushed against my skin, but my mind was too lost in a tornado of thoughts to pay much attention to the fires it caused. I was part angel? My mom told me Dad was a Guardian, but there was never any mention of angels. Did she even know?

"There must be a mistake. I'm merely a Guardian. There's no way...I mean, there's just no way. How do you even know this?"

"Uh, uh, uh, Cassandra," he chastised. "We had a deal. No questions about how I know."

"Yeah, well, I made that deal before you told me I have freaking angel blood, Hunter. I'd say that deserves a minor adjustment to the rules, don't you think?"

"No, I don't. The deal stands."

I stood, furious he could tell me something so devastating and not share any of the details. Maybe I needed to try a new tactic. "So, what? You're using my *hot commodity* status as leverage for something in your shallow life? Or, wait. You're going to drain my blood yourself and sell it on the demon market. Is that it, Hunter? You're protecting me for your own selfish, sadistic purposes?" I was in a complete rage, my entire body shaking.

Hunter shot up, grabbed my shoulders, and pulled me hard against him. His expression was grave as I fought against his rough handling. "Maybe I am protecting you for my own selfish purposes. Here, let me give you a taste of how selfish I can be." He smashed his lips hard against my mouth as his hand moved behind my head, angling it so he could devour me more.

After forcing his tongue between my lips, it violently mated with mine. The pressure was too much; I couldn't breath. But as I pushed him away, screaming how much I hated him, I longed to feel it again.

He didn't let me get far, grabbing me by the waist, forcing the lower halves of our bodies together. His erection pressed against my core, and, God help me, I wanted more.

"Maybe I'm protecting you because I don't want to lose you to anyone else." His eyes were in complete contrast to the aggressive way he'd handled me. "Maybe I only want you for myself. Would that be so horrible for you to believe?" He searched my eyes for his answer.

I didn't know what to think...or do. My heart and body were telling me one thing, but my mind was warning me not to listen to it. I couldn't make any decisions; I couldn't even think straight.

The silence seemed to gain weight between us. His expression turned hard, his lips, a thin, grim line. He pushed me away. "If I wanted to drain you, Cassandra, it wouldn't be your blood you should be concerned about."

I stared as he walked away, still too stunned to say anything. Dropping down into the couch again, I put my head back and let the world spin around me, helpless to try and sort it all out.

CHAPTER FIFTEEN

I breathed in the scent of a fresh spring morning by way of soft, clean sheets covering my nearly naked body. Shaking off the last dregs of a deep sleep, I blinked open my eyes and became completely disoriented. Glancing around the room, I tried to piece together where I was. The arrangement of the room looked slightly familiar, but I definitely did not know whose bed I was in, nor whose T-shirt I was wearing.

The sun was fighting to spread its rays throughout the room, but the blinds on the window only allowed a few slats on each side to filter in, giving the room a meager glow. The bed was huge, with four bedposts at each corner stretching toward the ceiling. I was lost in a sea of endless pillows propped up against the beautifully carved, cherry wood headboard. The patterned maroon comforter lay in a heap at the bottom of the bed, probably kicked off sometime during my sleep.

Noticing a nightstand next to the bed, I sat up, hoping to see a clock, but there was only a small lamp and a glass of water. As I peered around again, I spotted two large dressers, one on each side of the room. The dresser on the left was longer than it was high, a mirror affixed to the back, running the length of it, its edges softened by patterned wood. I caught a glimpse of my unruly, red waves in the mirror, and my attention was again drawn to the mystery of whose T-shirt I wore. I was pulling the sheet down to get a better look, when the door next to the dresser opened, and all of my questions were answered...with new ones taking priority.

Hunter stood in the doorway of a bathroom adjacent to the room. His chest was bare and my eyes were instinctively drawn to the smooth, sculpted muscles that ran from his shoulders down to his waist, where they leveled out beneath the waistband of the faded jeans he wore. Conscious of my eyes lingering a bit too long on the wonders of what his jeans covered, I brought my gaze back up to his. The smirk on his face was proof he'd caught me eyeing him too closely.

"You like?" His voice was low and husky.

As he moved closer to the bed, I pulled the sheet over my chest in a meager attempt to protect myself from his predatory gaze. He sat on the bed and rubbed his hand over the spot next to me. "I meant the bed," he said with a chuckle. "How did you sleep?"

Pissed that he was playing with me already, on top of the fact that I was disoriented and half naked, I decided the best defense was a good offense. "What the hell happened last night? How did I get in here, and *where* are my clothes?"

"Don't worry, Cassandra, your virtue is safe. If something had happened between us, you would remember it. You passed out on my couch, and I thought you might be more comfortable in the bed, so I carried you in here. Unfortunately, for me, that was it."

"And you changed my clothes?" I asked, hoping by some miracle I did it myself.

"Yes. I didn't want you to ruin your dress, so I gave you one of my T-shirts to wear. Your dress is hanging in the closet." He motioned toward a door near the bathroom.

"You...undressed me?" My heart pounded at the thought of him touching my skin while taking my clothes off.

"I closed my eyes the entire time. I was a complete gentleman about it." His face feigned innocence, but I knew he wasn't the type to worry about being a gentleman.

"Liar."

He laughed. "Okay, you caught me. But I've already been punished by the torture I was put through doing it."

I flinched from the insult.

"Do you know how hard it was to not to kiss that delectable mole you have right below your—"

I slapped his hand, which had managed to creep up and pull the sheet from my chest. The curses I threw at him only helped to fuel his laughter.

While he carried on, I glanced down to check that the sheet was secured once again, and I realized the hand I'd used to slap him was the same one I'd injured the night before, but it was no longer wrapped. The cut had healed significantly, leaving only a tender red scarring.

"The cut wasn't nearly as deep as we thought it was," Hunter said, watching me. "I cleaned it up before I left you last night."

"Uh...thank you."

I asked him the time. He told me it was close to nine, which was much later than I usually slept, but that was before my conscience had the added weight of a monstrous demon sent to take me to Hell. Brought back to the reality of the situation, my thoughts automatically went to Nora. I bolted out of bed.

"*Shit.* What if Caleb got to Nora while I was sleeping? I should have been there for her in case something happened."

I made for the closet to get my dress, but Hunter's hand caught my wrist, and he spun me back to face him on the bed.

"Nora is fine, Cassandra. Caleb hasn't been around."

"How do you know?"

"I can sense him."

"But how—" My words were cut off by the sound of my phone ringing from inside my purse, which was sitting on the dresser. I wanted to go to it, but Hunter still had my wrist. "I have to get that, Hunter."

Reluctantly, he let me go, but by the time I grabbed it, the ringing stopped. The display said the call was from my mom, and, within a minute, there was a voicemail notification. I listened to her message telling me she was back in town and needed to talk right away. She was on her way to my apartment.

I was about to call her back when Hunter came up behind me.

"Everything all right?" he asked.

"Yeah, it was my mom," I told him after turning to face him. "She's on her way over. Sounds like she has something important to talk to me about."

"I can't wait to meet her."

"What?" I thought he might be joking with me again, but seeing the serious look on his face, I was clearly mistaken. "No way, Hunter, you are not coming home with me."

"Yes, Cassandra, I am." He stepped closer in an effort to intimidate me. "I, too, would like to know what Mom found out on her trip."

Sidestepping him, I moved to the closet. "Well, then you are just going to have to wait to hear it from me. I already have too much to tell her, I'm not about to try and explain you too. Not that I have much to say on that subject anyway, since you refuse to tell me anything about yourself." I said the last part under my breath, because I knew it would be wasted on him. I realized if there were something Hunter didn't want to tell me, I wasn't going to get it out of him...yet. I'd find his weakness though, even if it killed me.

"Anyway, she'd freak—" I glanced in the closet and saw my dress and shoes, but they weren't what brought me up short. My favorite pair of jeans and black tank top were folded nicely on an upper shelf. My sandals rested on the floor next to the devil shoes from last night. "How...never mind, I don't think I want to know."

Grabbing the clothes, I went toward the bathroom to change. I almost made it in the door, when I heard Hunter pointedly clearing his throat. Turning toward him, my mouth dropped when I saw him sitting on the bed, dangling my bra from last night in one hand, and a pair of new panties in the other.

"These are my favorite," he said with a devious smile.

How in the hell had he gotten a pair of my panties? He must have gone into my apartment while I slept. Not only was I royally pissed that he'd broken into my apartment, but I was embarrassed as hell he'd raided my panty drawer.

Straightening my spine, I stomped over to him. "Give those to me." I went to snatch them from his hands, but he pulled them out of my reach, causing me to lose my balance and fall forward. Momentum took us both down on the bed, with me on top, and my legs between his.

"Have you no shame at all, Hunter? What are you, a child?" I tried to push myself up, using his chest as leverage, but he'd locked his legs around mine. It was too awkward a position to allow me to stand completely, so I remained over him, palms flat on his chest.

"Oh, no, I'm very much a man. Would you like to find out?" He pushed up on his forearms, bringing his upper body close to mine.

"Grow up, Hunter, and let me go."

"You must be forgetting one of our lessons already," he said. I narrowed my eyes, confused. "I always get what I want, Cassandra, and today, I want to meet Mom. Do we have an agreement?"

I couldn't believe he was ransoming my clothes to get me to agree with him. What a low, slimy move. But it was one that wouldn't work on me. There was no way I'd let up when it came to protecting my mom.

"You know what? Do whatever you want, Hunter. Keep embarrassing me with your innuendos, steal my clothes, ravish me, I don't care. I am not letting you come over."

Oh, shit.

Faster than I could replay the words in my head, I was on my back and crushed into the bed beneath his body. His arm pushed into the bed, raising him enough to gaze down at me. "See now, Cassandra, I told you you'd give me permission."

His words registered, but my protests were killed when his mouth came down on mine. His tongue wasted no time exploring my mouth, sensually entangling itself with my own. It made me forget any remaining protests that may have been lingering from my sense of morality. He tasted of a sweet wine, and my tongue relented, matching his hunger.

As he groaned into my mouth, my hands went to the back of his head, frantically rubbing my fingers through the short strands. Lifting his hips from mine, he nudged my legs apart and settled back down between them. His arousal pressed between my thighs, sending waves of pleasure through my body as he moved rhythmically against me. Moans tried desperately to escape my throat, only to be smothered by his wonderful mouth. I'd lost all sense of who I was, or the reality of what I was doing. There was only him and the thrill he was creating with my body. Nothing else mattered.

The back of his knuckles brushed against my naked skin as he grabbed the bottom of my shirt and pulled the trapped material up between our bodies. There was a tearing sound and I broke from his lips in an attempt to assess the damage. Hunter leaned up and peered down with me. I let out a gasp when I saw the T-shirt I wore was torn up the front. He moved a piece of the material aside to reveal my stomach and gave me a lecherous smile.

"I never did like this shirt," he said hoarsely.

Before I knew it, Hunter ripped apart the rest of the shirt, baring my breasts openly. He gazed at them, devouring them with his eyes. His smile was gone, replaced by a look of complete rapture. "You are the most tempting woman I've ever seen, Cassandra."

I took a deep breath as his hands lightly moved up my stomach, teasing me as he rested them right below my breasts.

He gazed into my eyes, and I couldn't help the rapid breaths that escaped, tortured by his lingering touch, wanting more, but unable to form coherent words to tell him so. Bringing his fingers to his mouth, he licked them with his tongue, and lightly brushed their wet tips against my nipples. My back arched in its effort to bring my chest closer to his hands. A moan escaped my lips as he finally cupped my breasts, his touch feverish on my skin.

Hunter's breath heated my chest. I waited for the sweet descent of his mouth, but it never came. When I could no longer stand the torture of waiting, I glanced down and became transfixed by his hungry gaze.

"Tell me you want me, Cassandra," he breathed. "Say the words. I want to hear you beg for me."

With each word, his hot breath caused my nipples to harden to the point of pain. I had to get relief. My entire body was on fire with need for him. I wanted nothing more than to beg him to take me completely, but somehow my conscience wormed its way into my head.

"Hunter," I said breathlessly. "No...please—"

His mouth was on mine again, choking back my rejection. Jailing my head between his hands, he caressed my cheeks with his thumbs, before pulling away to capture my gaze. "If you can look me in the eyes and tell me you don't want this...want me...then you can leave, and I'll never touch you again. Is that what you want, Cassandra? Do you want me to stop touching you?"

Staring deep into his eyes, I searched for an answer I knew he could not give me. The only thing I saw in them was pure desire; they were glowing with it. Did he see the same in my eyes? Could he see the lust I had for him? Could he see my fears? The ones of being with him, my careless actions around him, my need for him...and my latest...the fear of what would happen between us if I let myself go.

As he waited for my answer, his fingertips slid down the side of my body, leaving a trail of goose bumps. When his hand came up the inside of one thigh, I could barely catch my breath.

"Tell me, Cassandra," he whispered.

I was in a state of pure torture and utter pleasure, and it was unbearable.

"Hunter...Hunter, don't st—"

One minute I was in the throes of passion, the next I was in the back seat of a speeding car.

Scenery raced past through the window, but I recognized the city streets as nearby neighborhoods. I looked in the front seat and saw my mom intent on keeping control of the car at the high rate of speed she was driving. But it wasn't her dangerous driving that sent ice through my veins. Leaning toward her was the man I'd seen in the previous car crash; the one who'd disappeared. As he grinned, his glowing eyes stared back at me. My stomach dropped.

His gaze returned to my mom, and then he whispered in her ear. Her neck twisted to peer out the window. When I tried to spot what she was searching for, the man pointed out a bicyclist waiting at the light up ahead. That's when I realized what was about to happen.

I pulled myself up toward the front seat, screaming at my mom, warning her, but well aware my words would never reach her. With tears streaming down my face, I kept my eyes on the bicyclist, while shaking my mom's shoulder to get her attention. The light turned yellow, and the man whispered into my mom's ear again. The car jerked forward as it gained more speed. I lost it. I flung my fists at the man, but he disappeared before they hit their target.

My mom finally spotted the bicyclis,t and veered the car to the right to avoid him. When I looked up, we were headed straight for a light post. I screamed, and everything went black.

***

Hunter was rubbing the side of my face when I opened my eyes. "Cassandra, can you hear me?"

Attempting to sit up, I realized I was lying in his lap. A sheet covered my body, but it couldn't keep the chill from my skin. Hunter called to me again. I scrambled to get out of his arms, yelling for him to let me up, but he held me tight.

"Hunter, please," I cried. "It's my mom."

"Cassandra, calm down. Tell me what happened."

"There's no time. He was there with her. He's going to kill her." I managed to get out from his arms. With the sheet wrapped around my body, I rummaged into a drawer, searching for something to cover myself.

Hunter held out a T-shirt for me. "Who was there, Cassandra? Who's trying to kill your mom?"

I grabbed the shirt from him, turned and hastily put it on. Remembering my jeans in the closet, I grabbed them and put them on too. When I was finished, Hunter took hold of my shoulders and turned me around to face him.

"Who, Cassandra?" he yelled.

"It was him; the same man from the car crash by Luke's. I saw him right before the driver crashed his car into a pole and died. He was in the car with my mom too. He was—"

"A demon," he said flatly. "It was one of Caleb's."

The name hit me like a shockwave. It had been him all along, trying to get to me, playing with me. And now he was going after my mom...while I'd been selfishly concerned with my own pleasure.

"Damn it, Hunter. You said you were looking out for her. You said she'd be all right." I motioned toward the bed. "And now he's going to get to her because I...we...*this*. I knew I shouldn't have given in to you. I never should have trusted you."

Pain flashed in his eyes, but it quickly faded to an angry resolve. "I promise you, Cassandra, if anything has happened to your mother, Caleb will pay."

With fire in my eyes, I stood tall in front of him. "Don't you get it? She's all I *have*. If something happens to her, it's *already* too late."

"I will not allow you to face Caleb on your own," he said, as if it was the end of the conversation.

My blood boiled. "You know what, Hunter? I'm not asking for your permission. I can take care of myself."

"We'll see about that."

Snatching my purse from the dresser, I moved to leave when my phone rang. I scrambled to get it out of my purse, and when I did, the display showed it was the hospital. My heart dropped. I looked at Hunter with tears in my eyes, knowing exactly what the call was going to be about. With shaky fingers, I answered...and I was right.

CHAPTER SIXTEEN

Mom was taken to Park Hill Hospital and admitted to the ER. Jessi, one of the nurses, who also happened to be a friend of mine, was kind enough to give me some details over the phone as I made my way to the hospital. From what she told me, Mom had a few cracked ribs, a sprained arm, and a nasty gash on her head. More than likely, she also had a concussion, but they were running internal tests to make sure there wasn't more damage.

My mom was alive. I could breathe a sigh of relief over that much. I only prayed the test results would come back with more good news.

Hunter and I fought about how I would get to the hospital, but when he grabbed my purse and threatened to carry me to his car, I lost the battle. On the way over, however, I was adamant about him staying away from my mom once we arrived. He didn't respond to my demand, but I decided to deal with it later.

Once we got to the hospital, I rushed to the ER. Jessi was at the front desk waiting for me. She gave Hunter a curious glance, so I told her he was my driver, feeling a little redemption in the lie. Jessi appeared confused; Hunter was livid. With a self-satisfied smirk, I told him to wait for me in the lobby. Thankfully, he didn't fight me on it.

As Jessi led me to my mom's room, I remembered I hadn't called Nora to tell her what happened.

Hunter eyed me curiously as I walked back over to him. "Could you please call Nora and make sure she's okay?" I asked timidly. "She'll want to know about my mom too." My ego was brought down a notch, needing something from him so soon after I'd humiliated him.

He fed off my shame. "Of course, my lady," he said extravagantly. "Would there be anything else I can do for you?"

I gave a grunt and a barely audible *thank you* as I turned and walked away from him.

"Is she awake?" I asked Jessi as we went down the hallway.

"Yes, she's awake, but very groggy. We got her on a morphine drip to ease the pain. You'll be able to talk to her. She's very lucky, you know."

We reached mom's room, and I peered in the window to find her lying frail in her bed. Tears watered my eyes. She was there because of me. I wiped my eyes and turned to Jessi. "Thanks, Jessi. Who's her doctor, by the way?"

"Dr. Lambach. She's in good hands, Cassie." She smiled and put a comforting hand on my shoulder.

Jessi was close to my age. We'd known each other since I started working at the hospital. She treated her patients like family. When she lost one, she took it hard. I knew she'd take good care of my mom. Dr. Lambach was new to the hospital, having transferred in from out West. I didn't know much about him, but I trusted Jessi's judgment completely.

I went into the room and closed the door behind me. Mom slowly turned her head when she heard me come in. "Cassie," she said, her voice hoarse.

"Oh, Mom." I rushed to her side, crying openly. I thought I'd lost her, and I still couldn't shake the dreadful feeling it gave me. Pulling the chair up against the side of the bed, I sat and held her outstretched hand. Her head was bandaged, along with her left arm. She was lying stiff, which, more than likely, had something to do with her cracked ribs.

"Mom, you scared the hell out of me. How are you feeling?" I checked her over more closely. "Do you need anything? Can I get you some—"

"Cassie...Cassie, stop. I'm okay. Just a little banged up. Well, a lot banged up, but I'll be fine. I feel so stupid about the accident. I'm not even sure what happened. One minute, I was driving to your apartment, and the next, I was going through a red light. Then this bicyclist came out of nowhere..." Her voice broke, and I squeezed her hand. The guilt weighed on me, knowing I was to blame for all of it. If it weren't for me, Caleb wouldn't have sent his demon after her.

Mom composed herself, and then her eyes grew wide. "Cassie, there's so much I need to tell you. You...you're...your father..." Her words came fast, as if she couldn't get them out quick enough.

I thought I knew what she was struggling to tell me, so I held out the ring on my necklace, showing her the jewel. "Mom, are you talking about this? Did you find out about our bloodline?"

She stared at the ring and slowly nodded. "But how did you know? I found out from the Elders. I thought they were the only ones who knew?"

"The Elders? Who are the Elders?" I didn't think she knew any other Guardians but my dad.

Mom glanced around, as if checking to make sure no one else could hear. Turning back, she leaned slightly forward. "The Elders are a group formed to watch over the Guardians of Fate. You could call them the *senior* Guardians. They do not age and have watched over us for thousands of years. Now I know why. It's because they were created by the Heavenly Council. Angels, Cassie...like your father...and now, you. You are the descendent of Handraniel and Anael, both very powerful angels." She stopped and stared at me. "But you already know. How?"

Hunter told me about the angelic bloodline, but he never gave names. For some reason, hearing them made it more real. I was...important all of a sudden, like my life had more meaning. I wasn't simply a Guardian anymore; I was a Guardian with angelic blood. It made me different, but I didn't know how. Well, except for the fact it sent more powerful demons after me.

I ignored my mom's question, not ready to explain Hunter and Caleb until I knew more about the Elders and what else they may have said. "How do you know about the Elders? You never mentioned them before."

She sighed, leaning back against the pillows propped up at the head of the bed. After fumbling for the button on the control box near her hand, she eventually found it and hoisted the bed up so she was level with me. "I never told you about the Elders because your father told me not to, and that I was only to go to them if I thought you were in trouble."

I jumped out of my chair. "So, you knew? Dad knew? I'm confused. You told me you just found out about our bloodline."

"I *didn't* know. Your dad never told me about the bloodline. One day he sat me down and said he had to leave in order to protect us. He told me to watch over you, and made me promise that if anything ever happened, I would go to the Elders right away. It was the first time he'd mentioned them. After he told me how to find them, he left."

My mom watched me, waiting for a reaction.

I could feel how wide my eyes had become, but their display of shock was nothing compared to how the news affected me. "You told me Dad died. Does this mean he's still alive somewhere? Is he with the Elders? Oh my God, Mom, did you see Dad?"

"No, Cassie. Your dad is dead, or at least, the Elders told me he was when I went to them after he left. I couldn't stand not knowing what was going on, where he was, if he was in danger somewhere. When I finally gave in and went to them, they told me he was gone from this Earth." Her chin fell, and she sat silently for a moment as if re-living the dreadful time.

Taking her hand back in mine, I asked, "How did he die?"

Mom gazed back at me, her eyes wet from unshed tears. "I don't know," she whispered, her voice sad. "They wouldn't tell me. I'm sorry. I don't have that answer for you, Cassie. At the time, I was devastated. It was like losing him twice. I hated myself for not standing up to him or refusing to let him go. I hated myself for allowing him to die alone. But I was also grateful for what he'd done. Whatever got to him, if that's truly what happened, it didn't get to you too." She squeezed my hand.

With a smile, I leaned down and hugged her. "It's okay, Mom. I don't blame you. You did the right thing. I'm thankful I have *you* in my life, at least."

I sat back in the chair, and my mom reached out to grab my hand.

"We have to go to them now, Cassie. They told me you're in danger. There are powerful demons after you."

Attempting to ease her tension, I covered her hand with mine. "I know. They've already tried. And they failed." I'd told her more to calm her fears, but I also wasn't sure how I felt about going to the Elders for help. I needed to know more about them first.

"What? When?" she asked, terror shining in her eyes.

"Not now, Mom. You need to rest. We can talk about all of this when you feel better."

The door opened, and Nora walked in. My mom smiled at her, but the smile faded quickly. When I turned to see what had caused the change, I noticed Hunter watching us through the window. I looked to Nora, silently asking her how he'd gotten there.

"He wants to talk to you," Nora leaned in to me and whispered. "Says he's not leaving until he does."

"Cassie? Who is that? What does he want with you?" My mom was no dummy, and Hunter was far from subtle in the way he was staring at me. I'm sure it shocked and frightened her to see this force of a man waiting for me outside the room, especially with what she'd learned from the Elders. Seeing him through the window, so big and powerful, I probably should have been scared too.

"I'll tell you everything, Mom, I promise. I just have to do this...thing real quick. I'll be right back." I went to the door as

Nora took my place in the chair next to the bed. Mom called out to stop me, but I left the room and closed the door.

Not wasting any time, I grabbed Hunter by the wrist and forced him to follow me down the hallway. "I told you to wait for me in the lobby. Now, my mom saw you, and she's wants answers I'm not ready to give her. Do you have to defy everything I ask you to do?"

"Not everything, Cassandra. But it's harder for me to watch over you from the lobby. You asked me to stay away from your mom for now. I'm, at least, giving you that."

"You call lurking outside the window, staying away?" My voice had risen, causing a nurse walking past to glance our way. I took a deep breath to calm myself. "Look, my mom knows there are...*things* after me, so, I'm sure she doesn't trust anyone right now. Could you please just, I don't know, go buy a coffee or something? I won't be much longer because she needs to rest. We can go over what needs to happen next after that. Please..." I put my hand on his forearm and peered up at him.

Hunter regarded me for a moment, and then cupped my jaw with his hand, brushing a thumb across my cheek. I tilted my head into his palm, and softened my gaze on him, playing coy in order to get him to leave. Fighting with him only seemed to make him more stubborn.

After exhaling a deep breath, he removed his palm from my face, and rested both hands on my shoulders. "In the future, it will take a lot more than your beautiful eyes to get me to do something I don't agree with, Cassandra." He squeezed my shoulders. "I'm only giving in to you out of respect for what you and your mother have been through. Don't expect to win so easily next time."

"Thank you." I decided to let his ego go for the time being.

"I'll be back in half an hour." Before I knew what was happening, he placed a hard kiss on my lips, released me abruptly, and then turned and strolled down the corridor.

Grumbling, I headed back to the room.

When I reached the ER station, the nurse who'd passed Hunter and I in the hallway stood behind the desk, smiling at me. "Making up is so much better than fighting, don't you think?" she asked.

"Yeah, great," I groaned, shoving open the door to my mom's room.

I barely made it in the room when the interrogations began. "Cassie, Nora and I are both confused as to why you are here with that...Hunter guy. Actually, I'm extremely concerned. From what Nora tells me, you only met him a day or two ago. What if he's..." She stopped short, glancing at Nora.

"It's okay, Mom. Nora's a Guardian too." I grabbed another chair and sat next to them.

Mom's gaze snapped to Nora. "What?"

Nora nodded. "Yes, Mrs. Cosgrove, I am. I lost one of mine last night and got so upset I blurted it all out to Cassie."

My mom's shocked features turned sympathetic. "I'm so sorry, Nora," she said.

It wasn't long before the conversation turned back to Hunter.

"Why is he here?" Nora asked. "I mean, it's obvious his coming into your life is not a coincidence."

"He says he's here to protect me." I sounded naive as hell, but I felt the urge to defend him.

"And you believe him?" my mom asked.

"I guess, in a way, yes. I don't know. It's really just a feeling. He's the one who told me about everything. And he's already protected me once from Caleb." Remembering the scene at Celestino's, I added quietly, "I think."

"What do you mean, *you think*?" my mom and Nora asked at the same time.

I decided the best way to make them understand would be to tell them everything from the beginning—the night at Luke's,

Celestino's, and all Hunter had explained to me about my bloodline. Of course, I left out all the physical encounters between Hunter and me. I was pretty sure they wouldn't understand how any of that fit in.

They listened in awe, stunned by how much had happened to me while they'd only known bits and pieces. But those bits and pieces—Nora, losing someone, Mom with her accident— made them realize the role they'd played. They knew then, it had to be Caleb. Or, at least, I thought they knew.

"I still don't trust him, Cassie, and neither should you," my mom said about Hunter. "It's only us three now. We can't trust anyone else. How do you know he's not the same as Caleb, trying to lure you to him so he can turn you into one of them? I would think the Elders would have said something to me if they knew someone was here to protect you from these demons."

"You know the Elders?" Nora asked my mom. "That's where you were?"

"Yes, I went to them when Cassie started seeing these demons in her visions. Why do you ask? You know about the Elders?"

Nora stared at my mom, as if waiting for her to say more. "Yes, I know of them," she finally said. "I thought all the Guardians did."

"Anyway," Mom continued, "the Elders told me we needed to get Cassie to them, and that is what the three of us are going to do as soon as I can get myself out of here. Only us, Cassie. I don't trust this Hunter guy. He's not coming with us. I won't put you in danger without knowing who he really is. We'll ask the Elders about him when we get there."

I nodded. She was right, but I also felt less safe without him.

"Nora? Do you agree?" my mom asked.

"Yes, absolutely. We stick together on this."

Mom nodded, as if the plan was confirmed. "Okay, then. I'm going to call the doctor, and get myself out of—" She looked up as the door opened. "Hi, Doctor," she said with a smile. "I was just telling my daughter how much better I feel. I'd like to check out now."

I spun to gauge the doctor's reaction to the news. My stomach dropped. Caleb stood inside the room, adorned in a doctor's lab coat with a stethoscope dangling around his neck. His hands hung on each end of the instrument as he shook his head. "I'm afraid I can't let you do that, Sara. In fact, I can't let any of you leave right now. Not before we take care of business."

CHAPTER SEVENTEEN

"Caleb." I uttered his name with dread as I stood and positioned myself between him, my mom, and Nora. I wasn't sure how I could protect anyone, including myself, from a demon, but I was ready to put up a hell of a fight trying.

He moved closer to me, his smile turning more sinister as he watched my feeble attempt to play heroine. "Ahhh, Cassie. I've missed you. *Really*. I'm sad our date didn't go quite as planned, but here we are, together again."

I stood, undaunted, or at least I pretended to be, as he came less than a foot away from me.

"Well, here we *all* are now," he said, glancing over my shoulder. "I guess its true, good things *do* come to those who wait. I'm getting the three-for-one deal here."

"No," I shouted, bringing his attention back on me. "It's me you want. Leave them out of this."

"You do have a point there." Caleb's hand came up to caress my face.

I cringed at the familiar electricity his touch sent through my body. Not long ago, it was a pleasurable sensation. Now, it made my skin crawl.

"So what are you saying, Cassie? That you'll come back with me willingly if I spare the others? Will you? Because it's really not as bad as you think. You'll belong to me there, and I will give you anything you desire. Those tender moments we shared before were not a complete farce, you know. You ignite things in me that...well, let's just say I wouldn't mind keeping the flame going with you for the rest of eternity. What do you say, beautiful?" His fingers trailed lightly down my neck, his gaze following their motion. My eyes closed as the sensual touch sent shivers down my body.

"Cassie, no," my mom yelled. "Get away from—" Her words faded as Caleb waved his free arm behind me, fingering my collarbone with the other.

I turned at the sudden silence and was horrified. My mom and Nora had vanished. They didn't get up and leave; they were simply gone, just like the patrons in the restaurant. Whirling around, I went at Caleb in a rage, my fist aimed to strike. He anticipated my attack, grabbed my fist, and forced me against the wall, pinning my arms above my head with one powerful grip.

"Let's close this deal in peace, shall we?" he whispered. Before I could respond, his lips crushed down on mine.

The sudden force of his body against me, along with the pressure of his mouth, suffocated me. I needed to find a way to gain control, but I couldn't even take a breath, much less get him off me. Finally, a surge of energy swept through me, and I used all of it to free my hands from his grip. He pulled away, trying to wrestle my arms back again, and I used the opportunity to shove at his chest with everything I had. I'd never felt so much power inside of me. It burst through my arms and smashed into his chest. When he flew across the room and landed in a heap in the corner, I stared in disbelief.

I was stunned, wondering how in the hell I'd managed to send a demon from hell clear across the room. Then, out of nowhere, my body was yanked around. Instinctively, I struggled against the powerful grip on my arms, when the sound of Hunter's voice broke through my haze of confusion.

"Cassandra, are you all right?" He shook me as I stared blankly at him. "Cassandra, are you hurt?"

"I'm...I'm..."

"She would have been just fine if you wouldn't have gotten in the way again," Caleb said from the corner, standing back up. "In fact, I think she was beginning to like it." He winked.

Hunter flung me behind his body and faced Caleb. "Touch her again, and I swear to you, I will make sure you rot in Hell." His words were filled with such venom, I cringed. "You may already live there, Caleb, but I will personally make you suffer for the rest of eternity."

As I held onto Hunter's arm, I peeked over his shoulder. Caleb's sneer was pure evil, one that would make the Devil himself proud. He didn't seem concerned with Hunter's threats.

"We shall see who suffers in Hell, brother. Soon, very soon."

He disappeared while I was still shuddering from his warning.

I should have been relieved, but Caleb's final words refused to evaporate along with him, reminding me of the dream where he used the same moniker—brother. I let go of Hunter's arm and stood in front of him. His expression was unreadable.

"Why did he call you brother?" I asked, not sure if I was ready for the answer.

He stared at me, his blue eyes searching my face for something I was oblivious to. Was he looking for trust? Understanding?

"Oh my God. What just happened?" Nora cried out from over by the bed. Her and my mom had reappeared as if they'd never left.

As relieved as I was to see them, I couldn't help but be disappointed by the interruption. I kept my eyes on Hunter for a second longer before going to my mom and Nora. In that split second, Hunter let out a barely perceptible sigh.

"Cassie, are you all right? Did he hurt you?" Mom asked. She attempted to sit up, wincing from the effort. I got to her before she hurt herself any further. "I'm fine, Mom, just a little shaken up. Are you two okay?" I looked them over. "Caleb made you both disappear. Where did you go?"

My mom shook her head, but it was Nora that answered. "I didn't go anywhere. I feel like I lost time, though." Mom nodded in agreement. "How long have we been gone? Where'd he go?" She glanced around.

"You weren't gone long. I think we scared him off for now."

"Did he hurt you, baby?" Mom asked.

I reassured her I was fine again, that he'd only bruised, but my toned down version did nothing to ease her nerves. "How could he make us disappear like that?" she asked.

"It is one of the many powers of a Seeker." Hunter moved to the foot of the bed. "They remove all distractions to get the Guardian they hunt alone. Then, they seduce and turn them. Seekers have the power to make anything disappear. Those objects, or *people*, do not cease to exist, however. They are merely...on hold, if you will."

"And how would you know this?" my mom asked.

Although my mother's tone was accusatory, Hunter's demeanor appeared unfazed. "I've had experience with Seekers."

"I bet you do," she said. "I don't trust you, Hunter. And I want you to stay the hell away from my daughter...from all of—"

"Mom," I shouted over her. "Hunter's the one who scared Caleb off. He's the reason I'm still here right now. Stop this." Even though I didn't completely trust him myself, it felt wrong to let my mom attack him.

"What if he did it to have you for himself, Cassie? You don't know him any more than you know Caleb. No, I want you out of here, Hunter." She pointed at him. "Get out...*now*."

My mom winced, putting a hand to her side. She was stressing herself out too much for the condition she was in.

I went over to Hunter and placed my hand on his arm. "Go, Hunter. Wait for me in the hallway."

"Cassandra—" he started, but never got the chance to finish because Dr. Lambach came into the room. He assessed my mom's state and ordered us all out to tend to her.

Hunter left the room while Nora and I said our goodbyes, promising to be back as soon as she slept. My mom made me promise I'd stay away from Hunter, which I obliged with crossed fingers, so she'd calm herself enough to get some well-deserved rest. As soon as she was better, we'd leave and go to the Elders, hopefully with no surprises along the way.

As I left the room, I contemplated what I was going to do about Hunter. I still didn't know whether I could trust him. My mom was right; I knew nothing of who he was or what he wanted from me. He could be staying close for his own evil purposes. But there was a nagging piece of me that refused to believe that. I felt safe with him. *I was an angel, right? Wouldn't an angel be able to feel when someone was evil?* Regardless of how I felt, both my mom and Hunter were two very stubborn people. I wasn't sure I could persuade either one of them to do anything.

My head hurt from thinking about everything, and I decided I wasn't going to deal with any of it until I refreshed with a shower. I'd talk to Hunter after I recharged, tell him everything my mom told me and gauge his reaction. I walked up to him in the hallway, told him my mom was resting, and I was going to ride home with Nora.

"I really need someone to watch over my mom. I can't leave unless I know she's going to be safe while I'm gone. Will you stay?" I asked him.

"No. I stay with you, Cassandra. But I will have someone else watch over her. Someone I trust completely. Let me make a call, and then I'll follow you two back."

"She'll be okay?"

"It will be as if I were watching her myself. This man is very loyal to me."

"Great, more mystery men," I mumbled.

Motioning to Nora, I made my way down the hallway. "C'mon, Nora. Let's go home. I need a shower to wipe Caleb's scum off me."

Nora and I sat in silence on the way home. I imagined she was trying to sort out everything, same as I was, only from a different perspective. As we neared the apartment, I stole a glance at her, and my heart felt heavy from the pained expression she wore. I knew I'd probably lost some trust from my best friend. I lied to her about much of what had happened the last few days. Sure, she'd kept being a Guardian from me, but that is what we, as Guardians, had to do. I, on the other hand, outright lied to her.

Hunter stayed true to his word of following us home. There was not one car that came between us during the whole ride. We all entered the building and went up the staircase without speaking a word to one another.

"You need to give us space right now, Hunter," I said once we reached our apartment. "Give me a chance to explain everything to Nora. I owe it to her." The tone of my voice made it clear there would be no negotiation on it. He nodded and told me he'd be in his apartment if anything were to happen.

Once Nora and I were inside, I sat with her and told her everything—from my first visions of Hunter to everything he told me in his apartment.

"And you've been dealing with all of this by yourself?" she asked.

"To be honest, I really haven't had time to deal with anything. It's all happened so fast. And Hunter has been with me every step of the way."

"Cassie, do you really think you can trust him? I mean, what if your mom is right?"

"I've thought about that so many times, Nora, my head is spinning. I don't know how to explain it, but I feel this connection with him. The visions I've had of him for so long make me feel like I've known him forever, like he's always been with me. I know this must sound crazy, and believe me, I still have my doubts about him, but I have to go with my gut right now. So far, he hasn't done anything to hurt me, and I don't think he will."

Nora was thoughtful for a moment. "Is there something more to your connection with Hunter? I see the way he looks at you. Has something happened between you two?"

I cast my gaze down at my lap. I didn't know what to tell her. *Yes, when he touches me, my entire body melts into his?* How do you explain something like that, especially when it's about someone you don't know if you should trust? Love at first touch doesn't happen in the real world. Was it lust? Maybe.

Looking up at her through my lashes, I said, "We may have kissed a couple of times. But before you ask me if I think he is just seducing me like Caleb, I don't. It's like there's this power surge I can actually feel when he's near me, and I think he feels it too. It's as if we're being pulled together by some invisible force." I studied my lap again, embarrassed. "God, that sounds so corny."

After a few moments of silence, Nora put her hand on mine. "What you feel is not corny, Cassie. Feelings don't lie. I only want you to be safe. Trust is an easy thing to give until it's taken away from you."

"I know," I answered her. "I will."

"Good, because we're all in this together now," Nora said with a smile. I squeezed her hand in agreement. "Okay, then." She stood. "I refuse to sit around and wait for something to happen while your mom rests. I'm going to try and go about things as normally as I can, until we can go and get her. So, I am going to study for an exam I'll probably never end up taking." She giggled. "I suggest you do the same. Go take your shower. Refresh and relax. I'm sure you need it."

"Okay," I said. When she turned to go, I called her back. "Nora, thank you...for everything."

She returned my smile. "Together, Cassie. No thanks needed."

After Nora went into her room and shut the door, I sat on the couch for a while, going over everything we had talked about, my feelings for Hunter front and center in my mind. I was driving myself crazy with my mixed emotions. I knew there was not much time left before I'd have to leave for the Elders. I knew I wanted Hunter with us, to keep watching over us. To be honest, I simply wanted to be near him.

I needed to do something normal, like Nora said. Wipe the slate clean and start with a fresh mind. The shower would be a great start. Caleb's touch made me feel dirty.

In my room, I noticed my jogging shorts and tank from the other day lying in a heap on my floor. The idea of a run compelled me. Something about the fresh air and the real world around me convinced me a jog would be the most normal and refreshing thing for me. Nora and Hunter would kill me for going out on my own, but I'd make it quick and be back before they knew I was gone. It was dangerous, but I desperately needed to feel some semblance of normalcy to keep my sanity. I pulled on a new pair of running clothes, stopped to write Nora a quick note, and went out to the park.

CHAPTER EIGHTEEN

The run was as refreshing as I thought it would be. I was free of all the burdens I had to bear, if only for those few moments. I imagined myself as someone normal running down the path. No powers, no demons chasing me to Hell, no angel bloodlines. I was merely an average college girl out enjoying the invigorating elements around her.

My average Jane Doe persona was mentally knocked on her ass as I neared the turn where I'd run into Hunter the day before. The memory of his kiss burned into my mind, slashing through the nothingness I'd accomplished when I first started my run. My eyes instinctively went to the bench where we'd sat so close together, the waves of electricity pulsing between us.

I tried to shake off the reverie by speeding up on the path, determined to bring myself back to the comfort zone I had been in. As I ran past a big bush on the side of the path, I was grabbed from behind. Before I could scream, a large hand covered my mouth. Next thing I knew, I was pushed against a large tree, pinned between it and a hard body behind me. I struggled to free myself, but the arms around me were solid and locked.

Anger fused with regret as I thought about the chance I'd taken going out alone. I wondered if there was anywhere I could go Caleb wouldn't hunt me down.

The hand over my mouth relaxed enough to allow me to breathe through my nose, and when I did, I smelled him. There was no mistaking the scent of lavender and musk. It was intoxicating. My chest rose and fell in fast gasps against the tree, every inhalation bringing with it the sweet scent of Hunter.

His hand yanked my ponytail to the side, forcing one cheek into the tree, his other hand only partially shielding me from the bark. Within a second his lips brushed against my ear. "Is this what you want, Cassandra?" he asked in a throaty whisper as his tongue flicked over my lobe. "Tell me. Can you not wait to get to Hell? Can you not wait to feel Caleb use your body for the rest of eternity there?"

The hand covering my mouth slid down my chest and roughly squeezed one of my breasts. My breath caught, but the energy that flowed from it was surprisingly erotic.

"Hunter, let me go." I struggled with less force than I should have, caught up in the sensual feelings he was igniting in me.

Hunter loosened his hold on me, but only enough to spin me around until I was facing him. After jailing my hands above my head against the tree, he pressed his body into mine. The thin material of my shorts did little to buffer the contact of his hard sex with my core, causing my chest to pulsate against his with every rapid breath I released.

"Isn't this how he held you?" The anger in his eyes cut into mine. "Did you enjoy him pressed against you like this? What about his kiss?" His mouth smashed against my lips as his tongue forced its way through them. Just as quickly as he'd started the kiss, he pulled away. "Was it like that? Maybe you didn't want me to rescue you in the hospital, after all. Is that why you snuck out here on your own? So he could find you again?" He was breathing as heavily as I was.

"No," I shouted. "*God no*. How could you even think that? I hate Caleb."

Hunter stared at me for what felt like hours. I couldn't speak. I was hypnotized by the glow of his eyes on me.

"Like you hate me, Cassandra?"

"*No*. I don't hate you, Hunter. I lo—" My eyes widened as I caught the words that came out of my mouth of their own free will, not even sure why I would have said such a thing.

Hunter's eyes glazed over. A slow, steady breath passed through his lips as he lowered his head to mine.

"No, wait...Hunter...wait. I didn't mea—"

This time his lips were soft against mine, caressing them tenderly. He released my arms and gently cupped the back of my neck. His tongue tickled my lips, as if requesting permission to go in. I opened my mouth willingly and met his tongue with my own. The sexual current the contact sent through my body was overwhelming. My legs gave out, forcing me to lean into him, my palms pressed lightly against his strong chest.

The deep growl he let out rumbled in my mouth. When he tore his lips away and trailed them over my jaw and down my neck, my body was lost to me, given over to the ecstasy that now controlled it. As he made his way to the sensitive spots below my ear, shivers ran down the side of my body, where they met with shock waves of pleasure from his erection rubbing against my core. He pulled my leg up to rest on the back of his thigh before his hand found its way into the back of my shorts and gently molded the tender skin. I let out an audible groan as I let him take advantage of my body.

His hot breath caressed my ear as his lips lingered outside of it, the anticipation of them causing my skin to tingle uncontrollably, until I almost screamed at him to continue.

I barely heard his whisper through the haze of my euphoria. "I'll never let him have you, Cassandra. I'm going to make you mine, right here. There will be no turning back."

Comprehension of his words was futile because his touch melted away any source of interpretation. The sensations he sparked throughout my body were all my mind could process. I had no control. My body was his slave.

Hunter continued to make love to my mouth as he lifted me into his arms and carried me. I was oblivious to where we were going, until I felt soft grass beneath me. He put me down and lay on his side next to me, half his body covering mine. His thigh moved to open my legs, rubbing the very core of my sexuality, making me wet for him.

Suckling my neck, his hand caressed my bare shoulder, playing with the strap of my tank top, until he peeled it down. Reality hit me. He was going to make love to me. Right here. Right now.

"Hunter," I gasped. "We can't...not here...there's too many peop—"

He placed his finger over my lips, cutting off my protests. "There's no one. No one but you and me."

I gazed into his eyes. They held no doubt.

With his eyes on mine, his finger lightly stroked my lips. "You want it to be me, don't you, Cassandra?"

I was scared. Being so caught up in the feelings of his touch, I hadn't been able to think about any consequences of what we were doing, of what we *might* do. I wanted time to make sense of it all, but his eyes were promising me so much more than mere sensual pleasure. It was as if our magnetic connection was about to be bonded. But then what?

"Say yes, Cassandra," he whispered as his finger lightly traced a path down my neck.

Certain I would hyperventilate if I didn't give in, I slowly nodded.

"No," he said. "I want to hear you say the words. Tell me it's me you want." He moved over me and held my head, his face inches from mine, his arousal against my belly as he straddled me.

"Yes, Hunter. It's you I want. It's always been you."

His urgent lips came down hard, and I met his force with my own need for him. We became one as our tongues fought desperately with each other. His hand slid up and down my body, teasing the places that begged to be touched. Instinctively, I grabbed at his hair, pulling hard at it when he tickled my nipple with his fingers. Lightly caressing the skin right below my tank top, he broke our kiss and gazed down at me once more.

His heavy lids barely covered the sleepy passion that twinkled from the blues behind them.

Sitting up as he continued to straddle me, his hand slowly lifted my top. I pushed up from the ground and raised my arms, allowing him to take it off completely. As I lay back down, his gaze darted back and forth from my eyes to my breasts. The wind against my skin caused my nipples to tighten even more than they were. He placed his hands around the fullness of my breasts, lifting them up as he lowered his mouth to them. I raised my chest, wanting to get even closer. His groans mixed with my own sighs of pleasure as he devoured me. A twinge of pain came as his teeth pulled at my nipple, only to lavish it away with his tongue. He took his time on both of my breasts, making sure they were both equally consumed.

I sat up; my eyes in line with the sculpted chest I knew lay underneath the shirt he wore. Frantically, I scrambled to release the shirt from his pants, desperate to feel his skin against mine. Once his shirt was off, I watched my hands as I slid them over his chest and down his stomach, following the smooth valleys of toned muscle. I did it once again, tracing the path with my mouth. His head went back as he let out a breathless moan. I brushed the top of his jeans with my hand and let it linger there, my boldness surprising both him and me. His hand went behind my head, grabbing my hair, and forcing me to meet his gaze.

"Cassandra, if you continue, I won't be able to stop myself. I *will* be inside of you." He kissed me, his lips bruising mine with the pressure of it. Pulling my head back again, he said, "And I want to taste all of you before that happens."

Before I could say anything his body pressed against mine, pushing it back into the grass as he laid over me. His kisses left my lips and quickly moved to my breasts, sending me back into a whirlwind of indulgent satisfaction. Slowly, he moved his mouth down my stomach. His hands skimmed up my thighs, resting his thumbs on the inside, teasing my most sensitive area with their mere presence.

With one swift movement, Hunter made quick work of my shorts, ripping them down the length of my legs. He spread my legs with his hands, slowly making his way between my thighs. Gazing up at me, his blue eyes glowed with the promise of sheer sexual pleasure. The smile he gave before lowering his head to the center of my desire, told me he was planning to enjoy every minute.

His tongue gently lapped at the sensitive bud before his mouth suckled it. Back and forth he tormented it, sending waves of pure pleasure up and down my entire body. The tightening sensation grew inside until the pressure was almost unbearable. I cried out in painful ecstasy as I rose and pulled Hunter up by his shoulders.

"Now, Hunter," I panted. He sat between my legs, and I quickly reached for the button on his pants, but he stilled my hand with his.

"Cassandra..." There was a warning in his tone.

"I want you inside of me. Please."

"No," he said with finality. "Not until I hear you scream from the pleasure I'm giving you."

He began the sweet torture all over again, taking me to a level of bliss I never imagined possible in my best fantasies. I pulled at the grass in an effort to get a grip on something in order to control my writhing body. Finally, release came as explosions erupted within me, sending wave after wave of sexual delirium through my entire body. Unconsciously, I screamed his name over and over again until the waves subsided and left a dull throb in their wake.

When I opened my eyes, he was leaning over me, his eyes clouded with desire.

"God, Cassandra," he whispered. "Do you know how good you taste?"

He kissed me again as he pushed his sex between my thighs, causing the throbbing to burn again in anticipation of him.

"This is what you do to me. I want you to feel me."

Grabbing my hand, he placed it over the large swell in his pants. I gripped him, and he let out a low moan. His hand quickly moved over the zipper of his jeans. "I need you now." His pants disappeared in one fluid motion. With a thrust of his hips, he was inside of me, filling me as we both cried out from the pleasure of it. With his lips pressed to my ear, he said in a labored breath, "You're mine now, Cassandra."

Kissing my neck tenderly, he slowly pulled out of me, only to slide back in, creating shocks of pleasure deep within me. His thrusting hips became a steady rhythm as our bodies melded together. Cries of ecstasy became our verbal communication, while our bodies moved perfectly together speaking their own language, as if they'd done so a million times before.

Hunter's drives came faster and harder as his breathing grew heavier against my neck.

"Tell me your mine," he demanded, gazing into my eyes as he gained speed.

The intensity grew as he became harder inside of me with each wonderful push.

"I'm yours, Hunter. I'm all yours," I told him breathlessly.

He tensed with one last powerful thrust as he arched his back and let out a loud, low growl. The sensation was so deep and strong inside me that it put me over the edge. I climaxed with him, my inner walls clenching around his shaft, a pleasure encompassing not only my body, but my mind as well. I no longer cared that I didn't know who Hunter was, or what his ultimate goal was with me. There was only this, him and me, in this moment. I wasn't sure of what my future held, or how much of one I even had. All I knew was that I wanted him to be there with me for it.

He remained inside of me as he came up on his elbows, his face flushed from the efforts of our lovemaking. His eyes roamed over my face as he brushed aside strands of my hair. Lowering his lips to mine, he kissed me softly, sweet flutters from one corner of my mouth to the other. When he was done, he raised his head to look lovingly into my eyes.

"You're beautiful, Cassandra," he said in the barest of whispers. The backs of his fingers lightly brushed my cheek, causing my skin to tingle from the touch. "I'm afraid you've created an addiction in me. I can't get enough of you. I already want more. I think I will always want more."

Every inhibition I had seemed to escape its prison with every explosive wave of pleasure he brought out of me.

"Then take more." I moved beneath him.

Passion reignited in his eyes before they slowly closed. When he finally opened them, the passion was gone, replaced with...*regret*?

"I'm afraid there's no more time," he said. "I must go."

CHAPTER NINETEEN

"What?" I cried in disbelief.

Up until now, I couldn't do anything without Hunter under my heels. Now, after we'd been as close as two people could get, he was going to leave? My anger spiked and lashed out through the palms of my hands as I shoved at his chest.

He rolled off me. I stood, intending to let out a litany of questions and accusations when he held his T-shirt out to me.

"I must go away for awhile, but I promise, I'll come back to you. Here, put this on. Quickly, Cassandra."

I was about to protest when three huge men appeared out of nowhere and stood before us in the park. Two of the men wore steel armor over their torsos and wielded swords at their sides. The other was dressed in a T-shirt and jeans.

The two armored men ogled my nude body. Hunter shot up in front of me, in all his naked glory, to block their view. With shaking hands, I scrambled to put the T-shirt on.

"Awww, c'mon, Hunter. Move aside and let us get a peek of the little beauty. After all, she'll be famous for this," one of the men said, laughing. His armored twin laughed along with him. The third man didn't seem to share in the others' humor, as he stood with a grim expression.

Hunter glared at the men. "If you even think of looking at her, I will gut you both. You'll be praying to let me end your immortality. She's mine."

Their smiles faded. The one who'd spoken became red-faced as he caught the third man unsuccessfully hiding a chuckle. Tersely he said, "Yeah, about that, you've been summoned back. We are to escort you at once."

Hunter peered over his shoulder at me. Seeing I was covered, he grabbed his jeans and put them on. The escorts must have taken his words to heart because their eyes never once wandered toward me. They continued to eye Hunter's every move. After getting dressed, he walked back to them, and I gasped as they brought out a pair of chains, metal shackles hanging at the ends. Hunter said something to them I couldn't hear, they nodded, and he walked back over to me.

I didn't give him the chance to speak. Clapping his chest with my hands, I barraged him with questions. "Hunter, what's this about? Who are these men and why do you have to go with them? Where—"

He grabbed both of my hands in his and squeezed. "Cassandra, shhh. Listen to me. I have to go with them, but I will be back."

I was about to protest, but he cut me off again.

"No negotiations. This must be done. See the man in black? He's one of mine. He'll watch over you while I'm gone."

"I don't need a babysitter, Hunter."

"Yes, you do. Caleb can show up at any time. When are you going to accept that?" Gripping my arms, he pulled me hard into his chest. "You're mine now, Cassandra. I won't let anything to happen to you. Eric will take care of you. He is completely loyal to me and will do whatever he can to protect you. I promise, you'll be in good hands."

I cast my gaze down at the ground, both scared and sad at the same time. "But I want to be in your hands," I whispered.

Hunter's fingers lifted my chin. "I've wanted to hear you say that since I first met you." He brushed his thumbs across my jaw. "I need to take care of something, but I'll be back for you."

"But where are you going? What do you need to do?"

Hunter shook his head. "I can't explain it right now."

Before he could say anything more, the men flanked him, and then pulled his arms behind his back to shackle them. "All right, that's enough. Time to go, Hunter. Let's make this nice and easy for her, eh?"

Hunter showed no resistance as they finished with their mechanical prisons. Eric came over and stood next to me. I gazed up at him with anxiety, but his friendly face managed to put me at ease.

I could only watch as the men pulled Hunter away. But before all three of them disappeared, Hunter looked me in the eyes and said, "Trust me, Cassandra. I'll be back for you."

And I did.

***

The walk back to the apartment was awkward, to say the least. Eric wasn't very talkative. I attempted to get him to tell me where Hunter was going and who had summoned him, but all Eric would tell me was that it was up to Hunter to fill me in when he returned. I even tried to ask him how he knew Hunter, but apparently, that information was classified as well. Much to my dismay, the old adage about guys sticking together was true no matter what worlds they were from. The only information he gave was that he was there to protect me from Caleb, and he'd be staying in Hunter's apartment.

When I got back, Nora's door was closed. I peeked in at her and saw she was fast asleep, sprawled out amongst her books on the bed. I quietly closed the door and went into the bathroom to take a shower.

I turned on the shower, and then pulled Hunter's T-shirt over my head. The smell of lavender and musk caught me off guard as the shirt rubbed against my face. I held it to my nose, breathing in the heady scent. Closing my eyes, I relived the glorious events in the park. I pictured Hunter laying over me, his steel eyes penetrating mine as he made me feel things I'd never imagined. As I washed, I remembered his hands in all the places that made me burn for him. Everything was perfect, as if fate had finally brought us together.

But as wonderful as it was—the way he felt, the way he looked, the way he touched me, the beautiful things he said—I worried if this was fate's final act. Would we ever have those wonderful moments again?

The reality of Hunter being gone hit me hard. Would I ever see him again? He told me he'd be back for me, but it didn't appear as if he had a whole lot of control in those shackles. Did he only say it to keep me from arguing?

Eric was the only one who had the answers, and as I left the bathroom, I vowed to get them from him.

"Hello, Cassie."

I jumped. Caleb was sprawled casually amongst the cushions of the sofa. My body tensed as his eyes roved over me, stopping at the lacy bra and panties I tried to hide with my hands. His lecherous smile proved I was unsuccessful.

"I've got great timing lately," he said, sitting up straighter.

I glanced toward my bedroom, gauging the distance it would take me to get in and close the door before Caleb got to me. He must have recognized my intentions because as soon as the thoughts were out of my head, he flashed over to the room and leaned his arm casually against the doorway. Shaking with fear, I pushed back against the wall in the hallway, as if it would somehow allow me to melt into it and disappear.

"Now, c'mon, Cassie. Let's be adults about this. I want you; you want me. I'll help you get over this phobia you have about going to Hell. No one has to get hurt, and we'll live happily ever after. We can start right now." He waved his hand toward my room, and candles appeared everywhere, creating a chillingly romantic setting. "I can make it the best night of your life, Cassie, but if you fight me, I can make it the worst." His easy smile turned into a grim, cruel leer.

I couldn't speak. I stood against the wall, panting in fear, trying to think of how I was going to get out of this. Would Eric sense Caleb? Would he come to my rescue? I twisted my neck, looking at the door to the apartment, as if willing him to burst through it.

"Forget about Eric." He dismissed my hopes with a lazy wave of his hands. "He's got his own problems to deal with over there, thanks to my associates. Oh, and if you're waiting for your knight in shining armor to save you again, he won't be coming this time either." He shook his head, tsking at me as if I were a child. "See, he's got quite a bit of explaining to do to our boss as to why he hasn't completed his mission. He's going to be there a while."

I jerked my head at Caleb's assertion. "You're lying."

"Oh, c'mon, Cassie. I thought you were smarter than that. Did you think he was different from me?" He laughed, but when he noticed my shocked expression, his eyes grew wide. "Oh my, you really did. Wow, I guess he hasn't lost his touch after all. He's a Seeker. You know, like me."

I refused to believe him. "I know what you are, but Hunter is *not* like you. Why would he be protecting me from you if that were true?"

Caleb sauntered over and leaned his hands against the wall on either side of me. I cowered back. "Because *you* are the ultimate prize in Hell, Cassie," he hissed. "A Seeker with angel blood. Can you imagine the damage you could do for Hell? And, well, the one that turns you is sure to be richly rewarded for it. Hunter and I have a little competition going on. You know, may the best man win and all that good stuff."

My mind was processing everything he was telling me, but my heart refused to listen. All I could do was shake my head in denial.

"It's all true," he continued. "Hunter is a Seeker. He was sent here to turn you. Look, I'm sure he told you that I was one, right? Did he tell you how we get Guardians to trust us? We seduce them. Tell me, Cassie, how far has he gone to seduce you?" His finger slowly made a trail down my cheek and continued down my jaw until it stopped under my chin. When I grimaced from his touch, he yanked my chin up to face him. I glared into his glowing blue eyes and realized I'd seen that radiant hue in someone else's—Hunter's.

No. I refused to believe I could have made such a mistake. I was a Guardian with angelic blood, *damn it*. My instincts would have warned me. What Hunter and I shared in the park was real. There had to be another explanation for the similarities between Caleb and Hunter. Caleb was merely trying to get me to Hell any way he could, right?

But there was an inkling of doubt now, and it pissed me off. After the park, I thought I knew whom I could trust, but Caleb had planted a seed. I didn't want it, but it was there, and I was angry it had invaded my one source of security. The anger inside of me was different than ever before. It built up and found its own momentum, until I shook with the urge to release it.

Caleb was the perfect recipient.

"Get. Back." I stared him down.

"Awww, don't be that way, Cassie. You had to know. I'm only sorry I had to be the one to tell you." He pasted a fake frown on his face. "What do you say we do this nice and easy? Get it over with?"

"I said, *get back*." A beast within me let loose as I shoved at him with a force I'd never possessed before. I watched in awe as he sailed backward through the air, clearing my bedroom doorway. He hit the far wall hard and slid to the floor in a heap. I stood rooted to the spot in the hallway, trying to comprehend what happened. Where had that power come from? I glanced around, wondering if Eric had come in and used some type of telekinesis or something, but there was no one else in the room. Nora's door was still closed. The only other explanation was too unbelievable. I simply didn't have that kind of strength. Or did I?

Caleb remained motionless against the wall in the bedroom. Was he faking? Was this a trick? I had no choice but to check. I searched around the room for a weapon to defend myself with, but realized how futile that was. How did one even go about killing a demon from Hell? So, I trusted and prayed at the same time, that the newfound power I'd exhibited wasn't a fluke. Slowly, I made my way toward his lifeless body.

When I reached Caleb, I leaned back as far as I could and kicked my foot out, hitting him hard in the side. He didn't move, except for the jostling my foot caused. But as soon as I let my guard down, Caleb's hands shot out and pulled me into him.

"No," I screamed.

Adrenaline rushed through my body. Instinct that seemed to come from deep in my soul took over my entire being. Straddling Caleb, I watched my own movements in confusion and horror as my hands became strategically placed at opposite sides of his head. He screamed for his life as I imagined twisting his head with such force it snapped right off. My murderous intent might have played out if a female voice from behind hadn't stopped me.

"Cassandra, no."

My hands stilled by a force outside of my control. A breeze filled with the sweet smell of roses wafted around me. Twisting my head, I gasped when my eyes fell upon one of the most beautiful women I had ever seen. She stood a few feet away, her pale skin amplified by the stark contrast of her long, fiery red hair and a black, flowing dress. Her shape was that of a model's dreams, perfect in all the right places. But it was her eyes that drew me in, the green hue so vivid and intense, they appeared hypnotic.

Those beautiful eyes were on me, penetrating me, controlling me. There was a familiarity in them I couldn't put my finger on. I stared at her, mesmerized, as she came toward me. My hands relaxed on Caleb, and I feared he would use the reprieve to escape, or worse, turn the tables on me, but when I glanced down, he seemed just as spellbound by the woman.

"Anael," Caleb whispered.

My gaze snapped up. Could it really be her? An angel, herself, had come to stop me from killing Caleb? *But why?*

"Yes, Caleb, it seems I've come just in time for you. It would be in your best interest to remember that after Cassandra releases you. I have a special interest in this Guardian, and I will deal with her alone. Do you understand?" Anael's steel resolve was such a contrast to her soft, beautiful air, but it held a force that left no room for argument from him.

I, however, was not so ready to give in to her demands.

"I'm sorry. Anael, is it? It's nice to meet you, but I have a big problem with the whole releasing him part. See, I've been through hell with this demon, and I'm not about to let him go only to have him come back and torture me again. I'd rather end it all right now, if you don't mind." I continued straddling Caleb, my hands pushing against his chest to keep him down. I was still surprised at how much power I suddenly had.

Anael regarded me, as if considering my proposal, but then she turned her gaze to Caleb and said, "You will obey my orders or suffer the consequences." Without waiting for his answer, she waved a hand, and I fell to the floor as Caleb disappeared from underneath me.

"What the hell?" I yelled as I scrambled to sit back up.

"I'm sorry, Cassandra, but I couldn't allow you to kill him. If you had, the Devil himself would be after you, and trust me, no one would be able to protect you then. Caleb won't come after you anymore. I've given him an order. He will obey."

"Why would Caleb obey the orders of an angel?" I asked.

"Because I'm not an angel anymore. I live in Sheol now—Hell. Caleb has to obey me. I am technically his Queen."

I fell back against the wall as if I'd been thrown at it. Anael, my ancestor, was some kind of fallen angel? I swore the hole I'd been sinking in couldn't get much deeper. Until now, apparently.

CHAPTER TWENTY

"I don't understand. I thought you were an angel. They told me I had your blood, angel blood," I said, as if I could convince Anael she was wrong.

She sat on my bed and motioned me over, but I stayed where I was, leaning against the wall.

"I was," she said. "But a long time ago, I betrayed a powerful angel. Because of my disloyalty, I was banished from that world and forced to live eternity in Sheol. I've been the Queen of Sheol for many generations now."

I shot away from the wall, panicked. "You're a demon? Are you here to take me to Hell yourself? Is that why you got rid of Caleb?"

"No, Cassandra. I'm here to protect you. You are my last descendent, and I will do everything in my power to keep you mortal. Our bloodline must not end with you. If they turn you, it will die along with your soul. You must keep the line going. The fate of Heaven and humanity depend on it. You are more important in this war than you realize."

My body trembled as she continued to tell me about the huge responsibility I was to assume in a war I didn't even realize existed. How had it come to this?

"But I don't want any of this. I don't want the fate of the world on my shoulders. I can't possibly fight this war. I'm just...me."

"You're stronger than you think. Look at what you did to Caleb. It's in you to fight against evil. You simply need to embrace your power. I will help you as much as I can, but you must know, the King of Sheol is a much stronger force than I. If he finds out I am betraying him, he'll...well, I won't be able to protect you anymore. So, you must go to the Elders as quickly as you can. They will help you. They'll know what to do. Do you understand, Cassandra?"

"No, I don't," I yelled, louder than I intended. "To be honest with you, I don't understand any of this. In the last week, my life has been turned upside down. People...*things*...are after me to take me to Hell because I'm some lethal weapon, or some shit. I've heard so many lies I don't know whom to trust anymore. I just...I..." Overwhelmed, I broke down and cried. With my hands over my face, I bent my knees and slid down the wall to the floor.

Instantly, Anael was at my side, her arm around my shoulder. "Shhh...Cassandra. I know this is a lot to take in, but you're a fighter and *will* get through this. It's in your blood. Trust your heart, it will help you find the way."

Gazing into her bright green eyes, I realized we both carried a heavy burden that neither of us had asked for. Anael was forced to live in a world she didn't belong in, enduring an eternal punishment. Was this her way of righting that wrong?

"Anael, are there others like you? I mean, is it possible some demons can actually be good?"

She looked at me with kind eyes. "You're talking about Hunter, aren't you? You want to know if a Seeker can truly fall for a Guardian," she said, reading my mind.

"So it's true, he really is a demon." I hung my head in disappointment. My heart ached from the betrayal. I wasn't ready to let go of the feelings he brought out in me. "Was Caleb telling the whole truth? Was Hunter only protecting me so he could turn me himself?" I felt sick even thinking about it.

"Yes, Hunter is a Seeker, Cassandra. He's actually the highest ranked Seeker in Sheol, second only to King Nergal."

My heart sank even lower hearing how important he was to Hell.

"But, not anymore," Anael added.

I jerked my head up, confused. "What do you mean?"

"He broke the rules when you two were together in the park. That is why he was summoned back to Hell. He's being punished for his betrayal."

Oh my God, they knew we made love in the park? Embarrassed, I asked, "But how? How did they know? And why is it such a big deal to them? I thought that's what Seekers do. They seduce the Guardians, and then turn them."

"Yes, they do, but the seduction cannot involve being intimate the way you two were. It can never go that far. There have been other Seekers who have gotten too close and went, how do you say it? AWOL. Nergal realized what was happening and forbade it. The punishment was severe enough to prevent other Seekers from losing their way...until now. Caleb was watching you, he saw everything and reported back to Nergal."

I lowered my eyes; utterly horrified Caleb had seen everything that happened in the park. It was such a beautiful thing to me, but the thought of him watching made me feel dirty about it. I couldn't worry about that, though. I had to know what was happening to Hunter.

"What is the punishment?" I held my breath, waiting for her answer.

Anael peered back at me with sympathy and maybe even remorse in her features. *Was it shame for having any association with their world?* "Hunter is being held in a Sheol prison. They will torture him there for the rest of eternity."

My hand shot up to my mouth as I gasped. Images of him restrained, bloody, and in pain, tore through my mind, causing me to tremble. Bile came up my throat, but I held it back.

"No," I cried out.

I didn't want to believe it. It was incomprehensible to me. He'd risked eternal punishment to be with me? It felt like a knife was slicing through my heart as I thought about the torture he was enduring.

"It's not fair," I said, my eyes welling up. "He doesn't deserve to be punished. It was all me; I let this happen. It's all my fault."

"He knew what the consequences were."

"But why would he do that? Why would he risk it?" I asked, knowing she couldn't really answer.

"Sometimes fate cannot be controlled, Cassandra, even by us immortals."

The irony of her words did not go unnoticed by me. Here I was, bound by my blood, trying to change the fate of countless lives, only to be restrained by the fate of my own heart.

"You must help him, Anael. *Please?*" I asked, not knowing whether it was even possible. I was still mad as hell at him for not telling me he was a Seeker, but how could I deny what he'd risked to be with me? It killed me to know he was suffering.

Anael put her arms around me and held me tight. I felt comforted and safe in her arms.

"I'll do whatever I can for him, I promise. He helped protect you and that means more to me than you know."

I wasn't sure how much power she held in Hell, but it helped to know she'd be there for Hunter, and would try to help ease his suffering.

"Thank you," I said.

"I must go. I can't be away too long. It'll draw attention. Go to the Elders like we talked about. Now, Cassandra. Get your mom and Nora and go. Be careful. And remember, you have a power within you that is very strong. Find it and use it when you need to."

I nodded, but was scared out of my wits of what lay ahead for me. We stood together and hugged once more. Before Anael disappeared, she kissed me on the forehead and whispered, "Goodbye, my child. I'll be back for you. Until then, remember I am a part of you, here." She put her palm over my heart. I could almost feel the heat from her touch, but wasn't sure if it was real or imagined. Either way, I felt her with me.

***

I remained against the hallway wall after Anael disappeared, dreading my next move, imagining what Hunter was going through, and knowing I'd probably never see him again. But I also knew I *had* to go on, if only to spare the lives of those I *did* have around me. And, of course, there was that whole fate of the world thing.

Nora came out of her room just as I'd gathered myself together. "Oh hey, Cassie—"

The front door burst open, and we both screamed as Eric charged in. "Cassandra," he yelled before noticing me in the hallway. Nora continued to scream as he bounded through the room toward us.

"Nora, it's okay," I told her. "He works with Hunter." I could tell she was still leery, though, and it was understandable. Eric was a big bear of a man to begin with, but to come charging toward us, his whole appearance disheveled, was quite terrifying.

"Eric, are you okay?" I asked when he was near enough. I put my hand out to touch a cut on his face, but he flinched away from me.

"I'm fine," he said. I stared in awe as the cuts on his face and arms slowly receded as if being sucked into his skin. "Where's Caleb? What happened?" There was murder in his eyes.

"Caleb was here?" Nora asked, confused. "Cassie, what the hell is going on? And who is this guy?" She eyed over Eric's massive frame.

I was still recovering from all of the information I'd received from Anael, so the flood of questions had me reeling. I took a deep breath in an effort to calm my beating heart enough to answer them. "Yes, Caleb was here, but he's gone now," I said

~ 166 ~

to both of them. "Anael came and sent him away. Hopefully, for good."

Exhausted, I moved between Nora and Eric and headed for the couch. Peering over my shoulder, I said, "Oh, and Nora, this is Eric. He's a Seeker watching over me while Hunter is being tortured in Hell for the rest of eternity. Nora, Eric. Eric, Nora." I sank down into the sofa, defeated.

"*Holy shit*. What?" Nora exclaimed.

"Anael was here?" Eric asked with the same amount of intensity and confusion.

They came around and sat with me as I explained what happened with Caleb and Anael. Nora's features displayed many of the same emotions I had gone through during the events that had taken place in our apartment. Eric, on the other hand, showed no emotion at all. His calm demeanor reminded me of Hunter's.

After answering all the questions I could, I got up from the sofa and gazed down at Nora. "We need to get my mom and go to the Elders as soon as possible. I have a feeling that even if Caleb won't be back, others will. Apparently, I'm pretty high up on Hell's hit list, and by association, so are you."

She nodded blankly and got up. "I just need to pack a few things."

"You coming?" I asked Eric, once Nora was in her bedroom.

Eric stood and came so close I was forced to look up at him. He was a handsome man, with dark, thick hair and features, aside from the familiar blue eyes. His strong build was as intimidating as Hunter's.

As he gazed down at me, his calm expression changed to one of humility. "I'm sorry, Cassandra. I have failed you. Hunter will surely kill me himself for letting Caleb get near you." He broke eye contact and hung his head.

"I don't think you have to worry about that, Eric. You knew they were taking him to Hell. Anael confirmed it. He won't be back." My heart broke having to say the words.

Eric's head came up, and the grin on his face was one of pure confidence. "You don't know Hunter very well then. If he wants something, he will do everything in his power to get it. No amount of metal in Hell can stop him."

My heart skipped a beat with the hope that what he said was true. Remembering one of Hunter's lessons, I said, "Yeah, I've heard that somewhere before."

***

Eric, Nora, and I rode in Nora's car in silence, each of us in our own world of thoughts. When we arrived at my mom's hospital room, the man Hunter assigned to watch over her was standing in the same place he'd been when we left. He nodded my way, and I returned the acknowledgement. Nora and I went into the room while Eric talked with the guard.

My mom was sitting up in her bed, and relief swept over her face when she saw us. "Oh Cassie, Nora. I was so worried about you when I woke up. I tried to get that Neanderthal to come in and tell me what was going on, but he just stood out there the whole time."

I glanced out at the guy. *He must have some major patience.*

Mom looked much better. The color had returned to her skin, and she seemed to be moving around with more ease than before. Her arms felt stronger around me as I hugged her. I was relieved, knowing we were getting her out of there, but when I pulled away, she searched my face, and as much as I tried, I was horrible at hiding my distress from her.

"Cassie, what's wrong? Did something else happen? Did you get rid of Hunter?"

Her words stung, even though she didn't know how close she'd gotten to the truth about Hunter, and how much it hurt me.

"Yeah, Mom, he's gone," I said, dropping my gaze. I didn't want to answer any more questions. I only wanted to move on and get to the Elders safely. "We're getting you out of here. Today. *Now.* We have to get to the Elders. Do you think you're strong enough, or should I send Eric in here to help you?"

"No, no. I'm much better. Let me just get some clothes on, and we can go. I'll need to stop at the house...*wait*, who's Eric?" She glanced at the two men outside the room. "But they all look so similar," she said, almost as if to herself. "They look like..."

"Hunter, I know. They work together, and they're here to help. You're going to have to trust me on this, Mom. We need them. And I'm sorry, but we won't be able to stop by your house. We have to go now. We can pick up anything you may need along the way if we have to. Go ahead and get dressed, and I'll have one of the guys make sure the hospital staff stays away so we can get out of here."

I didn't wait to hear any of my mom's protests as I left the room. I was determined to be in control, going off my instincts. Anael told me to trust what's in my heart, and I was listening.

Realizing I had never even met the man who had been diligently protecting my mom, I went up and introduced myself. His name was Matthew, which was the extent of any information I got from him, but it didn't matter. What did matter was getting my mom out of there. I told him and Eric about my plan, adding that there would probably be some objections to it if any of the doctors or nurses saw us leaving. They promised to take care of it, and I had no doubt it would be effortless for them.

When I peered back into the room, my mom was dressed and Nora was getting her personal items from the closet. They were ready to go. I put the guys in motion and went back into the room. We got my mom out without anyone noticing. In fact, there seemed to be no one anywhere in the hospital at the time, thanks to the two demons I had working with me.

It should have felt wrong. When it came down to it, I was working with the Devil. In the end, would Hell have my soul for it? The calm that seemed to come over my nerves was so odd considering what I was up against, but, at the same time, it felt natural. I was hardening inside, the last bit of softness within me now imprisoned with the man, or demon, I'd so easily given in to. Would I ever get it back? Did I even *want* it back? I wasn't sure about anything anymore.

Mom, Nora, Eric, and I piled into Nora's car and set off for the Elders. Matthew informed me he would attempt to get in touch with Anael and help with Hunter. I told him, as much as I wanted Hunter out of that prison, I didn't want anyone else to suffer the same fate. I didn't get an agreement or denial, but from the determination on his face, nothing I said would matter. He was loyal to Hunter, just as Eric was. I wondered what it was that held the three together so tightly.

Nora drove, and my mom directed her where to go from the passenger seat. Everyone was on edge. The tension in the car was thick. My mom was yelling at Nora for not following her directions, when Nora's outburst took us all by surprise.

"Back off, Sara. I know where I'm going," she shouted.

Awesome. More surprises.

CHAPTER TWENTY-ONE

"Nora?" I prodded. When she stayed silent, I lost it. "Look, I've had it with people lying to me, keeping things from me, fighting me, and trying to kill me today, so spill. How is it you know where the Elders are, and why haven't you shared this fact until now?"

"I'm sorry, Cassie," she said, sounding defeated.

Leaning over the front seat, I could only make out her profile, but I could tell she was struggling to hold it together as she drove.

"I was sent here to watch over you by the Elders. It wasn't by chance that we met. I found you, and basically, threw myself into your life."

I fell back into the seat, floored by her confession.

"I'm so sorry," Nora continued. "Please believe me when I tell you, you're like a sister to me now, and I care so much about you. And you, Sara, you're family too." She glanced back at me with anxious eyes through the rearview mirror.

"Watch me do what?" I asked, my tone not so forgiving.

Did everyone I know have an ulterior motive with me? Was I merely a pawn in everyone else's games? Well, not anymore. I was done playing innocent, naïve little Cassie. From that point on, I would trust no one.

"You are Anael's last descendent. They knew it would be dangerous for you if anyone found out. So, they sent me to keep an eye on you, make sure you were safe. I was to report to them the minute anything out of the ordinary occurred, but your mom went to see them before I even knew what was happening to you. I guess I got so caught up in being your friend that I forgot what I was really here for. I failed them, and you. I'm so sorry."

She was crying, and I wanted to comfort her, but the deception hurt too much.

"Why is it that it's supposed to be this big secret that I'm Anael's descendent, but everyone seems to know but me? Can someone tell me that? Hey, Mom, did you know too?" I asked, lashing out.

My mom gasped, and then reprimanded me, but I dismissed her when I heard Eric say, "And you thought *we* were the bad guys," under his breath.

"Really, Eric?" I turned on him. "You've been mute up until now and you come up with that?" He turned away from my glare, but not before I saw the grin on his face.

Leaning back in my seat, I let the steam roll off me. When I was calm enough, I said to no one in particular, "Let's just get to the Elder's, okay? Unless there is anything else I need to know?" The silence was my only answer. Even Mom held back, which was saying a lot.

Laying my head back against the seat, I tried to put everything out of my mind, but the non-stop circus of events kept circling through my head. Finally, I closed my eyes and let my thoughts go until my brain grew tired.

I was running through the forest I'd grown so familiar with; running for my life from a presence I both loved and feared.

Hunter caught up with me, kissing me with a gentleness that didn't seem to fit his strong physique. The familiar dread came over me as I asked him, "Will you kill me now?"

"No, Cassandra, I do not need to kill you," he whispered, touching my cheek with his fingertips.

A relief passed over me, and a new hope ignited as I thought fate may finally be smiling upon me. Would I be free from the invisible bonds I felt, once and for all? With my eyes closed, I smiled and leaned my face into his palm, feeling the contrast in textures of our skin.

Slowly, he raised my face, and I opened my eyes. His luminous blue gaze hypnotized me.

"Cassandra, I do not need to kill you because you are already dead."

I pulled away as the hand, which moments before caressed my cheeks with love, held up a chalice. Somehow, I knew it contained my final destiny.

"Drink, my love," he urged.

I shook my head, refusing the offer.

"Drink, Cassandra."

Closing my eyes, I prayed to myself for him to leave me, but then I heard the words again. "Drink, Cassandra." Only the voice that said them this time was not Hunter's. I opened my eyes, shocked to see Caleb's face in place of Hunter's, urging me in the same way, as if he'd been the one standing there holding me all along. As I continued to refuse, the face flashed back and forth between the two demons, their eyes being the only thing that remained constant.

I was about to scream at them to stop torturing me, but the words were halted when I stared into my own face. The breath caught in my throat as I watched my hazel eyes fade to match those of my sadists.

"Drink, Cassandra," the clone told me.

And then I did scream.

***

My scream was powerful enough to wake me. My mom and Nora were in a panic, asking me what was wrong, as I slowly came out of the haze, still trembling from what I'd seen and heard in the dream. I glanced around. We were pulled over to the side of the road. The car door opened next to me, and Nora leaned in, grabbing my shoulders and shaking off the remaining images of the dream.

"Cassie, talk to us," she cried. "C'mon, honey, you're scaring the hell out of me."

Tears streamed down my face as I stared back at her. "I'm all right," I said, wiping away my tears. "It was just...it was a dream. I'm okay now." I was still in shock, trying to process what the dream meant, but I sat up straighter in order to put the others at ease.

"You sure?" Nora asked. "It must have been pretty bad. You scared the crap out of all of us, screaming like that."

My mom was leaning over the car seat, practically in the back with Eric and me. Her face was pale, a look of horror on it that I'm sure reflected my own. I put my hand over hers in comfort. "I'm fine, Mom, really. It was only a dream. Nothing more." I prayed my words were true. Mom seemed to relax from my reassurance.

I realized Eric was staring at me, and the blue of his eyes sent my mind plummeting back to the terrifying faces I'd seen interchanging. My breathing escalated. I couldn't get it under control.

"That's it," Nora said, slamming the car door shut.

She got back in the driver's seat, and the car lurched forward, only to stop a minute later. Back at my side, she urged me out of the car, whispering comforting words I only caught pieces of. My mom stood behind her, the concern on her face enough to push me to take control of myself. I got out of the car and took several deep breaths.

"We're going to stay here for the night," Nora said. "You need to relax. We'll get some rest, and then get back on the road tomorrow morning. Stay here with your mom, and I'll go get the room."

Nora moved me against the side of the car and stood before me, while my mom continued to hug my shoulders from the side, her touch more comforting than I thought I needed. I glanced at the motel and nodded, simply relieved to be out of the car.

"Wait," Eric yelled, getting out of the car. "Nora, stay there. I sense someone else here."

We all froze.

"Where?" I asked, fear icing my veins as I frantically searched the surroundings.

"In one of the rooms."

As Eric stalked toward the line of rooms, one of the doors opened. I let out a gasp as Hunter marched from the room, his stride determined on its path toward me. When he reached me and pulled me into his arms, I was a rag doll, limp and compliant. So sure I would never see him again, I struggled to get my emotions under control. It was as if he'd come back from the dead, his presence not quite real yet.

"Let go of her," my mom yelled.

"I'm not going to hurt her, Sara."

"What are you doing here, Hunter?" I stared back at him, still in awe over his appearance at the motel, or anywhere that wasn't Hell, for that matter. "How...how did you get out?"

"I'll tell you everything, but I want to talk to you alone. Now." There was a determination in his voice that told me there was going to be no other way about it.

"Hell, no," my mom started in again. She pulled me out of Hunter's arms, with a strength I didn't even realize she had, and stood between us. "There is no way I'm letting you take her anywhere. You think I don't know what you are? Where you come from? Stay away from her, Hunter. She's been through enough."

"Why don't you let Cassandra decide what she wants to do? She has the right to make her own choices." While Hunter appeared angry and steadfast, his eyes sent me a silent plea. This wasn't merely a stand against my mom. It was a choice between trusting him and turning my back on my own family, after everything I'd learned. Even as my emotions warred with each other over what I'd found about him, I needed to hear him out. I knew in my heart that what we shared in the park was much more than a conquest to him as a Seeker. I wanted to hear him say it. I needed to know he felt the same pull, the same connection with me as I did him.

"Mom, I'm going with him," I said. "I'll be fine. Trust me."

She turned to face me, surprise, disappointment, and worry masking her attractive features.

"He's not going to hurt me. I'm going."

Pain flashed through her eyes before she moved aside in defeat.

I took a step toward Hunter and locked my gaze on his. "Besides, if he even tries, I'll make him wish he was back in Hell."

CHAPTER TWENTY-TWO

I made my way into the room Hunter had come from without checking to see if he was behind me. If I hesitated for even an instant, I would lose my nerve. I wasn't afraid of him, so much as not being in control of my body around him.

The door shut behind me, the click of the lock sounding like the world beyond was being shut out completely. Moving further into the room, I glanced around, more to avoid looking at Hunter, than any interest in the decorative nature of the space.

The large bed loomed front and center, its scarred headboard set against the pale floral wallpaper that lined the walls. Stark white sheets peeked out of a blue bedspread. The linen gave off a fresh detergent smell, which would be inviting enough to want to dive into the stack of fluffy pillows at the top of the bed, if I didn't have to worry about a demon from Hell hovering behind me.

With not much to look at, besides a television set and the nightstands flanking the bed, I moved to an old wooden desk in the far corner of the room. I intended to sit on the chair behind it, putting space between Hunter and I, but before I got a few feet, Hunter gripped my arm, stopping me.

"Cassandra." The sultry way his whisper caressed my name had heat traveling through my veins. It was a battle trying not to throw myself at him and let my emotions go, forgetting about the world around us and the problems that came with it.

I refused to turn around, needing to be in control of my mind and body before confronting him. When I made no movement, he tightened his grip and forced me to face him, his other hand immediately under my chin, as if it were ready for me to avoid his gaze. But it turned out it wasn't my gaze he was after. His lips came down so fast I only had seconds to catch my breath before they were pressed into mine, demanding they open and allow his tongue inside. His hand moved from my chin to the back of my head, gently angling it to fit his needs.

"Cassandra," he said again, this time against my lips. His soft plea rendered me helpless to keep the moan from escaping my lips, allowing his tongue entrance. When it did, my moan grew stronger and more encouraging, melding with his. Electricity sparked as our tongues collided, crashing and sliding against one another as if in urgent battle.

I was about to wrap my arms around his neck in an effort to bring us even closer, when my conscience found its way through the sensual haze and warned me that going any further would render me helpless to get the answers I desperately needed. I teased at the thought of never knowing those answers, giving over to the desires of my body rather than my mind. But then I remembered how scared and vulnerable I'd been in the last week, lost and worried about what was happening to me. As phenomenal as Hunter made me feel, it wasn't worth losing control of my life.

"Hunter, please," I said, pushing against his chest and taking a step back. "We need to talk. I have so many questions—"

He placed a finger over my lips. "Shhh. I know, Cassandra. And I plan to answer all of them. I just...had to feel you. When I found out Caleb came after you...I almost went crazy knowing his hands were on you."

"How did you know?"

"Anael told me."

"You saw her? Did she help you get out?"

"Yes. I don't know how she did it, but she made it happen. I only hope Nergal doesn't find out she had a hand in my escape."

"You mean there's still a chance she could be caught? Is she still there? Hunter, Caleb knows she came to me. He could expose her at any time. Why didn't you bring her with you?"

"As much as I urged her to, she wouldn't come with me. Believe it or not, you and Anael are very much alike. Being stubborn must run in the family."

I hadn't realized his fingers were mindlessly playing with my hair as he talked, until they brushed down my neck. I moved out of reach of his touch and sat on the edge of the desk. I needed to breathe, and standing so close to him seemed only to take that away from me.

He sighed, but conceded to the distance I needed. "Anael told me Caleb knows nothing more than that she stopped you from doing some serious damage to him, and that she wanted to deal with you directly. She feels confident he will obey her orders."

"Are *you* confident?" I asked.

"Caleb is a loose cannon right now, so I'm not sure. Either way, there is no forcing the Queen of Sheol to do anything against her will."

"I hope she'll be okay," I whispered, more to myself than for conversation. Talking about Anael reminded me of what she revealed to me about Hunter. Now was the time to hear it from him. "Why didn't you tell me you were a Seeker, Hunter?" My voice was even, but I couldn't meet his gaze. "I trusted you. I made love…" I couldn't finish; unsure if I wanted to bare my heart to him after how much he'd hurt me.

I continued to stare at my shoes when he moved closer. He pushed my legs apart and stood between them. When I still wouldn't look up at him, he placed his palms on the sides of my cheeks and gently urged my face up.

"You made love to me because you felt how right we are together. I made love to you because you were meant to be mine."

"We can't be right, Hunter. We're on opposite sides of this war. You're a Seeker, and I'm a Guardian. Good versus evil. For

God's sake, you were sent to kill me. How can I ever be *right* with that?"

"Not kill you, turn you. But once I saw you, I knew I could never do it. And once I tasted you, I knew I could never be without you again. And I won't. I don't care what side of this war we are on. I would go against Heaven or Hell to be with you. I told you, you're mine now, and I won't lose you to anyone or *anything* else."

His words cut straight to my heart. It swelled with feelings I'd never experienced in my life. I wanted to hear them. I wanted him to say them over and over and over again. And I wanted to say them back. But it could never work. It didn't matter what we felt for each other. Life and death didn't stop because of feelings. It was a classic Romeo and Juliet story. There was no happy ending.

"I have to go to the Elders," I said. "I don't know much about them, but I'm pretty sure they won't want you around."

"Stay with me."

"You mean in Hell?" I pulled away, fear taking over me.

Hunter straightened and crossed his arms, the black material of his T-shirt stretching over the defined muscles of his chest and biceps. He squinted, flames of anger shooting from his eyes. "You really can't get past what I am, can you? I didn't ask to be who I am, Cassandra. You of all people should understand what that's like."

The disgusted look on his face before he turned away hurt more than I expected. I felt like I would lose a piece of my heart if I let him take one more step away, so I grabbed his arm and tugged him back to me. His eyes challenged me to prove myself. I reached up and pulled his head down to mine.

"I know who you are," I whispered, "and I want all of you."

He let me kiss him, my mouth silently claiming its devotion of love to him while holding back an explosion of longing to have more at the same time. My hands went to his face as our kiss became more urgent, his mouth creating as much fire as mine between us.

With a hand at the back of my head, he eased me back on the table, as his tongue led a trail down my neck. He leaned over me, and his arousal rubbed against my aching core. As waves of pleasure matched the friction of our bodies, I moaned in ecstasy. Running my hands through his hair, I grabbed at the short strands when the powerful sensations overwhelmed me. His hands slid over my chest, down my stomach, and back up. As his palms cupped my breasts, his head lowered to them. Through the thin material of my clothes, he placed a kiss on my heightened nipple, before gently tugging at it with his teeth, creating a blissful agony within me as a strained tension mounted. He continued sucking, licking, and nipping at the tiny buds, making me arch my back and get closer to the source of my ecstasy.

My body screamed to feel his skin against mine. I reached down and ran my hands over his bunched biceps, feeling the muscles change as his hands continuously sculpted my breasts. But the contact only seemed to tease my senses. I needed to feel more of him. Reaching to his lower back, I clutched the material of his shirt in my fists and attempted to pull it off him, but it was trapped between our bodies. He groaned as he pulled away enough to peel away the obstruction.

Like magnets on iron, my hands instantly went to his beautifully chiseled chest, but before I was allowed to really appreciate his exquisite form, he raised my arms. I closed my eyes, caught up in the feel of his touch as he freed me of my shirt and bra.

With nothing between us, we came together and sighed from the contact of our bodies. We kissed frantically, neither one of us able to get enough of the other. Brushing his fingers down my back and sides, he left a trail of goose bumps in their wake from the whisper of his touch.

Hunter pulled back and locked his gaze on mine, his eyes glowing with liquid blue fire that seemed to lure me further into the trance he had cast upon me. His fingers stilled on the button of my jeans as he lowered his eyes, taking all of me in. When they came back up to meet mine, time stood still as he slowly unclasped the button and lowered the zipper.

A strong exhale escaped my lips. My heart beat rapidly in anticipation of what I knew was coming. As I raised my hips from the table, Hunter yanked off my shoes, and then my jeans. He kneeled in between my thighs, slowly sliding his hands up. My hips squirmed, my body tortured with his closeness. He moved my panties to the side, and I felt his hot breath on the sensitive skin.

"You're so beautiful," he whispered, before his thumb softly massaged the center of my essence. With my head back, I let out a small scream of pleasure as my hips lifted from the table, heaving with a will of their own, begging him for more. When his lips replaced his thumb, a surge of sweet energy shot through my body. His tongue swirled and suckled at the tender flesh as I writhed in complete rapture against his mouth, every muscle in my body tensed to a level I knew I couldn't withstand much longer.

I glanced down my body when a waft of air hit the skin where his mouth had so expertly played. He stared back at me, his face flushed with passion.

"I want to be inside you, Cassandra,"

His magnificent body hypnotized me when his jeans hit the floor. His stomach was lean and tight with muscles that teased my eyes to continue lower. My fingers were drawn to the hard lines of his nakedness, itching to follow the path my eyes had already created. I sat up and reached out to him, wrapping my hand around his large shaft. Hearing him growl, I gazed up at his face as I stroked him, my other hand lightly feeling the ripples of his stomach beneath my fingers. His arousal grew and hardened in my hand, and somehow I knew he was as close as I was to reaching the peak of release. He reached down and cupped his hand at the back of my neck, urging my head up as his lips came down on my mouth. We tasted each other with a renewed passion until he pulled back and rested his forehead against mine.

"Do you want me inside of you?" he asked.

"Yes. *Oh God,* yes."

As soon as the words left my mouth he filled me up completely, the slick walls inside pulsing from the throb of his arousal. Staying deep inside of me, he leaned over, his face inches away. "You were made for me, Cassandra," he said on a breath, his eyes so warm and tender as he gazed back at me.

I lifted my hand to his face and brushed my thumb over his lips. He kissed it sweetly and my heart burst with a love for him I didn't quite understand. I knew there was no way we could live the happily ever after fairy tale, but that couldn't stop what we were right then. And if all I had with him was this piece of time, then I was going to savor it, every last second of it. In this moment, I was made for him, as he was made for me.

I pulled his head down to mine and whispered, "Only for you, Hunter. Make love to me." I kissed him with everything I wished we could be after our *piece of time* was over. He kissed me back with the same fervor of emotion, our mouths bonding together as if they were one entity connecting our entire souls.

He moved within me as we kissed, picking up a rhythm filled with desire and sending wave after wave of burning pleasure with every thrust. My body matched his perfect tempo, somehow knowing exactly how to heighten the euphoria. He was so deep inside of me, deeper than I thought was physically possible, and it was sheer heaven. I had to pull from his lips, as my cries of pleasure grew too frequent. He drew back from me, slowly pulled one of my legs up, and rested it on his shoulder. Hugging the ankle to him, he passionately kissed the sensitive skin, his groans of pleasure vibrating against it. A tremor swept down my leg, met with the heat emanating from my core, and exploded into millions of electrical sparks that traveled to every part of me. He must have sensed my sexual tension at its peak because he thrust into me with a force. I cried out his name when my climax erupted. I lay on the table, in a state of bliss while the explosion settled into waves of throbbing pleasure.

He released my leg and leaned over me with a sexy smile. *God, he was beautiful.* I put my hands to the sides of his face and just looked at him, my eyes telling him everything I felt for him. As he kissed me, I reached around and ran my hands down his muscled back, enjoying the feel of his soft, firm skin. I continued lower, felt the tightness of his backside, and squeezed. He groaned in my mouth and moved inside of me again. The pace of his thrusts picked up, and he put his head in the crook of my neck, his lips pressed against it. His rapid breathing mixed with his moans as he continued to drive into me, his shaft feeling as if it were becoming harder with every push. With one final thrust, he let out a long growl as he pulsed powerfully inside of me.

We stayed that way until our breathing returned to normal. He placed small kisses on my neck as I lightly trailed my fingers up his back, and then down his arms. He grabbed my hand and brought it up to his lips, kissing the inside of my wrist and sending shivers up my arm. His head came back over mine.

Gazing into my eyes, he brushed the backs of his fingers against my lips. "I love you, Cassandra," he whispered.

My heart swelled in my chest, as I smiled at him. "I—"

A loud banging on the door of the motel room cut me off. "Hunter," Eric screamed through the door.

"I'm busy," Hunter yelled back, not taking his eyes off me.

"Uh, look man, we got a problem out here that can't wait for you to...uh...you just gotta get out here."

My eyes widened with dread at Eric's words. I pushed Hunter off me and was about to run to the door when Hunter grabbed my wrist, sending me spinning back.

"You stay here. I'm not letting you go out there looking like that."

I glanced down and realized I was still naked. With a nod, I frantically gathered up my clothes to get dressed.

Hunter went to the door.

"This had better be important, Eric, or I swear I will steal the Sword of Final Death and kill you myself." He opened the door a crack, blocking Eric's view of the room inside.

I'd just gotten my shoes on when I heard a scream coming from my mom on the other side of the door. I was terrified from it at first, until I realized Hunter was standing naked in the open doorway. I was quite certain her fear came more from seeing him in all his glory than anything else. I ran up to the door and shoved his jeans at him.

"What is it? What's happened?" I asked Eric and my mom.

Eric kept his gaze on Hunter. "It's Nora. She's gone."

CHAPTER TWENTY-THREE

"What do you mean, she's gone?" I screamed. "Where is she?"

Panic surged through my veins as my eyes darted between Eric and my mom, who was standing at his side, her features full of fear.

"She said she needed to get something to drink," Eric explained. "I told her I should go with her, but she didn't want me to leave your mom. She said she was only going to the vending machine by the office, and would be right back. I didn't like it, but she insisted. When she didn't come back, I woke Sara, and we went looking for her. We checked the vending machine, but she wasn't there. When I asked the office manager if he'd seen her, he told me the vending machine was out of service, so he directed her to the twenty-four hour diner across the street." He turned around and pointed at a small building with neon lights shining through its windows, promising the best home-cooked meals served twenty-four hours a day.

A knowing look passed between Eric and Hunter that made my blood ice over. I had a feeling sweet apple pie wasn't being served over at that diner.

"It's Caleb, isn't it?" I asked them both.

"Yes," Hunter said.

Without hesitation, I stomped in the direction of the diner, but Hunter blocked me after I'd only gotten a few feet.

"What do you think you're doing?" he asked.

"I'm going to get my best friend out of there. God knows what he might have already done to her."

"No, you're not. Think about it, Cassandra. He wants *you*. This is what he's waiting for. We need to come up with a plan."

"There's no time for that, and he's too unpredictable to plan for. Don't you think I know it's me he wants? That's why I have to go. There's no other way around this, and you know it. Please, let me go." I was determined and he sensed it. It may have sounded like I was asking for his approval, but he knew I'd go without it.

Hunter directed Eric to take my mom into the room and protect her with his life. My mom protested, of course, so I went over to her and grabbed her hands in mine. "Mom, Nora needs me," I said, staring into her frightened eyes. "I'm the only one who can save her. I'll be okay, I promise. Hunter will be with me. He won't let anything happen to me."

She turned her head toward Hunter and a wall disintegrated from her demeanor. "You take care of her," she told him. "I'm trusting you to take care of my baby. Please."

"I'll guard her with my life, Sara."

My mom gave me a hug, before following Eric into the motel room.

Once the door to the motel room closed, I took a deep breath and rubbed the shivers of fear out of my arms. "Before we go over there, I need to know something," I said to Hunter. "How do I kill the fucker?"

"You can't. Only the Sword of Final Death can do that to a demon. And the Sword belongs to the King of Sheol."

"Of course," I said sarcastically. "Well, I guess we just have to beat the hell out of him and send him back home then."

I sidestepped Hunter and marched toward the restaurant again.

"Cassandra," he called after me, stopping me once more. I turned back to him, waiting. He moved up to me and cupped his hand to my face. "Before we go, you were about to tell me something in the motel room before we were interrupted. Please tell me now."

I was no longer in the throes of passion with him, so a confession of my love seemed much harder. I wanted him to focus on saving Nora. I was afraid if I told him what my heart felt, he'd be more focused on me. That's the kind of soul he was. He protected what was his. And that wouldn't work with the plan I'd come up with.

"I'll tell you what, you help me get Nora out of that restaurant and away from Caleb, and we can pick up where we left off. Deal?" I stuck my hand out to shake on it.

Hunter smiled and even let a small chuckle escape his lips. He put his hand in mine, pulled me against him, and kissed me hard. When he backed away, he still had the smile on his face. "Deal," he said. Then, his expression became taut. "All right, let's do this. But I want you to follow my lead, you hear me? Let me take care of him."

"Yeah...okay," I said, spinning away from him.

Hunter yanked me backward into his chest. His mouth was in my hair, near my ear. "I mean it, Cassandra. I will not lose you."

"I got it, Hunter. Now, let's go before it's too late to do anything for her."

He released me, and we both crossed the street, dread filling my body with every step I took toward the restaurant. Would this be the last mile for me, my death sentence? I had no idea what lay in store for us behind those diner doors, but I knew I would do just about anything to save Nora.

We reached the restaurant without another word. I was too wrapped up in trying to picture how this would all play out and Hunter was...well, who knew what Hunter thought about at any point in time. I reached for the handle of the door, and his hand clamped over mine, preventing me from opening it.

"I go in first. You stay behind me."

I didn't argue with him because I knew I couldn't win, and I must admit, I was secretly relieved. My bravado lessened as we walked over, to the point that fear had pretty much won out by the time we reached the diner. Fear of what may have already happened to Nora, and selfishly, what might become of me.

After nodding my agreement, he let up on my hand, and I removed it from the door. Standing behind him, I held my breath as he inched it open. I followed him into the dimly lit room, glancing around for Nora, but Hunter blocked my view of anything but the empty booths and tables alongside of us.

"Ahhh, Hunter," Caleb welcomed. "So nice to see you again. I knew you'd come. It was so good of Anael to help set you free so you could join my little soiree."

There was a pause, and I tried to step to the side to see what was going on, but Hunter anticipated my move and pushed me back behind him before I even got a peek.

"Surprised I knew she was your liberator? Don't be. I've watched you for quite some time now and I've seen...*everything*."

Bile rose up in my throat at the thought of him watching Hunter and me together. My heart dropped as his face peered around Hunter from across the bar, locking his gaze on me.

"Hello, Cassie." His voice was seductive as he gave a small wave in my direction. The courtesy cooled my skin, making me want to cozy up closer to Hunter. "Oh, now, don't worry your pretty little head about your great, great, great...well, whatever. You don't have to worry about Anael because your secret is safe with me. Well, I guess I can't really say that, since her fate really depends on you."

I lurched back and to the side of Hunter before he could stop me again. Caleb was in clear view, sitting on a diner stool in front of a long laminate countertop. There were several empty stools lined up along the counter, but I gasped when I spotted Nora seated on the one next to Caleb. She didn't appear injured. There were no ropes, tape, or anything else holding her in place, but the look of terror on her face told me they weren't needed. Caleb must have been holding something over her to keep her there.

Caleb noticed the direction of my eyes and glanced over at Nora. "Oh, right. Then there's her." He waved in her direction as if she were a pesky fly to be swatted. "See, I like to give myself a lot of leverage. You can never be too detailed in the ways to achieve your goals."

"I'm so sorry, Cassie. I never meant—"

"*Shut up.*" Caleb stood and grabbed Nora up by the throat.

I screamed, and Hunter took a step toward them, but slowed when Caleb pegged him with his gaze, his eyes glowing.

"Don't even think about it, Hunter, or I'll snap her neck before you get halfway over here." Caleb's voice was deadly calm.

I tugged at Hunter's arm. "Hunter, don't. Please."

"Let her go, Caleb," Hunter said. "You can take me to Nergal. You'd be promoted to second in command for bringing me back. I'll go willingly, no fight. Just let the women go."

Caleb set Nora back on the stool, none too gently, and laughed. "You're kidding, right? I don't give a shit about you, Hunter. You're his enemy now, so where do you think that leaves me? I'm already there, brother. I already took your place."

"There's no way I'm letting you do this, Caleb," Hunter said through clenched teeth.

"Well, now, the way I see it, you're not really going to have a choice." Caleb turned his attention to me. "Now, you, Cassie have a choice. It's really pretty simple. All you have to do is take Nora's place here"—he used his hands to indicate where Nora sat, like he was presenting a display—"drink this little concoction I've made, and I'll let her go."

I hadn't noticed there was a wine glass sitting on the counter in front of Nora until he pointed it out. Remembering what Hunter told me about turning Guardians into Seekers, I had a suspicion the red liquid inside was Caleb's blood.

"And if you act now," Caleb continued with his theatrics, "I'll even throw in my complete discretion over the fact that dear old grandma, or whatever Anael is to you, helped lover boy here go free. That's it. Easy, peasy, right? What'dya say, Cassie? Do we have a deal?"

I stood, motionless, except for my trembling hands and rapid heartbeat. This was it. This was my fate. I was to sacrifice my soul for them. Eight years ago, I was getting over the fact that I had a role to play in saving people's souls, and having to sacrifice living my life as an ordinary woman to do my duties as a Guardian. I accepted it and made it a part of my life. Never could I have imagined I would be so detrimental to the fate of others that I would have to sacrifice my own soul.

I was terrified of what I was about to become, but I didn't want those I loved to suffer. Hell was after me, not my mom, Nora, or Anael. They were only casualties in this war. It was only Anael's words that prevented me from running over and chugging down Caleb's blood. What if, by giving over my soul, the people I loved ended up being casualties anyway? Anael said having me in Hell would tip the scales enough for evil to win the war. It was hard to believe I held that much power, but was it possible?

It was a no win situation, but at least, if I took Nora's place, she had the chance to fight what Anael thought was inevitable. Hell, maybe *I'd* even have a chance. There was no way I could stand and watch Nora die right in front of me. I had to do something.

"How do I know you won't go after them again if I do this?" I asked Caleb.

Hunter snapped his head to me, eyes narrowed. "What the hell are you doing, Cassandra? You can't—"

"I can't just let her die here, Hunter." My eyes welled up with tears. "I just...can't."

He was quiet as he stared back at me. A tear fell down my cheek, and Hunter reached his thumb up to catch it. I closed my eyes, reveling in the feel of his touch, wondering if it might be the last time I'd ever feel it.

"Awww...How sweet," Caleb said. "While I'd love to let you guys finish this sappy goodbye scene, I've had my fill of bare tender moments from the two of you. Well, maybe not so much from you Cassie." His smile was smug.

I heard a growl come from the whirr of motion Hunter created as he charged Caleb, but he wasn't fast enough. Caleb snatched Nora up and held her body against his, his arm crossed over her jaw as his hand was placed strategically at the back of her neck. He was using her as his human shield.

"Any closer and this is all over," Caleb sneered.

Hunter stopped, but I used his preoccupation to my advantage and ran up to Caleb and Nora. Caleb's eyes were nervous as he moved to face me.

I put my arms up in surrender. "Let her go, Caleb, like you promised. I'm here now. I'll drink it. Just let her go." I could hear Hunter's protests, but I was focused on Caleb. I locked my gaze on his so he could read the truth in my eyes—I was giving in.

Nora watched me, terror in her eyes. "Cassie, don't do this. Save yourself."

I couldn't look at her. I knew if I did, I would lose my composure. I needed to be strong. I needed to swallow my fears and do this. It couldn't wait any longer. I wasn't sure how long my resolve would hold up.

"Call off your dog, and I'll let her go," Caleb said.

I turned to Hunter, who stood a few feet away and was, in fact, still growling. His eyes were fixed on Caleb as if he could kill him with their piercing glare. It took me several attempts at calling his name for him to break from the spell and acknowledge me.

"Hunter. Back. Off. I'm doing this, and there is nothing you can do to stop it now. If you want to help me, you'll look after those I love when I'm gone."

When he looked at me, the hatred in his eyes he'd directed at Caleb softened, but not completely. His chest pulsated in tune with his hard, rapid breaths. He was restraining himself from acting, his body extremely tense with the effort. Silently, he shook his head, and I thought for sure he'd argue with me, but he surprised me when he let out a sigh and stepped away.

"More," Caleb demanded.

Hunter's lip curled as he glared at Caleb, but he continued to step back a few more feet.

"Enough, Caleb. Let's get this shit over with," I said, my voice filled with hatred. "Let her go."

As if it were one continuous motion, Caleb pushed Nora away from him and grabbed my wrist, roughly pulling me into him. I turned my body around quickly in his arms, my back up against him, so I could watch to make sure Nora escaped.

"Hunter," I called out. "Take her back to Eric."

Nora stared, tears and regret in her eyes. "I don't want to leave you, Cassie."

"I'm not leaving," Hunter said.

"It would be easier if you guys left," I told them. "Please, it'll be easier on me."

They both stood unfazed by my desperate pleas.

"Hunter, get her out of here," I screamed.

Hunter grabbed Nora by the arm and forced her to the door.

"Okay, okay. I'll go," Nora cried as she opened the door. With one last glance back, she said, "I love you, Cassie," and went out the door.

Caleb continued to use his arms across my chest to barricade me into him, as his lower body got intimate with mine, grinding against me. I cringed as he nuzzled my neck, before his lips came up to my ear. "I can't wait to be inside of you, Cassie," he whispered. I let out a guttural sound of disgust, and he laughed. "I've fantasized about the day you would drink my blood."

An agonized roar came from Hunter, and he prowled toward us like an angry panther ready to pounce.

I put my arms out as much as Caleb would allow, palms out, warding Hunter off. "Hunter, no. I'm okay."

Peering over my shoulder at Caleb, I said with disgust, "Let's get this over with before I lose my nerve...or my dinner."

He laughed again, not put off by my insult. As we were, he led me over to the stool, forced me to sit, and picked up the glass filled with his blood. He lifted it in Hunter's direction, "Here's to the best man winning, brother."

I could almost feel Hunter's rage from across the room. "Damn it, Caleb." I grabbed the glass from his hands, spilling some of it onto the floor in my haste. Wanting to put an end to Caleb's torture, I quickly put the glass to my lips and lifted it up. The blood was thick in my mouth as it slid down my throat. I expected a metallic taste, but it was bitter, and almost burned, making me gag from the pungency. I fixed my gaze on Caleb as his blue eyes glowed back at me.

I had only gotten a few gulps down when I heard an angry cry and loud crash from across the room. Instantly, I knew it was Hunter, but before I could even turn my head to see what he had done, the wine glass was thrown from my hands, crashing against the wall at the end of the counter, its white tiles streaked with red.

For a moment, I was too shocked to do anything but watch those little red rivers stream down the wall. I finally came out of my trance from another loud crash next to me. Hunter had Caleb up on the counter, leaning over him, as the electronics of what I assumed was the computerized cash register hung ruined over the side, stretched wires the only thing keeping it from crashing to the floor.

"It's too late, brother." Caleb laughed. "I watched her swallow me. It's done. You were too late."

Hunter regarded me, and I saw the fear in his eyes. He watched me intently, staring directly into my eyes, as he continued to hold Caleb down. Caleb lifted his head and strained to see me around Hunter's broad shoulder.

Hearing Caleb's words and Hunter's reaction, a chill came over me as if a million icicles made their way through my body. I shook violently, not from anything internal changing, but from the fear of what I knew was now inevitable. I waited, anticipating something painful as I transformed into my demon state, but I felt nothing.

Caleb's arrogant smile vanished, his eyes squinted, and a grim line set on his lips. I glanced back at Hunter, my face apparent with all the questions I had, but he stayed as he was, merely eyeing me curiously. I think I was more nervous about their scrutiny at that point than my ultimate fate.

Impatiently, I asked, "So, what the hell? Am I a demon now, or what?"

CHAPTER TWENTY-FOUR

Hunter and Caleb stayed as they were, staring at me with the same confused expression on their faces. Finally, Caleb let out an angry growl, causing me to jump, and shoved Hunter off him. With murder in his eyes, he lunged at me, but Hunter quickly blocked the attack.

I was crouched behind Hunter, afraid and confused. Why didn't I feel any different? Shouldn't I have some evil thoughts going through my head? And why was Caleb coming after me now? He'd gotten what he wanted. Didn't he?

"You know what this means, don't you?" Caleb said to Hunter.

For a few minutes, I only heard the sound of their heavy breathing, then nothing, an *eerie* nothing. Hunter was still standing in front of me, guarding me from Caleb, or so I thought, until I stood, peered around him, and saw Caleb was gone. I stepped away, glancing around the room. Caleb was nowhere in sight.

Hunter's hands shot out and grabbed my upper arms, squeezing hard, making me wince.

"What were you thinking?" he yelled, shaking my entire body in rhythm with his words. "Did what we share mean nothing to you? Hell, I shoul—"

Before I knew it, his mouth was on mine, his tongue violently forcing its way in as if punishing me for how he thought I'd wronged him. My fervor matched his once I got a taste of what, moments ago, I thought I'd never have again. Our desperation for each other was frantic, and the world around me became lost again, until Hunter violently pushed me back from him. His jaw clenched and relaxed over and over again as he glared at me, his breath heavy. "We will discuss the hell you just put me through, Cassandra, but right now we have to get out of here." He pushed me toward the door. "Get moving."

"What's going on, Hunter?" I asked, struggling against him. "Where's Caleb? What just happened?" I tried digging my feet in, but it was no use. He was too strong for me. Moving in front of me, he grabbed onto my arm and pulled me through the door.

"It didn't work," he said flatly.

"What do you mean it didn't..."

I didn't bother finishing. It was no use trying to get him to answer my questions. He was dragging me toward the street in the direction of the motel. I yanked my arm so hard from him I thought I'd ripped it right out of the socket. It hurt like hell, and I screamed to prove it, but I was free. Hunter had already entered the deserted street in his stride to get us to the motel, but my feet remained planted firmly on the curb. He looked back at me, and I could tell he was surprised by my will not to follow him.

"I'm not going anywhere near my mom and Nora until you tell me what you mean by it not working. How could it not work?"

He stood below me on the street, his eyes level with mine, and I could see the impatience clear on his face. Brushing his hand through his hair, he let out a sigh of resignation. "Caleb's blood didn't work. He couldn't turn you with it and now he's *really* pissed off, so we need to get your mom and Nora to the Elders right now. I have a feeling his next step will be to visit Nergal and tell him everything."

"But how could it not work? I drank it. That's all it takes, right?"

He cupped his hand on my cheek, his eyes softening. "Cassandra—"

"Hunter," Eric yelled, running toward us from the motel.

Hunter spun around and gave orders to get my mom and Nora in the car right away. Eric never questioned him. He ran into the motel room faster than I'd ever seen a man run before, and was back with my mom and Nora in tow within minutes.

My mom and Nora ran toward me, calling my name, both of them crying. I met them on the other side of the street, Hunter alongside of me. They hugged and kissed me; bombarding me with questions I didn't know the answers to. I turned to Hunter for help, but him and Eric were deep in a hushed conversation. Eric nodded at something Hunter said and then they both looked over at me. From the expressions on their faces, I knew we had to hurry and get to the Elders. Whether they could protect us from the evil coming our way, I had no idea, but they were our only chance.

I ushered my mom and Nora toward the car, promising to tell them as much as I could once we were on our way. Peering back over my shoulder I watched Hunter shake Eric's hand, and then Eric disintegrated into the darkness.

"Nora, you and Sara, get in the back," Hunter said, marching up to the car. "I'm driving. Cassandra, you're up front with me."

"Where did Eric go?" Nora glanced around as she moved to the back of the car, where my mom was already getting in.

"He's going to try to warn Anael. Caleb won't hesitate to tell Nergal about her betrayal now. If Nergal finds out, he'll kill her. I asked Eric to find her and convince her to go to the Elders."

"But how can she go to the Elders?" I asked. "She's not an angel anymore."

"It's her only chance. If she stays in Sheol, Nergal will surely kill her."

Ironically, I said a silent prayer she'd be all right as I got into the car.

"You guys can die?" Mom asked. "How?"

"Not now, Mom," I warned, knowing damn well why she was asking.

For the first hour on the road, we discussed what happened at the diner. Apparently, Mom put up quite a fight trying to get out of the motel room when Nora told her what I'd planned to do. It took both Nora and Eric to hold her down and stop her from going over to the restaurant. It was heartfelt to know the lengths everyone was willing to go to in order to keep me safe, but it was also gut wrenching to know the danger they were all in because of me.

I did my best to explain to my mom why I drank Caleb's blood. Even though she argued, I knew she understood it was because of the kind of person she raised me to be. I was a Guardian, born to save people's souls. That kind of calling didn't discriminate. If anything, the drive was stronger to save those I loved. If she had been in the same position, I knew she wouldn't have hesitated to do the same.

After our arguments were exhausted, silence filled the car as we drove down the dark, deserted road. The forested earth passed by through the windows, and I thought about how calm it appeared from a distance, but in reality, the wild contained a life of its own. To the creatures inhabiting it, it was probably far from calm. Like us, they had their natural enemies lurking, waiting for the opportunity to strike, hitting them when they were at their weakest. Even when resting, they were required to stay attuned to the hidden dangers around them to ensure their survival. In truth, they could never really rest. They were always being hunted. I knew exactly what that helplessness felt like, and that we, too, would always be hunted.

I finally realized what Hunter meant back in the motel. I didn't have to go to Hell with him in order for us to be together. He was willing to run with me, however long and far we had to go, no matter how many demons we had to face. He was my best chance at survival because he loved me, and under his protection of love was where I'd be safest.

My mom and Nora would continue to be in danger if they stayed with me. Like the creatures of the wild, they could never rest with me around. Hell wanted me, and I wouldn't continue to lead it to the ones I loved. My mind was made up. I would leave with Hunter once we got Nora and my mom to the Elders.

"I'm going with you," I blurted, staring at Hunter across the seat.

His features changed from confusion to awareness when he glanced over at me. Then a warm smile softened his face and he nodded.

"Cassie, no." My mom came up between the seats and grabbed my shoulder. "You're coming with me. The Elders will take care of all of us."

"Not Hunter," I said. "He risked everything to be with me, Mom. And he's proven he can take care of me. I'm going with him." I turned in my seat to face her, tears threatening to spill over my lids. "You guys will never be safe if I stay with you. I can't bear knowing I'm putting you in danger. What I did in that restaurant? I'd do it again if I were put in the situation. You know they will keep coming after me, and that means they will keep coming after you." The tears escaped and ran steadily down my face. "I'd rather die than know I'd caused anything to happen to you. Please, you have to let me go."

Mom's tears matched my own as she slowly brought her hand up to my cheek to brush them away. There was so much love in her eyes and so much pain at the same time. It was killing me that I was hurting her, but if she remained safe, it was more than worth it.

"You're so much like your father," she whispered.

My body lurched forward and crashed into Hunter's arm, which had flown across my body, as he slammed on the brakes. The force with which my chest hit his arm knocked the wind out of me, and for a moment, I thought I might suffocate. Compelling my lungs to save me, my breath finally came out with a choke and followed with rapid shallow gusts of air that matched my heart rate. I glanced in the back to make sure my mom and Nora were all right. They appeared shaken up, but uninjured. I searched around for the cause of the sudden stop, when I noticed Hunter staring straight ahead. Following his gaze through the windshield, I couldn't see anything except the deserted road in front of us.

I leaned forward, squinting to try and get a better view of what had him so entranced. "Hunter—" Then I saw them. Just past the edge of the light coming from the headlights of the car were several people standing in the middle of the street. My heart sunk into my stomach as hairs rose on my arms.

With a jerk of his hand, Hunter put the car in reverse. He took his foot off the brake and we slowly rolled backward, but he stomped on the brakes again when the people ahead of us disappeared. I twisted around to see out the back window, but there was only darkness beyond the glowing red of the brake lights.

When I twisted back to face the front, I screamed. Standing directly in front of the car were several men staring back at us through the windshield, their blue eyes flashing with the illumination of the car's headlights. Two of the men moved toward the sides of the car, stopping right outside Hunter's door and mine. Their movements were that of soldiers ready for battle, the sheer size of them enough to scare any enemy away. There was no doubt these were the demons from Hell, and they were prepared for war.

I stared at the man outside my door, terrified as I anticipated him opening it and pulling me out. But they only stood there, as if on guard. Nora let out a loud cry, and I spun around in my seat, my skin prickling with fear. She was staring out past the windshield, pointing. When I followed her lead, my heart stopped at the sight before me.

Caleb stood directly in front of one of the headlights, but he was not alone. Anael was held against him. He had her by the hair, forcing her head up, lengthening the skin of her neck. As if in slow motion, I saw the sword in his other hand come up toward the base of her throat, his eyes piercing mine through the windshield with the movement. There was a sparkle of light reflecting off the hilt of the sword that caught my eye. Several blue jewels, almost identical in color to the demon eyes that stared back at me, were embedded into the gold handle. I'd never seen it before, but my gut told me it was the Sword of Final Death...and he was going to kill her with it.

"*No*," I yelled, as I moved my hand to the door handle. Hunter grabbed at my other arm, holding me back.

"Stay in the car," he said with steely reserve. "If you go out there, the rest of us are dead—your mom, Nora, me. I'll go out there and hold their attention while you drive away—"

"No, Hunter." I was the one to grab onto his arm now. "They'll kill you."

"There's no other way, Cassandra. This is the only way to get all of you out of here. They won't kill me."

He leaned over, and I closed my eyes as he pressed his strong lips to mine. The kiss was short, but everlasting as I thought again how this would probably be the last time I'd feel them.

"Trust me," he whispered.

My heart melted as tears flowed down my face. "Hunter, I love you," I told him quietly, but with every bit of my soul wrapped around those words.

His eyes closed as if he were taking my words into his body and vaulting them in his heart. He brushed my lips with the pad of his thumb. "I didn't think it was ever possible, but you're the one who's turned me. Maybe not my soul, but definitely my heart. I will always love you, Cassandra. I know now that I have since the day I came for you. Never forget that."

I pulled his hand to my lips and held on to it, squeezing it as if it would make him stay with me forever. Kissing his fingers, I nodded and released his hand with a devastated sigh.

His expression turned grave. "When you see I have their attention, slide over as fast as you can and hightail it in reverse. I'll keep them busy while you get as far away as you can, but make sure you get back on some other route to get to the Elders."

I nodded, even though every part of my being argued that there must be another way.

"Cassaaannndraaa..." came a deep voice, calling me as if from inside the car. I searched around, expecting one of the huge men to be seated in the back with my mom and Nora, but there was no one. They were glancing around in the back seat the same as I was.

Hunter opened his door to get out. The guard near him stepped back only far enough to let him out of the car. Once out, the demon grabbed Hunter's hands and pulled them roughly behind his back. Hunter dwarfed the guard in height and muscle. It was clear he was allowing himself to be taken.

"There you are, Hunter."

The voice was the same as the one that called my name. It was distinctive, the timbre seductive, yet deadly at the same time. I snapped my head in the direction of it, and stared into the face of a breathtakingly handsome man. His dark, finely chiseled features emphasized his eyes. They were blue like the others', but seemed much more mesmerizing as I gazed into them from behind the windshield. Thick, dark hair waved down to his broad shoulders, lying right above his naked, muscled chest. He was the biggest of them all. His attractiveness, however, could not hide the diabolical nature that seemed to emanate from his presence. This had to be Nergal, the King of Sheol, or, as I liked to think of him, the Devil.

"You already know how disappointed I am that you deserted your mission. Your punishment was nowhere near fulfilled, however, when my traitorous wife helped you escape."

Caleb yanked at Anael's hair, forcing her to face Nergal's glare, and she cried out in pain.

I ached at the inference to Hunter's torture in Hell. It killed me to imagine what they'd do to him now. Would they find a greater torture than he'd already gone through? Or would they simply kill him with the Sword of Final Death? I suspected Nergal took some sort of sick enjoyment out of watching people suffer.

Hunter stood his ground, appearing as relaxed as if he were talking to anyone else but the highest power in Hell. "Well, you have me back. I'll go willingly if you'll agree to let the women go, including Anael."

Nergal erupted in sinister laughter that chilled me to the bone. I held my breath, waiting. He sauntered up to Hunter, as two of the guards closed in behind. Hunter eyed Nergal as he moved. Nergal stopped inches from him, and then leaned in to get even closer.

"Have you forgotten who I am, Hunter?" he asked, spittle spraying over Hunter's face. "I'm the King of Sheol. Your *ruler*. You *will* come back, but it will be on *my* terms. And I promise you, your punishment will be much more severe than before." He stepped back and paced the length of the hood of the car. "I'm thinking I'll let Caleb help out this time. Yes, that's it. I'll force you to watch Caleb have his way with our dear Cassandra, day after torturous day. Maybe I'll even have her father watch the show. You know, kill two demons with one stone. He deserves to be punished for his betrayal just as you do."

My mind was still trying to get over the image of the torture he was describing, when it suddenly stopped processing all together at the mention of my father. Nergal's eyes were boring into mine through the windshield.

Did I hear him right? My father was alive?

CHAPTER TWENTY-FIVE

Hunter charged at Nergal, but the guards converged on him. It gave us an opportunity to escape, but I couldn't make myself move. Nora frantically whispered to me to get behind the wheel, but I was rooted to my seat. I was lost in my own thoughts, trying to piece my world together in a way that would invalidate Nergal's revelation. But there was nothing I'd been told of my father that could do that. All I knew was he left to protect me. My mom told me he died, but had it only been his soul? I'd never even played with the idea he might have been forced into Hell. I turned to my mom, hoping for some kind of sign from her that none of it was true, but by the blank expression on her face as she stared out the windshield, she was in shock too.

There was no way I could leave without knowing the truth. I got out of the car, despite the screams from Nora. One of the guards ran up to me before I reached the front of the car. He kept a small distance between us, but it was enough for him to react to any sudden movements I might be stupid enough to make. Hunter and Anael yelled at me to get back in the car, the guards and Caleb strong-holding each of them, but I kept my eyes on Nergal as he came toward me.

"Cassandra, I'm so happy you've agreed to join us," he said with a smile. "It saves us a lot of time not to have to chase you. It also saves you a lot of pain, I might add. Come"—he extended his hand—"take my hand and we'll do this the easy way."

I put my hands up, warding him off, and I was surprised when he stopped a few feet away.

"What did you say about my father?" I asked with unconcealed hatred.

"Oh, don't tell me you didn't know." Nergal looked over at Hunter and laughed. "You mean to tell me you shared...well...everything with our little Cassandra, but forgot to mention her father was enjoying his stay with us? How very...demon of you."

"You're lying," I screamed at him, refusing to believe my father had lived in Hell all of these years. I searched Hunter's face for some kind of denial, but my heart sank as he hung his head, refusing to look at me. I knew then that Nergal was telling the truth, and it was like someone had stabbed me right through the heart. The heat grew from the wound and emanated throughout my body, causing me to shake with pain and anger.

"You son of a bitch," I yelled as I stomped my way over to Hunter. No one blocked my path or held me back. "You knew and didn't tell me? Why? Why would you keep that from me?"

He still wouldn't face me.

"Look at me, *damn it*."

There was pain in his features when he finally raised his eyes to mine, but I refused to be affected by them.

"I trusted you."

"I'm sorry," he whispered.

"You're sorry? You're *sorry*? My father has been living in Hell for years while I thought he was dead, and you knew about it. I can't believe you kept this from me." I beat at his chest, tears streaming down my face, not sure where all the rage and violence was coming from, but needing to get it out.

"That's it," Nergal urged from behind me. "Let your demon out, Cassandra. It's in your blood."

The meaning of Nergal's words didn't register at first. I was facing Hunter, my fists flattened against his chest, using him as leverage, when I realized the implications. My head was down, and I didn't want to look up, afraid to see confirmation in Hunter's eyes. I shook my head in an effort to convince myself it was a lie.

It would mean that...no, it wasn't possible.

I shook my head violently, as if I could shake the horrible lies right out of it.

"It's true," Nergal said as he came toward me.

I didn't fear him. I didn't feel anything at that moment. "Why do you think Caleb's blood didn't turn you, Cassandra? It's because you already have the blood within you. You are truly your father's daughter."

"Don't listen to him, Cassie," Anael yelled, still trapped in Caleb's clutches. Caleb yanked her hair with such force her neck strained further than I thought physically possible.

"Shut up, you deceiving little bitch," Nergal threatened. "I've allowed you to live for far too long. I should have killed you when I tired of you. It's been a long time since you've been of any use to me. I think it's time you served your final purpose. Caleb, show our friends here what happens to those who deceive us." His gaze fell on me. "Or to the loved ones of those who don't cooperate."

"My pleasure, Sire," Caleb said with a sadistic smile.

As I watched Caleb raise the Sword back and aim it at Anael's heart, Hunter roared. He was struggling with his captors, attempting to free himself. He'd managed to pull them in the direction of Anael and Caleb, but I knew it wouldn't be enough. Reacting on impulse, I charged at Caleb.

No one, including me, expected the quickness with which I reached him. I launched myself at him, while attempting to pull the Sword from his grasp. We all went down from the impact. I fell on top of Caleb, cutting my cheek on the Sword in the process. My face felt like it was on fire, with blood running swiftly from the cut. The pain was unbearable, but I forced myself to overcome it as I glanced at Anael. She lay close on the pavement, dazed, but not seriously injured.

The Sword was between Caleb and me, both of our hands in a battle at the hilt. As I struggled to free it from him, a rage grew within me, along with the same unexpected strength I felt back at the apartment. His eyes grew wide as I started to force the Sword from his grip. The power continued to surge as I wrestled it from him. With it finally in my hands, a possession came over me, my body automated as I sat over him, holding the hilt of the Sword downward, the tip pointed at his heart.

A warrior-like cry escaped my lungs, and I was about to lunge the blade into his demon heart, when my mom screamed. With my arms straining above me, I twisted my head toward the cries. Nergal held my mom against him. His face was that of pure evil. On the other side of the car, Nora was in the clutches of one of the guards. I stared at them for a while, hatred emanating from my body at the demons that would tie my hands and force me to cooperate.

Nothing was said. Nothing *needed* to be said. I dropped the Sword next to me in surrender, my heart crashing down with it as it hit the pavement. Caleb pushed me off him and grabbed the Sword at the same time that he pulled me back into his chest. With his face next to mine, he licked the blood that flowed from the cut on my cheek.

"Mmm…you taste as sweet as I imagined. I can't wait to see if the rest of you is as satisfying."

I closed my eyes in disgust, bile rising in my throat.

An animalistic cry pierced the night, and I felt a surge of energy burst from where Hunter stood as he threw the guards off him, scattering them further than I thought possible. He charged, reaching us in seconds. Throwing me to the side, he slammed his body against Caleb's, and they went down in a heap of muscle. Something cracked against the ground. When I righted myself, all I could see was Caleb lying motionless beneath Hunter.

Caleb appeared lifeless. Was it a trick? Hunter told me the only way to kill a demon was with the Sword, but the Sword had not moved from the pavement. At least, not that I'd seen.

Hunter was so fixated on Caleb he didn't notice the guards had righted themselves and were now pulling him off Caleb. He didn't appear to put up much of a fight. One of the guards grabbed me as I watched Hunter fall powerless to the demons. Once we were all under their control, Nergal moved forward with my mom.

"Enough games. This is over. If you do not come with us, I will kill your mom and friend. You've run out of time and options, Cassandra."

I didn't want any more bloodshed. We were overpowered. They couldn't be defeated. I glanced down at Caleb, picturing his body as one of my loved ones if I continued to fight the inevitable. This was it. I'd reached the end of the line.

"I'll come with you," I told him. "But I want to say goodbye, and I want to watch them leave safely."

"As you wish," Nergal said.

While he released my mom, he motioned for the other guard to do the same with Nora. My mom didn't move, staring out at nothing in particular, until her eyes rolled back and her body went limp. Catching her right before she fell, I held her dead weight against me. Nora was by my side quickly, helping me get her into the car. No one else moved. I imagined they didn't much care what was wrong with her.

As we sat my mom in the passenger side of the car, I leaned her head back and lightly patted her face, calling her name. I knew everything she'd seen and heard had finally become too much for her mind to process. It had given up and shut down to recoup. Mostly, I assumed it was the information about my father and me being demons that had been the last straw. Finding out my father was still alive was hard. Learning he was a demon in Hell was even tougher. But knowing he had been tortured all this time was too much to bear. I made a secret vow to avenge us all if I ever got the chance.

"She'll be okay, Cassie. I'll take care of her. I promise," Nora said, looking at me with tears in her eyes. "I won't fail you. I owe you that much."

"You don't owe me anything, Nora. It's not your fault this happened. It's been me they were after. There was nothing you could do to stop it." Peering into her green eyes, the telltale sign of a Guardian, I felt so different from her now. If I had known all this time that part of me descended from Hell, would I be the person I was today? I hoped so. But it was fate that decided these things. I was grateful for being kept in the dark for as long as I had been.

"I only hope you can still see me for what you thought I was, Nora...what *I* thought I was. I don't want you to think of me as one of...them." I put my head down, hiding my shame.

"I *never* did," she said.

I jerked my head up, thinking maybe I heard her wrong, but seeing her face, I knew I hadn't. She'd known all along. For an instant, I was mad as hell at her for not telling me, but I didn't have the energy to be mad...or sad, or confused, or hurt, or anything else anymore. I was done with surprises. I'd had enough of them to be numb.

I nodded. "Of course you did."

"I'm sorry, Cassie. It was my job to watch over you and make sure you remained true to your Guardian blood. I was never to tell you. As long as you remained honorable, there was no reason for you to know."

I pulled her to me and hugged her hard. "It's okay, Nora. It doesn't matter anymore. All that matters is that you get my mom to the Elders. Take care of her for me. She'll need you. Especially after all this."

Nora nodded, and I knew she would keep her word. She walked to the other side of the car and got behind the wheel as I buckled my mom in. Leaning over, I kissed mom on the cheek and whispered into her ear. "I love you, Mom. I promise, I'll send Dad home to you if it's the last thing I do."

I stood and closed the car door when I noticed Nergal moving toward Anael, who was still lying on the pavement. He was dangling the Sword as if on a stroll swinging a yo-yo. When he reached down and pulled her up by her hair, she cried out and struggled against him. "Time to die, bitch," I heard him tell her. He raised the Sword, pulling his arm back as he aimed it straight for her heart.

My gaze darted to Hunter, hoping he'd stop Nergal's deadly intentions, but two guards held him securely. I opened my mouth to scream, but the words died before they reached my lips as a blaze of white light swallowed up the street. I closed my eyes against the blinding glare.

When the light slowly faded against my lids, I chanced squinting them open. Before I could make out the scene in the street, I heard a deep, powerful voice resonate in the night. "Release her, Nergal, or our war begins now."

CHAPTER TWENTY-SIX

When the light finally faded enough for me to see clearly, I blinked several times to make sure what I was seeing was really there. It could only be described as an army of men, their skin radiant with light. It was as if their bright souls were transcending their bodies for all to see. While each of them differed in appearance, they were all beautifully alluring, each and every one of them. Their only common attribute was the color of their eyes. Resembling the color of emeralds shining under a shimmering white light, they were mesmerizing.

Powerfully built, they appeared as angelic warriors standing on the street before Nergal and his demons. All were strong and at attention, their swords and shields positioned for battle. With steel armor covering their tunics, they looked untouchable.

One stood out in front, seemingly the leader. While he shared the fierce green eyes of the others, his features were sharp, more powerful looking than the rest. He had long, dark hair pulled back and held in place by a very regal headpiece, which was etched with an emblem and spanned his forehead. His silky white tunic was partially covered with gold armor, molded to his muscular build. Massive arms matched his bare shoulders, one of which held an intricately carved sword at the ready. His presence exuded respect and compliance, and, in that moment, he seemed to be demanding it from Nergal.

Nergal released his hold on Anael and dropped the Sword to his side. "Hadraniel," he spit out as if the name left a bad taste in his mouth. "Why do you presume to care for Anael now? You gave her up when you tossed her soul into the depths of Hell with me long ago."

Standing before me was, in essence, good versus evil, the good guys against the bad. Realizing the next few moments could potentially change the universe, I held my breath as I stared.

"The reasons for my actions are no longer of your concern, Nergal," Hadraniel said, his eyes boring into Nergal. "What need concern you is if that Sword scratches even a pore of her skin, I will consider it a challenge of war. I'm quite certain you do not possess the power or the strength in numbers to make that move yet. You are also forbidden to take another of my descendents to your putrid underworld. Cassandra will not step foot in Sheol."

I placed my hand on the car door to hold me up. I couldn't believe it. I was Hadraniel's descendent? How?

"But she is of our blood too now," Nergal argued.

"She has shown no tendencies as a demon or Seeker. Her Guardian blood is overpowering the poison of your kind. We've watched over her for quite some time."

I glanced at Nora, and she put her head down, a telltale sign she was their source of knowledge.

"She will remain in our world, with our rules," Hadraniel continued, "unless she starts displaying her evil lineage."

Talk about fate. Mine was dependent on whether I let the tiger out of the cage that inhabited my body. It was a terrifying awareness of what I was capable of. It was even more frightening to think about what the consequences would be if I were to change.

"You really have no choice here, Nergal. Pick up your dregs and take them back to Sheol, or we fight here and now."

Nergal looked to the demons surrounding him, which seemed like a small circle of friends compared to the army standing in front of him. He motioned the guards near him toward Caleb's body. "Pick him up and take him back to my quarters," he told them. "This isn't over, Hadraniel. We will face off again."

"I look forward to it," Hadraniel answered.

Nergal sneered. "I assure you, we will be ready for war. And we will win. Humanity will be ours, and all your angels will be our slaves."

"We shall see."

Nergal eyed Anael. "Useless bitch. I'm glad to be rid of you. Now, you can torture your old love for the rest of eternity."

She met his glare. "Go to Hell."

He gave her a devious smile. "Gladly." Turning to the guards handling Hunter, he said, "Bring him to me. I will personally see he gets where he belongs."

The guards moved him toward Nergal, and before thinking twice about it, I ran up and stood in front of them, blocking their path.

"Stop. I have something to say before you take him away."

The guards peered over my shoulder. I twisted around to face Nergal. "You have nothing to worry about. I don't want him. I only have a few things I want him to remember me by." Before Nergal had the chance to protest, I spun back and hurried up to Hunter.

I was so close I could feel Hunter's breath on the tip of my nose as I glared up at him. "I can't believe I was stupid enough to think I'd fallen in love with you. You lied to me, Hunter. I'll never forgive you for that. You'll never be more than a demon to me."

He closed his eyes and let out an aching sigh. Opening them back up, I expected to see anger, but all I saw was understanding and resolve. "You may hate me now, Cassandra, but someday you'll realize I kept those things from you to protect you. If you think *I'm* ugly for being a demon, how would you have felt about your father, or yourself? I know now, after loving you, how hard it is to accept who I am, while feeling the way I do about you. I'm a demon. I'm not supposed to love anything, *feel* anything, but lust for evil. But I love you, Cassandra. I lust for only you."

His words melted my heart, despite me wanting to hate him for what he'd done. He was right; I couldn't get past the fact that he was a demon. I'd pegged him as evil from the beginning, and when I found out he lied to me, it all fell into place; he used me for his own evil intentions. The times we were together, those beautiful moments when we were alone, I'd gotten past it and even thought he'd somehow overcome the blood that ran through his veins. But he'd never overcome it; he merely waged his own war with it for what he felt for me. I blinked back tears, not wanting to show him how he affected me, but I knew he caught it. He caught everything about me.

"When that someday comes, I promise, I'll be back for you," Hunter told me. "And when I do, you won't doubt me; or this—"

Before I knew what was happening, he'd escaped the guards. His hands captured my face, urging it toward his lips. There was no time to fight him off. His tongue was in my mouth, desperate to taste what he could before being pulled away. As quickly as he had assaulted my mouth, he was back in the clutches of the guards. I felt empty as I watched him surrender to his captors, like he'd ripped my heart out when they pulled him from me. They tried to maneuver him around me, but before they passed, he leaned in to me, close enough for me to hear him whisper, "I'll be back for you, Cassandra."

***

As the demons disappeared into the night, I stood in the middle of the street, immobilized by my emotions. Hunter's words twisted around my heart, circling like bloodthirsty sharks. After hearing about his deceit, I'd built a cage around it, but now the cage threatened to break open and allow those sharks to feed. I knew the love I felt for him was real, because it penetrated through the pain and overpowered it. My heart heard his reasoning and loved him all the more. The only pain now came from the fact that he was gone, probably forever. I would need to force my heart to beat again without him.

A hand rested on my shoulder and slowly, lifelessly, I turned around. Anael pulled me into her arms, and I rested my head on her shoulder, allowing the tears to flow freely. She didn't say anything, merely held me while my steady tears turned to sobs. Everything that had transpired in the last few weeks came crashing down on me, crushing me.

My mom's gentle voice called my name and I opened my eyes to look upon her loving, concerned face. Anael handed me off to her, and we hugged, crying together.

"Dad..." I started, but couldn't find the right words to express how I felt about what we'd learned.

"I know, I know. I can't believe it either. All this time I thought he was a Guardian. I never would have guessed. I mean, how could I not have known for all those years? I thought we were in love, but how could he have loved me if he was a demon?"

"I'm going to find him, Mom. I'm going to find him and make him explain everything. I swear it."

"No, you won't." Hadraniel's voice was deep and authoritative.

I whirled around, prepared for a verbal battle of wills, but the intensity of his eyes melted my resolve. He had a power over me I couldn't explain...or resist.

"I can't just let him suffer like that," I said.

"Cassandra, your father's fate was decided long ago. He was turned and belongs to Sheol now. I cannot help him, as his blood is no longer ours." He glanced at Anael, who was now at his side, and then back to me. "Nor can you, if you wish us to protect you. They will send many more Seekers after you. You are the last of our line and extremely powerful. The only way into Sheol is to allow the demon side to overpower your

Guardian blood. If you let that happen, you will fall from our graces, and we will deem you our enemy."

The realization of my demon blood hit me. Part of my soul belonged to Hell, as my father did. But I wasn't forced to drink the blood of a Seeker; I was born with it. My fate was at war with itself. At any point in time, it could switch its course. I needed to know how to gain control over it.

"You mean I can get into Sheol? How? I mean, I don't even feel like a demon. Shouldn't I have some evil thoughts going on, or something?" It was probably not the best thing to be asking one of the most powerful angels in Heaven, especially one that just sent the Devil back where he came from.

Hadraniel eyed me as if contemplating what he should or should not tell me. "Our blood in you is strong, Cassandra. You will be wise to keep it that way. You have the powers of both worlds. The Seeker is also in your blood, but you mustn't acknowledge it. If you do, there is no telling where your soul will lie. Live your life as you had before all of this happened. Continue to serve the angels as a Guardian, and we will watch over you. You can live the normal life you've always wanted."

I nodded in acknowledgement, but he wasn't finished. "This includes staying away from Hunter. If he manages to escape Nergal's tortures again, he will come for you. The bond you created with him is strong, almost as strong as your bloodline, but you must sever it. His fate was sealed long ago and does not include you. You are forbidden to be with that demon again, just as you are forbidden to enter Sheol. The consequences will be the same."

I wasn't about to argue with him, not after all he'd done. He'd been my Guardian, and I was surrounded by the people I loved because of it. It was time to concede to the path he was pointing me toward. I'd follow his direction...for now.

Before they disappeared, Anael explained she still had a special connection with me and would always know when I was in trouble. She wasn't sure what Hadraniel had in mind for her, but she promised she'd come to help if I ever needed it.

Nora ran up to Hadraniel and Anael as they moved away from the car, and I watched as they talked together. My heart was heavy, knowing she'd probably go back with them since her job with me was done. When they were finished talking, she turned and started back toward me. I stared wide-eyed until the brilliant flash of light from the angels forced me to look away. As soon as my eyes adjusted back to the darkness, Nora was standing in front of me, smiling.

"They let me stay," she said, a hint of nervousness in her voice. "I asked them and they said I could stay as long as—" she stopped, afraid of speaking what I already knew.

"As long as I don't get all demon on you, I get it."

Nora put her head down. "That was the deal. It's still my job to watch over you and report anything suspicious."

"It's okay, Nora. I'm glad. You're my best friend, even if you're watching for little horns on my head. I want you here with us. I love you, and I don't care what your job is. Besides, I'm going to need all the help I can get, trying to remember what normal is."

Tears slid down her cheeks, tugging at my heartstrings, creating a chain reaction in my mom and me.

All three of us stood there in the street, in the middle of nowhere, having no idea where fate would lead us. All we knew was that we were Guardians of Fate, and it was our job to save the souls of the innocent. So, that was what we intended to do.

Epilogue

It took me a few months to find any semblance of *normal* in my life. I went back to school, but the dream of becoming a psychologist felt empty, knowing our destinies were determined by far more powerful forces. The only reason I kept at it was to help others deal with life, as they knew it to be. Plus, sticking to an average person's routine gave me a way to stay under the Elders' radar while I contemplated how I would get my dad out of Sheol.

Yes, that was still forefront on my mind. My mom, even as tough as she was, went into a depression after everything happened, and I had to be strong for her, every day attempting to lift her spirits. But I knew how much it pained her to know my dad was in Hell, suffering for us. I knew, because it was killing me. She didn't get Guardian visions anymore. Maybe her mind was deliberately blocking them, or somehow the powers of Heaven knew her heart wasn't in it enough to save others. She went to work finally, after not leaving her house for at least a month, but everything she did was robotic. It was as if she'd given up on happiness and hope. I couldn't say that I blamed her.

I still got visions and did my Guardian duties by saving others' souls when they needed it. I wasn't about to let anyone else suffer on my account. The recurring dreams of Hunter and me, and even those of Caleb and me, stopped. They were replaced with me in Hell, always searching for something I could never find. My determination to find my dad led me to believe the dreams were about him, but my heart would hit me with sudden emotional flashbacks of Hunter. They were both in Hell now, or at least I thought they were. Would I ever find them? I was bound and determined to find a way, but it wasn't like I had a secret Seeker on my friend list to tell me how to go about it.

I had a feeling Nora knew something, but we had grown so much closer since everything came out that I didn't want to scare her by making her think I'd gone rogue demon on her, so I never mentioned it. The only thing I talked to her about was being a Guardian and our normal lives, which consisted of work and school. She told me more about the Elders, though. I'd thought the angelic army that showed up the night we were saved from Nergal was the Elders, but she told me only Hadraniel was one. The rest were merely angels serving under him as warriors. Warrior angels. Who'd have thought? The Elders, she told me, were a select group of higher-powered angels with special abilities. They kept Heaven functioning, constantly keeping tabs on the underworld and its intentions. Sounded to me like another terrifying group of beings who had the power to change the world.

That's why I had to be very careful musing about how to get into Sheol. I didn't want to be some kind of fallen Guardian, enemy of the Elders. They seemed to be the more powerful force, so I wasn't about to stick my neck out too far, only to get it cut off. I was afraid to tap into my inner demon, not that I knew how to, anyway. I feared somehow the Elders would sense it. But I didn't know of any other way to get in Sheol.

Every day that went by I lost more hope of ever seeing my dad again. I was simply too...guarded. But then one day, my fate changed course. I was running through the park, as I did every morning, when I noticed a man out of the corner of my eye sitting on the bench where Hunter and I kissed for the first time. I picked up speed as I passed it, trying to block out the images of Hunter. They only brought about an empty yearning now that I knew could not be fulfilled.

"Cassie," a familiar voice yelled as I passed the bench. I stopped so abruptly, I nearly fell over. Chills ran through my body causing my hands and legs to shake uncontrollably. I knew that voice. It was one I never wanted to hear again.

Turning slowly, hoping like hell my mind was playing tricks on me, I stared at the man sitting on the bench. My fight or flight reflexes decided they weren't taking the chance, and I spun around, set on getting the hell out of there.

"Cassie, wait. I'm not what you think I am."

As I ran, I could hear his footfalls behind me, catching up. I twisted my head as my feet picked up the pace. "Stay the hell away from me, Caleb," I screamed.

I wasn't fast enough. His hand grabbed my wrist, and I was yanked back to face him. "Cassie, look at me. I'm not a Seeker anymore."

While struggling to free my arm from his grip, I peered into his face. It was...different. Gone was the cynical air it usually held. It almost appeared softer, with fewer edges to it, less...evil. Eyeing him up, I searched for signs he had some trick up his sleeve, but I saw nothing. Nothing but his eyes pleading with me to hear him out.

I shook my head. "But...but how?"

He relaxed as I stopped struggling. "I'm not positive, but I think it was your blood. I think your blood turned me and gave me back my soul."

"You're lying." I tried to pull away from him, but he tightened his grip on my arm.

"Cassie, wait. Look at me. Look at my eyes."

I stopped fighting and focused on his eyes. That's what was so different about him. It was his eyes. They were no longer the mesmerizing blue orbs. They'd lost their glow entirely. Instead, their brilliant green hue matched my mom's.

Transfixed by the change and the meaning it represented, I stood and stared.

"Is that even possible?"

Caleb pulled me over to the bench, and I sat down mindlessly.

"I don't know how it's possible. I've never heard or seen anything like it. All I know is, after I licked your blood off the Sword, I felt heat running through my veins. I don't remember anything after Hunter knocked me down, until I woke up in a chamber in Sheol. I was completely different. I can't even explain it, but I knew I was no longer a Seeker. I felt...good. And then I saw my reflection...my eyes. I knew I was changed."

"Didn't anyone question what happened to your eyes? They must have thought the same—"

"I didn't give them the chance. After I saw my eyes, I hightailed it out of there. When I finally realized how it happened, I wanted to tell you right away, but I was afraid it might only be temporary. I waited for a little while, and when I didn't seem to be changing back, I came looking for you. "

I stared at him, my mind running on overdrive. I was afraid to trust him after all he'd done in the past, but the proof of his words was staring right back at me. Then a thought hit me.

"Wait. So, you knew how to get out of Sheol without being a Seeker anymore?"

"Uh, yeah. I went out the same way I always did. Well, except I had to avoid anyone seeing me. Why?"

"So, that means you remember being a Seeker? I mean, you haven't lost any memories of what you were?"

"Believe me, every last evil thing I did is stuck here," he said pointing to his head.

I knew then that fate had just handed me what I'd been trying to figure out for the last several months.

"Do you know where they are holding my father?"

"Yes," he said slowly, trying to figure out where I was leading the conversation. I could tell the moment he figured it out. His eyes became wary. "You want me to show you how to find him, don't you?"

"Yes."

He stood and paced in front of the bench with his head down. I watched him, knowing it was a big decision. I was asking him to go back to Hell with me, or at least show me how to get there. He was no longer a demon, and if he were found helping me, they'd kill him for sure. He'd just come back to this life, and I was asking him to put it right back on the line.

"I'll do it," he said stopping in front of me. "It's the least I can do after putting you through what I did."

This was it. I was going to Hell. Oddly enough, I felt hope surge through me like I hadn't felt in a long time. I had a mission, and the wheels turned on a plan to get my dad back. *And* I had a former demon laying out the blueprints.

It's funny how fate worked. I spent weeks running from the demons, and now, I planned to run right into them.

As we walked back to my apartment, a question lingered in my head. I had to ask it, so I simply blurted it out. "Did you see Hunter?"

Caleb stopped, and I waited with him. He wouldn't look at me, keeping his gaze straight ahead. "I won't help you get him out, Cassie. There was one thing as a Seeker that stayed with me—how I felt about you. I wanted you, more than turning you. I'm no longer a demon, and you have no need to fear me anymore. But he is."

His words of affection shocked me. I didn't think Caleb was capable of anything but greed as a demon. I especially didn't think he was capable of affection. Then again, how was he any different from Hunter back then?

I tried to hide the hope in my voice that Hunter was still alive. I needed Caleb to help me, and if he knew I had any intention of finding Hunter in Sheol, I risked that favor. "You said *is*. So, that means he's still alive?"

"No, Cassie, he's a demon, and demons don't live, they exist," he said, irritated. "But, yes, he's still in Sheol."

I turned and began walking again, leaving Caleb behind, watching me.

"That's all I needed to know."

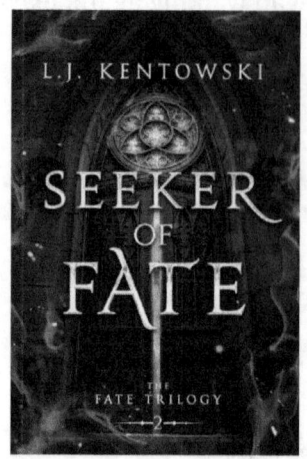

**CHECK OUT A SNEAK PEEK
OF BOOK TWO IN
THE FATE TRILOGY**

CHAPTER ONE

I am running through the familiar woods, fear pulsating through my veins. My eyes dart back and forth, scanning my surroundings, frantically searching for something in the dense foliage. My arms bleeding, I swipe at branches that feel as if they are made of pointed nails, but I forge on, slicing my bare skin. I will not stop until I find what I am looking for.

Finally, my fingers brush against cement beneath a feathery wave of vines that emerge from the mossy grass under my feet and extend beyond my sight. A pungent smell hits my nose, its smoky nature competing with the woodsy smell of the forest around me to overpower my senses. My heartbeat racing, my breaths cause short, quick plumes of transparent smoke to form. The tough vine stalks prove more tenacious than they appear, as I struggle to pull them from the concrete behind, using all my weight to bend and yank them away. After trampling the remaining pillared guardians, I step back to behold a huge mountain of stone, which to most might be confused with one of nature's natural formations, but to me, it is much more than that. I recognize the solid wall as the barrier that blocks the world we live in from the evil that lies below the surface of human cruelty and error. This evil has a home, one that is hidden deep inside the very forest I have been running through for years.

It is what I was looking for all along, but now that I've finally found it, my instincts conflict with my will to stay. Half of me wants to run from the mass I see before me, while the other half feels I belong somewhere beyond this wall. I place my hands against the cool stone, lightly rubbing its rugged surface, as if coaxing it into telling me how to enter its depths.

I close my eyes, imagining what I think Hell would look like. A ball of fire manifests in my heart, stretching, radiating heat throughout the rest of my body, until I feel like the flames will consume my skin. I know I have changed inside, I can feel myself hardening. But as I open my eyes, the only thing that appears to have changed is my impression of where I was going—home.

With pure force and determination, I pound on the wall. Slowly, it slides aside, accepting me, waiting for me to return to its fiery halls.

Hell welcomes me home.

***

I woke up the same way I always did upon having this dream: T-shirt drenched with sweat and stuck to my skin, while unruly, damp curls are plastered against my shoulders and face. Throwing the damp sheets from the bed, I got up and mopped the sweat from my forehead. Despite the perspiration glistening on my skin, my body trembled from chills that would stay with me for the remainder of the day. To most people, this type of dream would be unnerving, to say the least. But they would be fortunate enough to allow it to fade like the morning sun, with the comfort of knowing it existed purely on another level of consciousness. I didn't have that luxury. My dreams couldn't be forgotten. They were analyzed and deciphered because, in time, they would become my reality.

Two kinds of dreams controlled my world. My Guardian visions consisted of prophetic dreams, involving the death of a human, whose soul is stolen by the shadowy demons from Hell. As a Guardian of Fate, it was my job to take the information from these visions and use it to save victims from untimely and evil-induced deaths. Without my intervention, their souls would be destined to an eternity in Hell. I have learned to live with these kinds of visions. They are very much a part of my life, my responsibility.

There are other dreams that haunt my sleep. Even though they appear as deadly as the Guardian visions, they are more obscure to me and nearly impossible to comprehend. Just when the puzzle begins to unfold, they change, leaving me as confused as ever.

I went straight to the bathroom and shut the door to avoid waking my roommate, Nora. She was well aware of my visions, but since it was two in the morning, I didn't think it was a good time to bother her with my newest puzzle. Letting the water run cold enough to make me gasp, I splashed it on my face. Its iciness shocked my system from its fuzzy musings. After wiping my face with a towel, I gazed at my paled features in the mirror. The luster of my skin was no longer visible, as if it had washed out from everything I'd lost in the last year. The deep furrows weren't etched from an abundance of smiles, but rather, a hardened air I'd recently developed in my determination to get everything back.

Silently, I asked my reflection what this latest dream might be telling me. For the past few months, I was making plans to go to the very place my subconscious carried me. Did it mean I was on the right track? Or were my actions of late now dictating my subconscious? For years, I'd only dreamt of Hunter, and then one day he appeared in my life. But even that felt like a dream to me now.

"Stop it," I screamed at the mirror. "Get over him...it...and move on." Throwing the towel into the sink, I yanked open the door and walked face-first into a chin.

"Owww...*damn it*." I backed into the bathroom. "Caleb, what the hell are you doing lurking outside the bathroom door?"

"I wasn't lurking," he said, rubbing his chin. "I heard you get up and go into the bathroom, and then I heard you yelling." Concern came over his face. "Who were you yelling at, Cassie?"

Holding my forehead, which took the brunt of the impact, I looked at it in the mirror. I didn't really care whether a bruise formed or not, the bathroom merely seemed too small at the moment. I was searching for something to make me feel less claustrophobic.

Caleb came closer. I kept my composure in front of the sink, despite wanting to jump out of my skin and hightail it out of there. He was the only one who could help me with my plan, so I needed to keep him around. But when he raised his hand toward my face, I instantly flashed back to his rough touch months ago, and flinched away from his fingers. He held my gaze, but withdrew his hand. The look in his eyes told me he understood, although I didn't miss the sadness and regret that accompanied it.

"I'm not going to hurt you," he said quietly as he turned to leave the bathroom. "That's not me anymore. When are you going to realize that?"

"Look, it's going to take me a while, Caleb," I said. "I mean, it wasn't that long ago you were trying to take my soul to Hell and make me your love slav—" I slapped my hand over my mouth. I didn't mean for the harsh words to slip out. Everything that happened all those months ago was because he was someone different. But Caleb was no longer a demon. He'd been changed by my own blood, which now ran through his veins, and was a Guardian once again.

He swung around, stopping me mid-stride in the middle of the hallway. Leaning close, he grabbed my upper arm and whispered, "My soul status has changed, Cassie. *You're* the only demon here, but I've decided to overlook that. Maybe you can try and overlook what I used to be. And, by the way, I'm still working on making you my love slave."

His green eyes, recently changed from their *demon-blue*, stared at me while he waited for me to say...*what?* That I'd consent to become his love slave? No freaking way.

I pulled away from his grasp as I moved past him and out of the hallway. Nora's room was too close. I was afraid our banter would wake her before I had the chance to map out my plan to Caleb. He followed me into the kitchen. As I got a glass from the cupboard, I said, "Look, if I didn't trust you, I wouldn't have allowed you to stay here while we figure all this out. It's just hard for me to see you as a Guardian after everything we experienced. But I'm getting better." I moved to fill my glass with water and purposely brushed against him near the sink. It was a feeble attempt to show him I could still stand being close to him. "And for the record, I don't like what I am any more than you can endure thinking about what you used to be, so maybe in the future you could spare me the reminder."

"Deal," he said, leaning against the counter. "So, now that we've established once again who we are, will you tell me what you were doing yelling at yourself in the bathroom at two in the morning?"

Holding the glass in my hand, I leaned against the breakfast bar, blankly staring. I shook it just enough so the water swirled inside. I wasn't sure how much I wanted to tell him, this man, who deceived me once before, hooking me with his good looks, kindness, and charm. He was a Seeker then, whose sole purpose was to turn me into one of Hell's newest residents. As the last descendent of a high-ranking angel, I was a pretty hot commodity to the Underworld, so Caleb stood to climb substantially in the ranks if he claimed the turn. He was the epitome of evil, using my friends and family as bait to lure me into his trap. And he would have succeeded if I hadn't been half-demon already, another fact I'd only recently learned, along with my angel ancestry.

Thankfully, Caleb had since transformed back into a Guardian. He believed it was from tasting my blood the last time we fought. Was it be possible my blood, being half angel, was strong enough to transform the demons from Hell? Could their lost souls be redeemed by what flowed through my veins? With no proof he was right, I nevertheless desperately wanted to believe it because my plan depended on it. There was a chance, however, this was all some trumped-up scheme to lure me into Hell, and very possible that Caleb was performing his greatest role. For now, I'd have to take the chance.

"I had a vision."

"A Guardian vision?" He looked confused. "Why are you still here?"

"It wasn't that kind of vision. This one was about me. Specifically, me searching for Hell. I've had these dreams for the last few months and they're driving me crazy. Lately, when I wake up, I feel like I'm running out of time." I set my glass on the counter and got close to him, determination in my eyes, as well as my tone. "I have to go to Hell, Caleb. Soon. You have to tell me how to get in, so I can get my dad."

"Have you had dreams like this before? About you? About Hell?"

"No...well, not about Hell directly, but I dreamt about Hunter..." It was hard for me to think about him, even after so many months. Caleb's face fell after hearing Hunter's name. I knew it pained him to hear it almost as much as it did me to say it, only for a different reason. "I dreamt about him, and eventually you, before you came after me."

He looked thoughtful for a minute, then his face turned angry. "If you knew what would happen, why did you sleep with him?"

Hunter was another Seeker assigned to steal my soul. Although his mission failed, he did manage to claim my heart. I was still not quite sure how it happened, but I fell in love with him, and I believe he fell in love with me as well. At least, that's what he told me when our hearts bonded, along with our bodies. In the end, however, he betrayed me by not telling me my father was still alive and being tortured in Hell. After becoming intimate with me, he let me continue to believe my father was a Guardian, when he was, and always had been, a Seeker. My own mother, another Guardian, didn't even know. We discovered that fact together before Hunter was returned to Hell by the king of the Underworld. He was sentenced to an eternity of torture for abandoning his mission to turn me, not to mention sleeping with me, which was treason in the highest order to them. Ironically, he and my father held the same fate.

I didn't want to think about what happened to Hunter. It was too painful. Not because I regretted it, but because my feelings for him were still so strong. I wanted to hate him for deceiving me; God knows I did when I first found out. But for the last few months, it wasn't his lies that haunted my thoughts. It was the way he risked everything for me, the way he rebelled against everything he was to ensure I kept my soul—regardless of its purity. Although I'll never be able to forget his deceit, I learned to accept it. There was no rulebook for our love, especially for those who weren't supposed to ever experience it. Now, it was too late for me to tell him I understood everything, and the only way I could bear the painful knowledge that he was being tortured, was to keep my mind on my own mission.

I lifted my chin and stared into Caleb's accusing eyes. "Not that it's any of your business, but these visions don't work like that. I *didn't* know Hunter was a demon, just like I didn't know *you* were when we first met. The dreams are cryptic, and they never spelled out that you would both turn out to be liars."

"The difference being that you chose to be with him instead of me."

"No, Caleb. The difference being that Hunter tried to save me from Hell, while you did everything in your power to drag me there," I argued through gritted teeth.

Standing opposite each other in the kitchen, caught in our silent standoff, we glared at each other for our own reasons, both knowing nothing more needed to be said. We had become so used to preying on each other's weaknesses, knowing exactly how to hurt one another, that now the accusations flew easily. It would take more than the few months we'd already spent together to completely ignore the fact that we were originally trying to kill each other. At least, for me.

"Yeah, well, he's still in Hell," Caleb said. He closed the space between us and braced his hands on the counter behind me, jailing me between them. "But I'm here."

All I could do was watch as his face came down, stopping inches from mine. The Seekers were familiar with the use of seduction to lure the Guardians in. The power of attraction they held was undeniable and extremely hard to resist. Caleb still retained the beauty and charm that molded him into the sensuous weapon that originally attracted me to him. And during the last few months, he hadn't shown even an ounce of his previously evil self. But it wasn't any of Caleb's qualities that attracted me now, it was the position we were in that caused me to slowly close my eyes, and savor the body heat radiating from him. Behind closed lids, I pictured a time when Hunter and I were in the same position. I could feel his fingertips brush my face, trailing down my neck. My pulse quickened as I felt his breath against my skin.

"Cassie..." he whispered.

The way he said my name should have been enough to shake me out of my reverie, as Hunter would never call me that. With him, it was always *Cassandra*. And coming from Hunter's lips, it never ceased to tantalize my skin, as if his hands were caressing my entire body. But I didn't want the memory to stop. God forgive me, I wanted to shut my eyes against the reality of it all and pretend it was Hunter's lips now pressed against mine. So I did. I moaned when his tongue found its way into my mouth, and I sank into the arms that wrapped around me.

His solid body felt so familiar against me. I didn't notice his lips had abandoned mine, allowing me to breathe in his sweet, woodsy scent. It was another thing that should have reminded me it wasn't Hunter whose arms I felt around me, but I was too lost to care.

"Cassie, open your eyes," he whispered. "See me. I want you to know it's me you're with right now."

I tried to do as he said, but I didn't want my illusion to end. I didn't want to see the hurt in his eyes when he realized where I'd been. There were moments when I knew exactly where I was and who I was with, and I couldn't say I hated the feelings they evoked. I *was* still attracted to Caleb. Maybe I could pull it off. Maybe he wouldn't know.

I opened my eyes and instantly saw Caleb's face fall. He dropped his arms from me, turned, and stepped away. I reached out and put my hand on his arm in an effort to comfort him. It was all I could do, since I couldn't seem to find anything to say that would justify what happened.

"I'm not going to do this, Cassie."

"Caleb it's not you. I shouldn—"

"No, I mean I'm not going to help you get in to Hell."

"What?" I yelled as I forced him around to face me. "You promised."

"I promised to help you get your father, but I can see you're still longing for Hunter, and I don't want you anywhere near him. I'm sorry. The deal is off."

"You can't do this, Caleb. You're my only hope of saving my father. I can't do this without you."

"And I won't let you either," he said defiantly. "Not only won't I help you, but I'll do everything in my power to make sure you don't get to Hell any other way. I'll call on the Elders if it comes down to it."

The Elders were a group of top-ranking angels who oversaw everything the Guardians did, and the very ones who gave the Guardians their powers to begin with. I, however, had a special tie with the Elders, two of them anyway. Hadraniel and Anael were my ancestors. Their angelic blood ran through my veins, and I was the last of their line. Recently, Hadraniel explained to me that if I ever showed any demonic tendencies, they'd not only disown me as one of their own and lift any protection they previously provided me, but would also consider me a direct enemy of the angels. They already knew my father had been turned, and I was created with the bloodlines of both angel and demon; but they promised to watch over me as one of their own, unless I decided not to be.

"You can't do this. Over what? Your jealousy?" I glared at him.

He moved in closer, steeled in his reserve. I backed up into the counter again, but refused to break eye contact. "I'll do whatever I have to in order to keep you away from that demon. Do you understand me? I won't let him have you. Not ever again."

He wasn't going to budge. I knew that. I could see it. I could *feel* it. But I still intended to save my father. I never planned to seek out Hunter. Not really, but I left my options open to it. It was always in the back of my mind. Who was I kidding? It was in the forefront of my mind all the time. But right now I'd have to let it go for my father. He was what mattered most now.

"Okay, I'll do whatever you say, Caleb. I give you my word."

He studied my face, most likely looking for the loophole he thought I might have reserved for myself, but there was none. "You'll stay away from Hunter?"

"Yes."

"Alright." He reached up and caressed my cheek.

I flinched, trying to keep my emotions in check.

"I wish you could see how great we'd be together, Cassie. Maybe in time you'll finally realize I'm much better for you than he is. In the meantime, let's put together a plan."

"And what plan would that be?" Nora's asked from behind me.

Shit. I was so busted.

Reviews help readers decide if a book is right for them. If this story worked for you, please consider leaving an honest review. Just a few words make a real difference.

Thank you!

Seeker of Fate (Book 2)

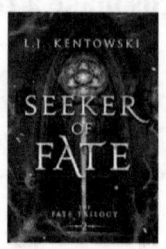

     The Fate Trilogy continues in Seeker of Fate. Grab your copy from Amazon.com today!

http://amzn.to/1Naq5Sb

More books by L.J. Kentowski

Fate Trilogy:

Guardian Of Fate (Book 1)
Seeker Of Fate (Book 2)
Angel Of Fate (Book 3)

Lexie Pearce Series:
Descended in Vengeance (Book 1)

Heart of Seeton Series:
Love Owned (Book 1)
Full Potential (Book 2)

Learn more about these books at
http://www.laurakentowski.com/

Get a FREE Urban Fantasy Short Story!

When you sign up for my VIP Newsletter, you'll receive access to release news, upcoming events, and exclusive content and giveaways!
As a thank you for joining, you'll also receive a FREE bonus short story companion to the Lexie Pearce Series!

Get started here:
https://preview.mailerlite.io/forms/1675703/160480288834586588/share

ABOUT THE AUTHOR

L.J. Kentowski lives with her husband and son in the Midwest, where to keep from freezing her tail off for nine months out of the year, she bundles up in front of a fire, writes stories, eats Twizzlers, and tries to ignore the Great Dane on her lap while she types.

Her first series is an Adult Urban Fantasy/Paranormal Romance trilogy, *The Fate Series*, filled with Angels, Demons, and the In-Betweens.

To learn more about L.J.'s books, visit her at the following places:

Newsletter (free newsletter announcing book releases and special contests)

Website

Facebook

Pinterest

Instagram